MINE TO CHERISH

Clarabella

Did I want to get married today?
It's hard to say when he proposed in front of over a hundred people.
Everything happened so fast, and I thought it was just nerves.
It was not.
The knock on the door showed me that what I was feeling was more than just cold feet.
I was a runaway bride.

Luke

The whole town was busy attending her wedding.
She was the one I let get away when I told her our night together was a mistake and then left town.
So I planned to spend the weekend getting drunk.

When she ran out of the church looking for a hideout, I opened the car door for her.
My one-bed-only cabin and longing looks don't mix well..
Somehow, I have to keep my heart intact and her reputation together.
Maybe she was just mine to cherish.

BOOKS BY NATASHA MADISON

Southern Wedding Series
Mine To Kiss
Mine To Have
Mine To Cherish
Mine to Love

The Only One Series
Only One Kiss
Only One Chance
Only One Night
Only One Touch
Only One Regret
Only One Mistake
Only One Love
Only One Forever

Southern Series
Southern Chance
Southern Comfort
Southern Storm
Southern Sunrise
Southern Heart
Southern Heat
Southern Secrets
Southern Sunshine

This Is
This is Crazy
This Is Wild
This Is Love
This Is Forever

Hollywood Royalty
Hollywood Playboy
Hollywood Princess
Hollywood Prince

Something So Series
Something Series
Something So Right
Something So Perfect
Something So Irresistible
Something So Unscripted
Something So BOX SET

Tempt Series
Tempt The Boss
Tempt The Playboy
Tempt The Ex
Tempt The Hookup
Heaven & Hell Series
Hell And Back
Pieces Of Heaven

Love Series
Perfect Love Story
Unexpected Love Story
Broken Love Story

Faux Pas
Mixed Up Love
Until Brandon

SOUTHERN WEDDING SERIES TREE

Mine To Have
Harlow Barnes & Travis Baker

Mine To Hold
Shelby Baker & Ace

Mine To Cherish
Clarabella & Luke

Mine To Love
Presley & Bennett

Southern Family tree
Billy and Charlotte
(Mother and father to Kallie and Casey)

Southern Chance
Kallie & Jacob McIntyre
Ethan McIntyre (Savannah Son)
Amelia
Travis

Southern Comfort
Olivia & Casey Barnes
Quinn (Southern Heat)
Reed (Southern Sunshine)
Harlow (Mine to Have)

Southern Storm
Savannah & Beau Huntington
Ethan McIntyre (Jacob's son)
Chelsea (Southern Heart)
Toby
Keith

Southern Sunrise
Emily & Ethan McIntyre
Gabriel
Aubrey

Southern Heart
Chelsea Huntington & Mayson Carey
Tucker

Southern Heat
Willow & Quinn Barnes

Southern Secrets
Amelia McIntyre & Asher

Southern Sunshine
Hazel & Reed Barnes
Sophia

Copyright © 2022 Natasha Madison. E-Book and Print Edition
All rights reserved. No part of this book may be reproduced or transmitted in any form or by any means, electronic or mechanical, including photocopying, recording, or by any information storage and retrieval system, without permission in writing.

This is a work of fiction. Names, characters, places and incidents are the product of the author's imagination or are used factiously, and any resemblance to any actual persons or living or dead, events or locals are entirely coincidental.

The author acknowledges the trademark status and trademark owners of various products referenced in this work of fiction, which have been used without permission. The publication/ Use of these trademarks is not authorized, associated with, or sponsored by the trademark owner.

All rights reserved

Cover Design: Jay Aheer Photo by Regina Wamba

Editing done by Jenny Sims Editing4Indies

Proofing Julie Deaton by Deaton Author Services

Proofing by Judy's proofreading

Interior Design by Christina Parker Smith

mine to CHERISH

Southern Wedding Series

NATASHA MADISON

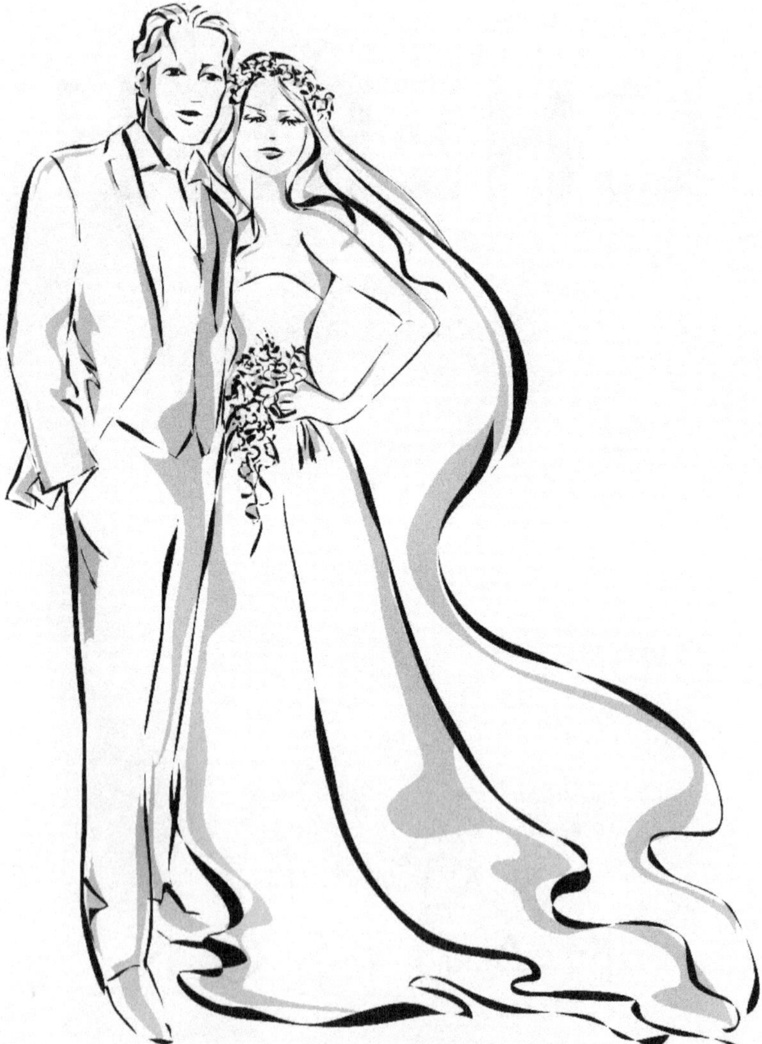

Prologue

Dearest Love,
Going to the chapel and we're going to get mar—
Hmm, are they going to get married?

Clarabella will soon be walking down the aisle. The flowers have been delivered, the food is prepared, and the champagne is chilled. Even the groom is on time. But...

The pesky little knock on the door makes all the cards come crashing down. It seems someone is keeping a little secret. An eight-pound, blue-eyed secret.

Will they get their happily ever after, or was she always meant for someone else?

Only time will tell!
XOXO
NM

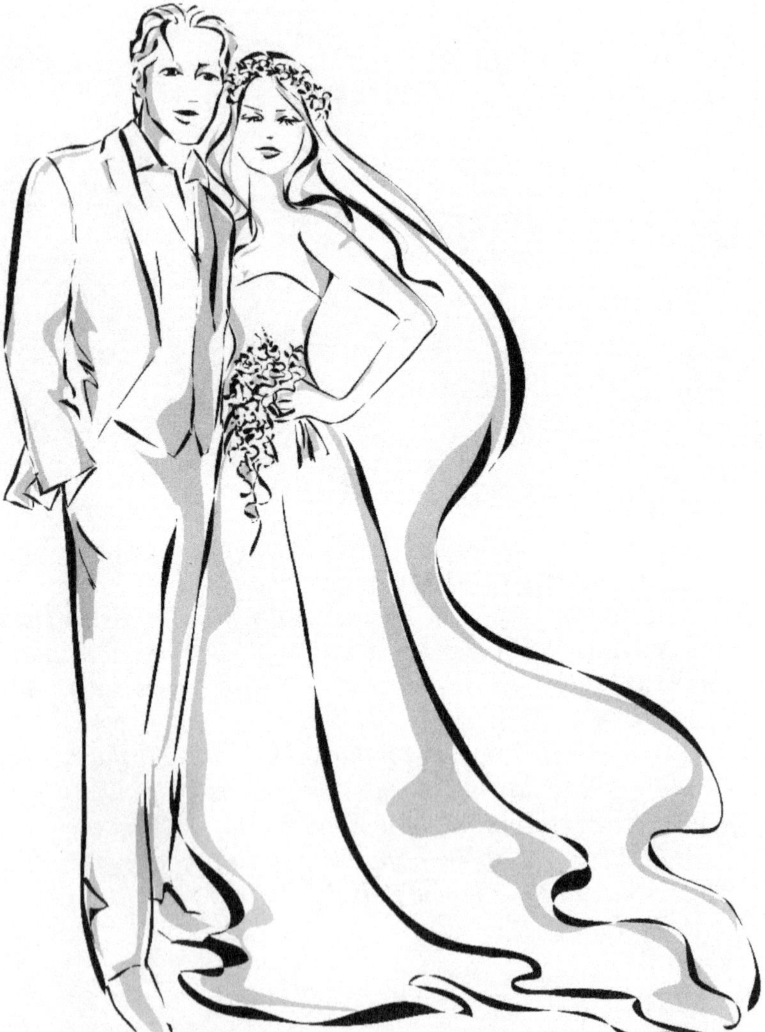

One

Clarabella

"This is stupid," I say when the car door opens. I feel someone grab my hand as she helps me get out of the car with a blindfold over my eyes.

"It's not stupid," Shelby, my sister, hisses, holding my elbow and guiding me down the pathway to the front door of our venue space.

"It's supposed to be a surprise," Presley, my other sister, says, and all I can do is laugh and secretly start to get hives. If there is one thing I hate, it's being surprised. Like, if I didn't know about this surprise, I would more than likely turn around and hightail it out of here.

"I helped plan it, for heaven's sake," I whisper but not

really at them. The clicking of our heels fills the night air.

"Well, no one is supposed to know about that," Shelby says. "But God forbid you let go of control for once in your life."

I stop walking and look over to where her voice was coming from, even though I still see black. "I didn't want this stupid party to begin with. I wanted dinner and maybe some drinks." I stop talking. "Okay, maybe a lot of drinks. But nowhere did I want a freaking party!"

"Well, tell that to Edward," Presley says of my boyfriend of the past two months. "He's the one who wanted this."

I grit my teeth together. "Why would you even entertain this ridiculous idea from him?" I shake my head. "Out of everyone else, you two should know better." I turn, but I'm still blindfolded, so who knows if I'm actually looking at them or not. I'm pointing at what I hope is one of them. "I'm very disappointed in you."

I can hear them snickering. "Good to know. Now lift your feet," Shelby says, and I know we've made it to the four steps. I huff out as my heart speeds up a notch after each step toward the front door.

"Just remember," Presley adds, opening the door for me, "we tried."

"I don't even know what that means." I'm pushed forward, and the blindfold comes off. I blink away the darkness, and all I see are bright lights until the focus comes to me.

"Surprise!" everyone yells, and I stand here stunned. This is not what I planned at all. My simple dinner party for twenty-five was no more.

It looks like my whole family is here, and as I look around the room, I see Travis, my brother, and his wife, Harlow, standing at the side, rolling their lips while trying not to laugh at me. Harlow's hand comes up to her mouth as she whispers, "Sorry," to me.

If I didn't have so many eyes on me, I would whisper back, "*You are dead to me.*"

"Oh my God," I say, putting my hand to my mouth when I see Edward coming to me, clapping his hands with a huge smile on his face. His blond hair is pushed back perfectly as he wears a tailored black suit and a white button-down shirt. My mother is right behind him with her hands in the air and a huge smile on her face as if she won the fucking lottery.

"Happy birthday!" He grabs my face and kisses me on the lips, then brings me in for a hug. My whole body is as stiff as a board, and I push back the anger bubbling over. His blue eyes shine so brightly as he smiles at me. "Are you surprised?" I can't say anything, or better yet, it's safer if I don't say anything. Instead, I just nod my head. "We have one more surprise for you." When he says that, my blood starts to boil, and I have to wonder if this is how the Hulk feels before he turns green and rips off his clothes. "She's stunned," he says, turning around to address the crowd that has now gathered even closer. I try to count the faces, but it stops after twenty.

"Happy birthday, sweetheart," my mother says, hugging me. I bend to hug her, but my arms stay limp at my sides. *Maybe I'm having a stroke*, I think to myself when the back of my neck starts to get hotter, and all I can hear is a deep buzzing in my ears.

"Do you want to say hello to everyone now?" Shelby asks me once my mother lets me go. "Or do you want to change?"

"I think she should change," Presley answers for me when I take way too long to respond, and all I can do is smile at everyone and wave awkwardly. I'm literally going to kill them all.

"Okay," Shelby says, putting a smile on her face. "We are going for a quick change, and then we will be out." She puts her arm around my shoulders and ushers me to the side, where the bride's room is located.

"What's wrong with what I'm wearing?" I look down at the pants and shirt that I thought would match my idea of what I thought my party was going to be.

"Um," Presley says, "it's a little more formal."

She opens the suite door, and black and white balloons are everywhere with the giant black 3-0 balloons. I walk into the room and see the bottle of champagne in the middle of the table. My feet move at the same time as my head is screaming at me to run. I grab the bottle and just bring it straight to my lips.

"Is she going to be okay?" Shelby leans over to whisper to Presley, who just looks at me with wide eyes.

"She'll be fine as long as we just keep feeding her booze." Presley walks into the room and closes the door, then turns to look at me. "On a scale of one to ten, how bad do you want to freak out right now?"

"A solid five billion," I reply honestly, then take

another five gulps of the champagne as if it's water. Knowing that this is a very bad idea.

"Okay, well, you can't do anything about it now," Shelby says, walking into the room and going over to the curtain that blocks the glam area. "So why don't we get you into your outfit and get this over with?"

I bring the bottle back up to my lips and try to calm myself down when I see the outfit. "Is that a fucking wedding dress?" I shriek, looking at the long-sleeved floor-length white gown.

"Pfft." Presley rolls her eyes. "No." I just look at her. "Fine, it might have been on the rack, but we were told it could be just a regular gown." I just stare at her. I don't even know if I'm blinking at this point.

"Are you out of your mind?" I try to keep my voice from rising, knowing that people can probably hear us. "If you say this is a surprise wedding, I'm going to throat punch you both." I hold the bottle in my hand. "And then shank you both with this." I move my wrist, looking at the bottle.

"As if," Shelby snorts. "If we did that, we wouldn't be telling you with a room full of windows that you could break through."

"Yeah." Walking to me, Presley grabs the bottle of champagne and takes her own drink. "If we did that, we would do it in a padded concrete cell so you wouldn't be able to run." She winks at me, and I grab the bottle away from her.

"Get your own," I say, taking another couple of gulps.

"Just relax." Shelby puts her arm around my shoulders

as she ushers me to the room. "We asked everyone to wear black so you would stand out." I look at both of them and take in their black dresses that I should have known were too formal for my dinner. "Now, why don't we get you dressed so we can get this whole thing over with. Then I can drink a lot of booze and take my husband home and have my way with him."

"I just threw up in my mouth," Presley says. "I'm going to go out there and make sure everything is set."

"I don't think this is a good idea." Those words come from me. "I don't do well with being surprised."

"Oh, trust me, we know," Presley replies. "It's why we pretended to have you plan it." She walks out the door, slamming it behind her.

"I hate her." I look at Shelby. "Ever since she gave up carbs, she's been a bitch."

"She isn't the only one," Shelby says to me and tilts her head to the side.

"They say that your weight at thirty is going to be your weight your whole life," I remind her.

"Who?" She cocks her hip to the side and crosses her arms over her chest. "Who says this?"

"Google," I say as she takes the dress off the hanger. "I even sent you the link."

"Clarabella, do you think I read everything you send me?" she asks as I drink more champagne. "Can you undress and drink at the same time?"

With a glare, I put the bottle down, undress, and slip into the white dress. The dress goes high to my neck and straight down to the floor. She zips up the bottom, then

mine to CHERISH

fastens the button at the back of my neck. It fits me like a glove, and when I turn around to see the back, it's got a diamond shape, leaving it backless. "Isn't it pretty?"

"It's white," I point out, turning to her. "I look like a bride."

"I promise you don't," she says, walking to the box of shoes on the counter. "Mom bought you the shoes." She opens the box and gasps.

"What's the matter?" I look at her as she takes the blue satin Manolo Blahnik shoes out.

"Fuck no," I say, shaking my head. "I'm keeping those shoes." I point at the shoes. "But I'm wearing my black shoes."

"Fine," Shelby concedes. "Now let's get out there." I grab the bottle and start to walk out. "You can't go out there like that." She points at the bottle.

"Fine." I shrug my shoulders, bringing the bottle to my mouth and finishing the rest of it. "Is that better?" I ask, and she smirks at me.

"You ready?" she asks, and my head is starting to get a little dizzy.

I take a deep breath and tuck my hair behind one ear and nod my head. She opens the door, and I start walking out. "This fucking dress has a train," I state when I look back. "I hate you both." I clench my teeth, but then smile when I see the photographer snapping pictures.

I walk back into the venue and hear some applause as I look around at the decorations I did not pick out.

A big 3-0 in bright lights is at the back of the room. Four long tables covered in white tablecloths form a square around the white dance floor and have place settings with black plates and black glasses. Five crystal chandelier candles sit in the middle of each table. High-top tables covered in black tablecloths are scattered around the venue with a black lantern centerpiece and a fake candle. Gold, white, and black balloons are everywhere.

"You look like you want to kill us all." Travis comes to stand next to me, and I just nod my head at him.

"I'm so sorry I was sworn to secrecy," Harlow tells me, kissing my cheek. "But in my defense, I did give you a hint." I look at her, confused. "I said what if they don't do what you say."

"That wasn't a hint," I hiss at her and pretend to be upset with a smile as I shake my head. I grab the glass of champagne from her hand and finish it, then hand it back to her. "How many people are here?"

"A hundred and twenty-five," Travis answers, bringing his scotch to his mouth to avoid laughing at me.

"I need a fucking drink." Looking around, I'm about to go to one of the bars set up in the corner when Edward spots me. He comes over to me. "Look at how beautiful you look," he says, kissing me on the side of my lips and then kissing my neck.

"Thank you," I say. I met Edward two months ago when we bumped into each other in a bar. It was tacky to say the least, but when he asked for my number, I gave it to him. We've grown extremely close in the past two months. "Can I have this dance?" he asks, and I look at him weirdly since no music is playing.

He holds up his hand, and as soon as he does, the music starts playing. Everyone looks around, and I don't say anything as he slips his hand in mine and brings me to the middle of the dance floor, where the words Clarabella's Thirtieth Birthday are printed on the floor. "Um, people are looking," I say, looking around the whole room as people gather around, smiling.

"It's just a dance," he says, wrapping his arm around my waist and holding up my hand in his. He brings it to his lips and kisses my fingers. "There, do you feel better?"

No, my head screams out as he turns us around. "Clarabella, these past two months have been a dream come true." I smile up at him.

"They have been amazing," I agree, and I'm not even lying. Being with him is so easy. It's also easy because he does whatever I say or want to do.

"I want to make you happy all the time." He smiles at me, and maybe it's the champagne in me, but I just nod. I mean, yes, every single time we have a disagreement, he just looks over at me and says what I want to hear, which then makes my blood boil. He's just so nice, and I feel like a big bitch. "Being with you every single day has been an eye-opener." I try to listen to his words, but I also start to see that everyone's, and I mean everyone's, eyes are on me.

It's almost like it's not happening. Like my body has left, and I'm looking down at the train wreck that is to come. He stops moving and lets his hand fall from my waist. He puts his hand in his pocket, and the music stops. Or maybe it doesn't stop. Perhaps it's because I've suddenly lost my hearing. I can see everyone look at each other, unsure what is going on. My heartbeat pounds in my ears, and all I can hear are the beats and not the whispers. He kisses me right before he gets down on one knee in front of me. "Being with you has made me see that I don't want to be with anyone else." He looks up at me and opens the small black ring box in his hand.

The gasps I hear are nothing compared to what I'm thinking right now. *This can't be happening. This can't be happening.* "Clarabella Baker, will you make me the luckiest man alive and be my wife?" My eyes go from him to the ring to my sisters, who just stand there in as much shock as I am. My mother is the only one who looks like she knew this was coming. Travis stares at me with his mouth open, and Harlow now grabs his drink from him and holds it up for me. "I love you."

I try to swallow, but it seems like my tongue is so thick that I can't. My mouth is drier than a desert on a summer day. My eyes are seeing little white spots, and I'm not going to lie, I'm expecting to pass out at any moment. But nothing happens, *nothing happens* except Edward just continues to look at me expectantly, his sweet face waiting for me to answer. "What do you say?"

There in the middle of what was supposed to be my thirtieth birthday party, I say the only word that will not make me look like a complete bitch. I also know at this moment that I might be making the biggest mistake of my life. "Yes." The minute I say the word, my head yells *what the fuck did you just do?*

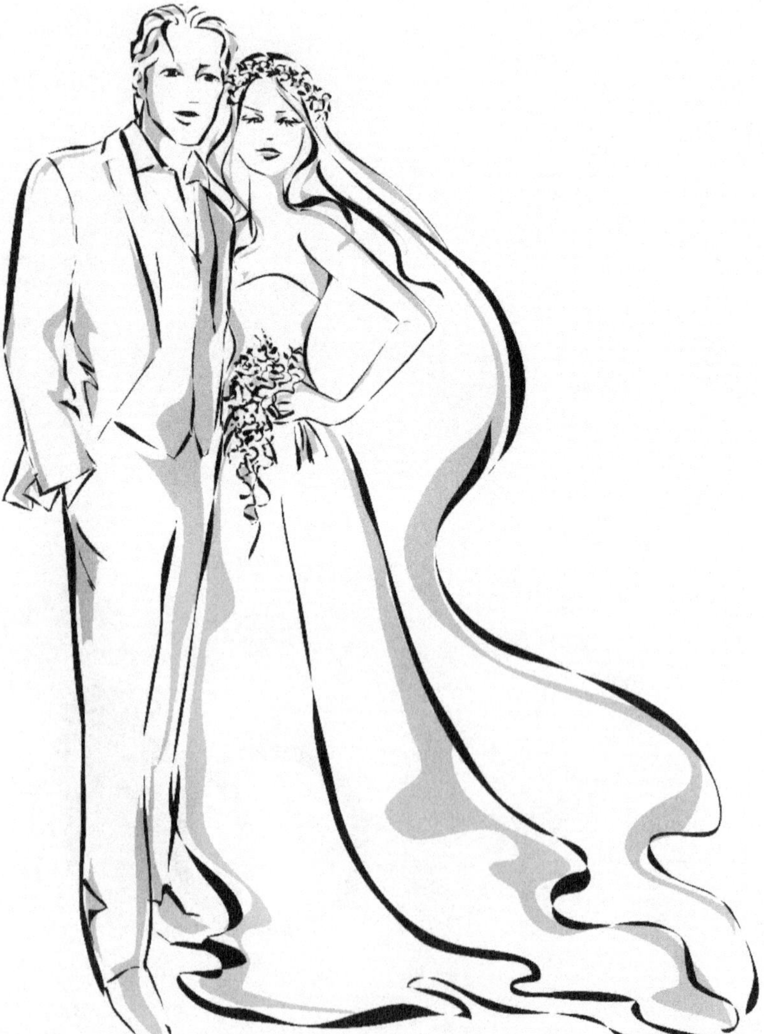

Two

Luke

Four Months Later

I pull up behind the restaurant and put the truck in park. "Why the fuck did I think it was a good idea to drive straight from New York home without stopping?" I ask myself, opening the driver's door and stepping out. My whole body is stiff from the fourteen-hour drive that took me seventeen hours because of the traffic getting out of the city and then an accident on the highway that delayed me for another hour. I put my hands on my back, stretching out when the back door to the restaurant opens.

"Well, well, well." I hear Mikaela say. I turn to see her

wearing her chef outfit and carrying a black garbage bag in one hand. "Look what the cat dragged in." She laughs, walking over to the dumpster and tossing the bag in. She rubs her hands together as she comes back. "Aren't you a sight for sore eyes?"

"I've been gone for six months, and you FaceTimed me twice a day to tell me how much you hated me," I remind her with a smile as she stands in front of me. The two of us met in culinary school, and when I decided to open my restaurant, there was no one I wanted to work with more than her.

"Oh, not past tense, present. I do hate you," she says, and I can't help but laugh, putting my arm around her shoulders as we walk toward the back door of the restaurant.

"What is that smell?" She looks at me, scrunching up her nose.

"I was in the car for seventeen hours," I say. "I left New York at four thinking that I would avoid traffic. News flash, there is always traffic in fucking New York." I put my hands on my hips.

"Well, go fucking shower before you come in my kitchen. Then you can help me with the dinner rush." She walks ahead of me. "Plus, I have a meeting with a bride and groom tonight for a taste test."

I look up at the blue sky and sigh. "I should have gone home first instead of coming here," I say, and it's her turn to laugh at me.

"I have your location on my phone." She walks back into the restaurant and the door slams shut behind her. I walk up the steps to follow her and open the back door. The smell of garlic hits me right away, making my mouth water.

Mikaela is behind the counter frying up something. "I'll get you something to eat," she says over her shoulder, and I walk past the counter toward the brown swinging door with the little glass circle in it. Pushing through the door, I see a couple of people are setting up for the night service. The bar in the middle of the restaurant is why I bought this place to begin with. It just was everything. It wasn't like this when I bought it. Fuck, it was a nightmare, and even the real estate agent asked me if I was sure. He didn't see what I envisioned in my head. He didn't see its potential. A perfect square so you can see every single part of the restaurant. The countertops are pure oak that I sanded down and varnished to a shine. The glasses hanging from the top wire racks give it a modern look with an old-school vibe. Barstools go all the way around and are always the first seats to be taken.

Booths line the far end of the restaurant, all with the same wood finish as the bar. The burgundy booths make everything look so rich. High-top tables are scattered throughout the rest of the floor, and I know this place will be filled with people within two hours. So much has changed since I bought this place. Luckily for me, I got it for less than asking, and then I got a small business loan for new business owners. I saved a fuck ton of money doing the construction myself. I also saved money when I lived here until it started picking up.

I walk to the back corner to the brown closed door

that says Office written across it. I open it and see that the shades are up, giving you the light you need. The couch against the wall has seen better days but is clear of my clothes that used to hang all over it. It faces the brown desk I put there when I wanted to be professional. I walk to the little bathroom with a shower, a toilet, and a standing sink with a mirror. The only thing in here is a tall hutch in the corner I bought from IKEA. I open it, grab a towel, then smell it to make sure it's clean.

I turn on the water, getting in and letting it run down my back. I've been gone for the past six months, and I have to say, it's good to be home. When Francois called me seven months ago, I didn't know what to think. I was in the middle of opening a second restaurant in town, this time a pub, and I was knee-deep in the final stages when he asked me if I wanted to partner with him. His partner fell through, and he knew I was opening my second restaurant, so to him, I was the first one he wanted to call.

It was a dream come true for me. Partner at a restaurant in New York City. It was also scary as fuck because the critics will eat your food and spit it out, and in a matter of a week, you can go from success to crickets. It was a challenge, to say the very least, and the minute I walked in, I knew a lot more work was needed than what he said. Not that I was afraid of work. I worked hard my whole life, from when I was fourteen and my parents thought they had given me enough support and decided that I should start paying my share. So I got two part-time jobs, and when I turned eighteen, I moved to a cheaper place and put myself through college for two years until I went into culinary school.

I turn the water off and get out of the shower, grabbing the towel and wrapping it around my waist. Wiping the steam off the mirror, I see that my eyes are bloodshot. I'm going to sleep so well tonight. I walk back over to the hutch and grab a pair of black pants and a gray T-shirt. I towel off my hair, leaving the bathroom and office to head toward the bar area when I see Mikaela coming out of the kitchen with a plate in her hand. "Right on time," she says, walking to the bar and putting it on the corner.

"The last thing I ate was pizza from a 7-Eleven," I tell her, walking behind the bar and grabbing a bottle of cold beer.

I see one of the bartenders setting up his station as he looks over at me. "Hey," he says, putting the white rag over his shoulder. "You back?"

"For now." I smirk and look over at Mikaela, who glares at me as I walk over to the stool sitting in front of the plate.

I take a pull of the beer and offer it to her. She shakes her head, and I place it down in front of the food. "I want a staff meeting tonight," I announce, and she nods her head. "We have to get ready for the dinner rush, but tomorrow, I want to check out the pub."

"I was there yesterday. It looks good." I nod at her, taking a bite of the burger.

"This is so much better than the pizza at the 7-Eleven," I tell her, and she gives me the finger. The front door opens, and I see a couple of the waitresses arriving. I look at the clock. "It's ten minutes past their shift."

"Oh, don't you know." She laughs, getting up. "We have to be thankful they come to work."

"Fuck that. I'll wait tables myself," I declare. "I'll be there in ten minutes." She gets up and walks to the kitchen. When I finish, I walk back into the kitchen and find her side by side with two sous chefs who look up and smile at me.

"Dad's back," Carson says, looking at me. "Playtime is over."

"Mom was mean to us," Kyle replies to us while Mikaela gives him the finger. I wash my hands and look at her.

"Where do you want me?" I ask, and she points at the table on the side.

"I want you at that table doing the taste testing for tonight." I grab an apron and walk over to the table with a white paper with Mikaela's writing.

"It's a whole page," I say, looking back down at it. "Like a full page. Who tastes this much food at a tasting?"

"It's an important client," she tells me. "So you better be on your A game."

"When am I not on my A game?" With a smirk, I look down at the list to get things going. "What time is this client coming?"

"Eight!" she shouts, and for the next three hours, I get lost in my cooking. I'm plating the last plate when I look over to see that it's almost eight.

"I'm done," I say, wiping my hands.

"I thought you being in New York would make you rusty," Mikaela states at the same time as the kitchen door opens and one of the hostesses comes in.

"The eight o'clock couple is here." She looks at Mikaela. "I will seat them at the booth."

"Sounds good," I say to her, and she turns and smiles at me before walking to the front. *She doesn't even know who I am*, I laugh to myself. She will have a rude awakening when we have the staff meeting tonight.

"You want me to come and introduce you?" Mikaela asks, and I just shake my head.

"I think I'll be good," I say, walking out of the kitchen and taking a look at how jam-packed the place is. There isn't an open seat, and I see the bartenders going nuts. I make a mental note to see if we can hire two more to help out. I walk over to the hostess stand where two girls are chatting together, and one is on her phone.

"Do me a favor," I tell the one on the phone. "Put the phone away. There isn't anything happening on Instagram that is going to change your life in the next hour," I suggest, and she just gives me a fuck-off look. "I'm Luke," I say. "You know, the owner." Her mouth opens in shock as I look at the other one. "Where are the guests?" She points her hand toward the back.

"Last booth on the left," she says, and I nod at her and make my way over to the last booth.

I approach the table, seeing the guy on the outside of the seat and both of them on the same bench. "Hi," I greet once I get there and finally look at the couple. I look at the guy dressed in a suit with his hair perfectly combed over. My eyes go to the woman sitting next to him.

Everything in me stops as she looks up at me in slow motion. Her eyes are even more blue than I remembered, her face even more beautiful. The smile on her face fades when she sees it's me, and the only thing that comes out of my mouth is her name. "Clarabella."

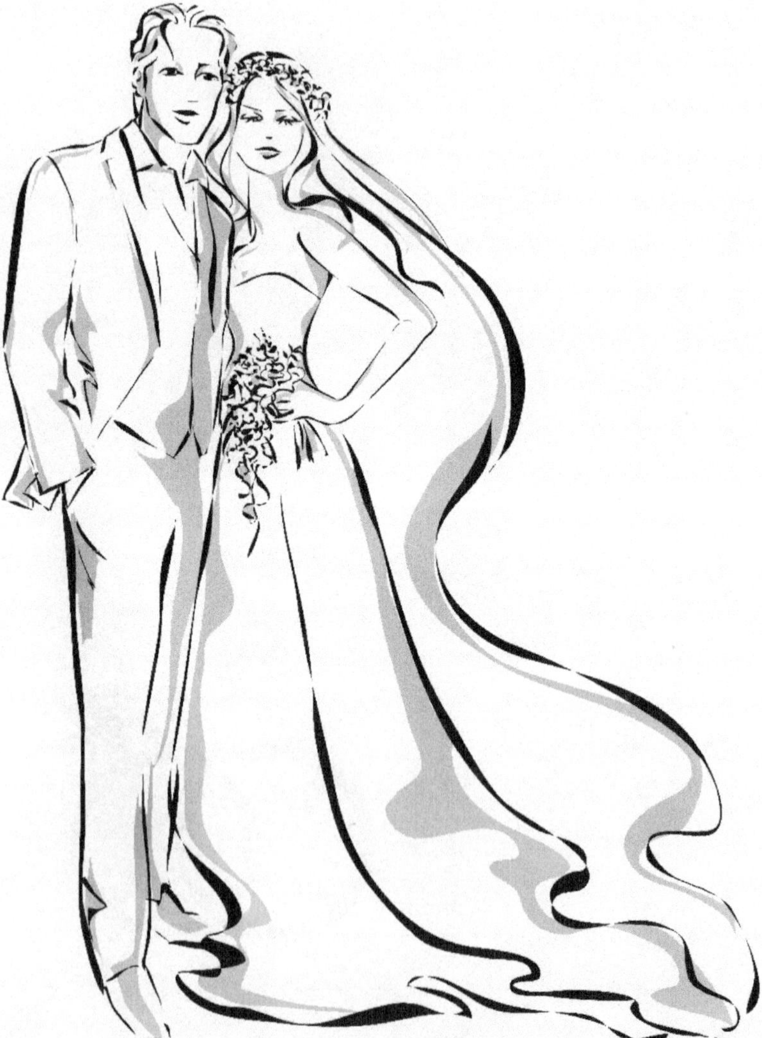

Three

Clarabella

One minute, I'm looking at Edward as he tells me about his day, and the next, I hear his voice. "Hi." At first, I think it's all in my head. I mean, it has to be because I know he's left town. I had no idea where he went, and I wasn't ever going to ask.

I close my eyes for a second, thinking I must have misheard before lifting my head. The clinking plates and laughing people sound far, far away. My eyes spot his hand as my head slowly lifts, or maybe it lifts fast. The only thing I know is I'm staring into his blue eyes. The smile on my face fades when he says my name. "Clarabella."

My heart speeds up in my chest, and I look over at Edward to see if he can hear it. I swallow hard, but my mouth is so dry nothing goes down. Edward smiles at me, so I put on my game face and look back up at Luke. "Luke." I say his name as if it's nothing. As if I'm not surprised he's here, and I'm not slowly freaking out on the inside. Okay, it's not slow. It's a full-blown freak-out. "I didn't know you were back." I want to kick myself the minute the words come out of my mouth. The last thing I want him to think is that I care he was gone or that I know he even left.

"Got back today," he replies. "So you're getting married." His face doesn't show anything as he looks at me and then at Edward. "We go way back." He smirks, and my mouth goes dry.

"Oh," Edward responds, looking at Luke and then at me.

"Not that way back." My voice comes out cracking, and I clear my throat. "We went to college together a long time ago." I smile at Edward. "He dated my best friend at the time. Then he came through when Travis was going to get married." I look back up at Luke. "Is Mikaela not here today?" I ignore my erratic breathing as I try to control it and press down the nerves.

"She is, but I'll be the one working with you tonight," he states. My head yells *fuck no,* and I have to bite down on my tongue to make sure that the words don't actually come out.

"Great," Edward says. "Someone who knows my girl."

"I guess that would be me." He just looks at me, and I look away, taking the glass of water and drinking it. Hoping that it goes down past the lump in my throat. "I'll be back with some food, yeah."

He walks away, and I make the mistake of watching his ass move. "Are you all right?" Edward asks, and I whip my head back to him. "You look a little flushed."

Putting my hand to my face, I can feel the heat from it. *Was I this flushed the whole time?* "It's a little hot in here." I look around and see that the entire restaurant is full. "I'm going to go to the restroom," I say, and he leans and kisses my lips. I smile at him, not saying anything. Grabbing my purse, I wait for him to get up, then scoot over to get out of the booth. Swinging one foot out, I stand, hoping my knees don't give out. "I'll be right back," I assure him, standing up in front of Edward and looking up at him.

I turn to walk away from him, making my way to the bathroom. I push open the brown door and head straight to the sink, looking at myself in the mirror. My cheeks look like I've been sitting in the sun too long or drinking too much scotch. "What the fuck is he doing here?" I ask myself, hoping that someone gives me an answer. The last thing I expected for tonight was running into Luke. I put my hand on my stomach when I think about the last time I saw him. I shouldn't feel this way. My body should not feel like this. "Traitor," I mumble, looking down at my heaving chest.

I'm engaged. I look at myself, reminding my brain of this. I have a fiancé who I love. *But do you?* When he proposed to me, all I could do was look around at all the faces staring at me. How could I have said no? My thirtieth birthday became our engagement party, which then led to the night I slept on my bathroom floor for the first time ever. When I woke up in the morning, Edward was there with a glass of water and two ibuprofen and a calendar.

If it was up to him, we would have been married within two weeks, but thankfully, my sister told him the earliest they could plan a decent wedding was four months. I knew they were giving me time, especially since we planned a kick-ass event in seventy-two hours. So for the past four months, I've been planning my wedding, even though it doesn't feel right. Even though I think we should take more time. From everything that I've read online and in the magazines, this is a normal reaction. It doesn't mean I don't love him. It means I'm not sure about giving up who I am. Even listening to my own words, I want to yell that it's a crock of shit. But instead, I grab my phone and text my sisters.

Me: We have a situation.

"It's going to be fine." I look at my reflection in the mirror and set down the phone. Turning on the cold water, I put my hand under the stream to make my hand cold before placing it back on my face to cool it down. I wet both cheeks twice when my phone beeps, and I pick it up, seeing that Presley answered.

Presley: I'm sorry, the person you are trying to reach about this situation does not care. Do you know why? Because the last time you had this type of text

message, it was because you couldn't get powder-blue napkins, which, I may add, is not a situation. Finding the groom fucking his best man? Now that's a situation. Finding the bride blowing one of the groomsmen? That's a situation.

I grind my teeth, my fingers flying over the phone.

Me: I'm not kidding. This is a huge situation.

I press send at the same time Shelby chimes in.

Shelby: Can the situation be tabled until tomorrow? Ace just got in, and he was gone all week.

Presley: Yeah, leave her alone. She's about to do the nasty.

Shelby: Do you think I would be doing the nasty and answering you at the same time?

Presley: Please, you think your little voice doesn't carry in your office. I heard in detail what you planned to do to his dick.

Shelby: Would you mind your business?

Presley: Trust me, there is nothing in this world I would love to never hear again than I'm going to take you so far in my throat your balls will slap my chin.

Shelby: THAT WAS A PRIVATE CONVERSATION!

I close my eyes and grip my phone in my hand, and to be honest, I wish I could smash it right now. I open them back up, not even bothering to answer my sisters. I take one more look at myself in the mirror before grabbing my purse and walking out. I smile at the girl entering while I exit, and when I get to the table, Edward is on his phone.

"Hey," I say, and he puts his phone down right away. Instead of sitting next to him, I sit in front of him.

"You feeling better?" he asks with concern all over his face, and I nod my head.

"Yes." I put my purse beside me, ignoring the beeping from it. "It must have just been too many people," I state as I spot Luke walking back to us.

"Sorry it took me so long," Luke says, putting down two plates on the table. "As per your request sheet, I made crab cakes with a mango salsa." I look down at one plate, my mouth watering. "And then I took the liberty of going out on my own a bit." He looks at me and then at Edward. "It isn't the South without mac 'n' cheese. This one is done with lobster." He looks at us. "I'll go get the other two." He turns, looking at the server beside him.

"I got you white wine," Edward says to me as the server puts down a crystal glass of chilled white wine. She places a beer bottle down for Edward, then nods at us before she walks away.

"I thought you were more of a scotch girl," Luke says as soon as my hand grabs the glass of wine. My eyes fly to his, and I can see his eyes light up. "I mean, it was a while ago."

"I prefer white wine," I say, smiling at Edward and ignoring the pull that Luke has on me. Bringing the glass of wine to my lips, I take a sip of it. "What do you want to try first?" I ask Edward, who just grabs one of the crab cakes and tosses it into his mouth. Luke keeps bringing out plate after plate, and I want to taste one thing that isn't good, but it's all melt in your mouth. Regardless of him being a grade A asshole, the man can cook.

"So what do you guys think you'll be going with?" Luke asks us, and I look at Edward, who just shakes his head.

"That's all her domain." Edward smiles at me as he puts up his hands, and I just shake my head.

"From what I saw, there are lots of different options on your list," Luke says. "And we are going to be able to do everything you need." I can't help but look at him, no matter how many times I tell myself I should look away. "When is the wedding again?" His eyes are looking into mine.

"Two weeks," Edward declares with a huge smile on his face, and I turn to look at him.

"How long have you guys been dating?" Luke asks, and I look at him, wanting to snap at him and tell him for as long as he's been gone.

But Edward answers him instead. "Six months," he says. "The best six months of my life."

"You're a lucky, lucky man," Luke says. I grab the glass of wine and take an even bigger sip this time.

"Hi," Mikaela greets, coming to the table. "I hope you are enjoying the food." She smiles at us.

"It's delicious," I confirm, smiling at her. "Thank you for doing this."

"We do it for all the other brides," she says. "It's only fair you get your turn."

"Well, it's always fun knowing when we will be working together," I reply.

"From now on, you'll be meeting with Luke more

than me," she states, and I swallow. "Since he's back, he's going to be handling it and leaving me in the kitchen where I'm happiest."

Oh, fuck no, the right side of my brain screams. *Out of the fucking question,* the left side of my brain answers. "We should get going." I look at Edward, who starts to get out of his side of the booth. He walks over to my side and holds out his hand for me. I slip my hand in his. "I'll call tomorrow with our decisions," I say to Luke and Mikaela. My eyes never go to his, and I can feel him staring at me. I can feel his eyes on me exactly like how a magnet would stick to a fridge.

"I look forward to hearing from you," Luke says. As I walk out of the restaurant, my heart thumps in my chest the whole time. The sound becomes louder and louder in my ears, and when Edward opens the car door for me, I get in and grab my phone right away.

Me: Tomorrow morning meeting.

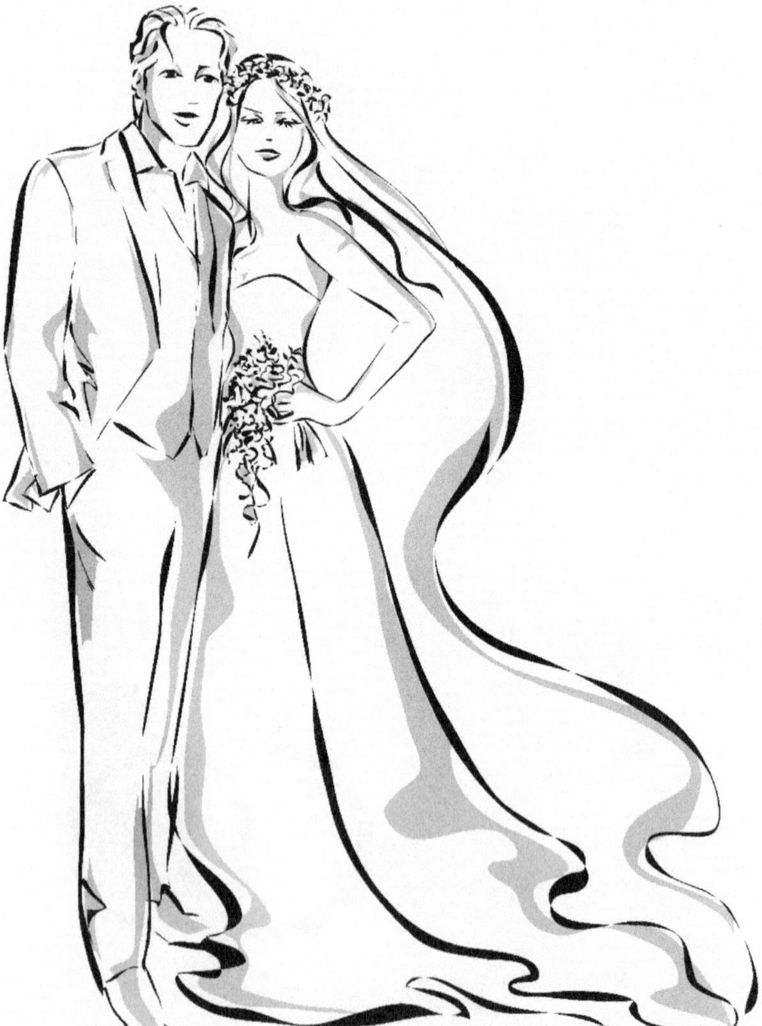

Four

Luke

I watch her walk out of the restaurant. My whole body has been one fucking vibrating nerve from when my eyes met hers. No matter how many times I tried to get her to look at me, she avoided me. But the times she did look at me, I was hoping she would give me something, anything to indicate she didn't hate me. But her shield was up. I knew it the minute she looked at me. It was a shield that took me a year to break down, and in the span of one second and a very fucking bad decision, it was back up again. "Are you going to be okay?" I hear Mikaela and turn to look at her.

"You couldn't have mentioned that the bride was

Clarabella?" I question while my hand grips the white rag that I used to carry out the hot plates.

"What difference would it have made? A bride is a bride." She puts her hands on her hips, shaking her head. "You've worked with her before."

"Yeah," my mouth says, but at the same time, my head says, *before you fucked up royally*. "Well, it's different working with her and working for her." I turn and walk away from Mikaela before I say something I shouldn't.

Instead of going to the kitchen and cleaning up my workstation, I head to the office. I slam the door behind me and toss the rag on the couch before going to the bathroom and turning on the cold water in the sink. My body feels like it's on fire as I cup my hands under the stream of cold water, splashing it on my face. When I close my eyes, all I see is her holding his hand and walking out with him.

She never looked back, not once, and trust me, I know because all I could do was stare at her. She was wearing tight black jeans that molded to her long legs, legs that I spent a whole night worshiping. Her ass fit perfectly in my hands when I picked her up. "You fucked up," I tell myself when I look at my reflection in the mirror.

I wipe my face with a towel. "She's getting married," I say in disbelief. "Fucking married." I shake my head, and the knock on the door has me turning my head. I don't know why, but for a split second, I think it's her.

For only one second before the door opens and Mikaela pokes her head in. "I come in peace." She's holding two glasses in her hand. She walks in and hands me one of the glasses with amber liquid inside.

"Thank you." I drink it down in two gulps, feeling the burn all the way down to my stomach.

"Jeez." She puts her own glass to her mouth. "Are you sure you're okay?"

"I'm fine." I put the glass down on the desk and then turn to lean on it. "When can we start the staff meeting?"

"In about thirty minutes." She takes a sip of her drink and goes to sit on the couch. "They are just cleaning up, the last customer left right now."

"What has been going on?" I ask. "Obviously, with me in New York, I wasn't hands-on like I was before I left."

"Everything is pretty much the same." She shrugs her shoulders. "Hostess girls have been hard to find." I nod my head. "We've taken a lot more catering jobs than we did before you left."

"That's always good to help us grow. Word of mouth is everything."

"It's also thanks to Clarabella for that," Mikaela says, and just hearing her name, my stomach sinks, and my heart speeds up. "She made us their top caterer at the venue."

"We were doing a lot of events before," I chime in. It was why I got so close to her, even though I knew it was a bad idea. But everything about her was amazing. Is amazing. She worked her ass off and never ever let you see her sweat. She was ballsy. She was sharp. She had an idea for how things needed to be. She never let anyone get away with talking down to her. She would nip that in the bud and make sure they knew she was not messing around. And she was absolutely drop-dead gorgeous.

"We were, but then she brought us in for corporate events, which then led to business booming every single day of the week," she points out, and I shake my head, wondering why she would do that after what I did to her. "It boosted sales, not just here but also at the pub."

My hands fist as she goes on and on about how amazing she is. Like I don't already fucking know. "Let's get this over with so I can get home and go to sleep."

She takes another sip, not caring that I just barked at her and that I'm taking it out on her because I'm pissed. "She also brought the pub in to do birthday parties and stuff."

I look over at her. "I'm going there tomorrow," I say. "Right before we go and visit the new place you were talking about."

"The one by the water?" she asks, and her eyes light up.

"That's the one," I confirm. When she called me a couple of weeks ago and told me about this place right by the water that was selling, I was hesitant at first until I saw the pictures. I saw what it could be, and it was a no-brainer. Nestled right over the lake near a marina, it is going to be a great summer spot for sure. "But I want to go in fifty-fifty," I say, and she just looks at me, shocked. "I know you don't have the capital right up front, so I'll put up the money, and you can pay me back."

"I don't know what to say," she whispers. It's no secret she's had a hard life. It's also no secret that for the past six months, she's run this place and the pub without taking one day off.

"You don't have to say anything," I reply, getting up. "You earned this." I open the door and walk out to see staff all around the bar. The hostess girls are on their phones, and I clear my throat. They don't even bother to look up.

"Can I have everyone's attention?" I raise my voice, and the girls finally look up at me. One of them even smirks at me. "For those of you who don't know me, I'm Luke, and I'm the boss."

Mikaela clears her throat. "I'm the second boss."

"Can we speed this up?" the blonde says, leaning back in her chair.

"We sure can," I say, crossing my arms over my chest. "You're fired." They both just look at me and then at each other, unsure of what to say or what the hell just happened.

"You can't just fire me!" the blonde retorts.

"Oh, but I can," I inform her. "You know why?" I wait for her to have one of her snarky comebacks. "Let me tell you why. One, you standing at that stand." I point at the hostess stand. "Which means when someone comes into this place, you are the first face they see. Do you think they want you to be on your phone and ignoring them?" I look at them, waiting. "Because if it was me, I wouldn't even give you a second thought and be out of here. Which means you're costing me money." They just look at me, and the other staff members avoid looking at them. "And if I'm not making money, no one is getting paid."

"It's not all the time," one of them says.

"Even one time is one time too many." I look over at Mikaela, who just nods. "If you're bored at the front, I'd rather see you walking around helping out by filling up water glasses than on your phone. So if those rules are too much to go by, the door is right there." I look around the room at everyone. "If demanding your full attention when you are working here is too much for any of you, now is your chance to speak up." I wait to see who will get up and who will stay. Even I'm surprised when no one moves, not even the blondes. "Good," I say, and Mikaela smiles. "With that said, I think we are going to be hiring more staff for behind the bar." The bartenders just nod their heads, and one puts up their hand.

"What about hiring someone just to deal with the tables?" he asks. "Lots of times, we are slammed with our own clients, and then we have the machine going nuts for the waitstaff."

I nod at him. "We will definitely be getting you some backup," I assure him. The rest of the meeting goes fast as I take the time to ask everyone what they like and what they are struggling with. It's something that I started in New York, and the workers just connected with you even more. If they think you're listening to them, they will work harder for you. Once the last person walks out of the door, I turn to Mikaela.

"I got to hand it to you," she says, smirking. "I thought those two were goners."

"Must be my charm," I joke, yawning and then

rubbing my hands over my face. "Let's go," I say, and we both walk out the back door. She locks it as I wait for her to get in her car before I get into my truck and head over to my house.

Pulling up in the driveway, I see that the front lights are on because they are set on a timer. I get out of the truck and walk over to the garage door, punching in the code. The door slowly starts to open. The beeping sound fills the garage, making me duck under the opening door and rush to the alarm panel to put in the code. The minute I finish putting in the last number, the beeping stops. I wait for the door to open before pressing the button to close it. I kick off my shoes once I walk up the two steps to the mudroom, not even turning on the light. My bedroom is right off the mudroom, and when I step in, the only light coming in is the reflection of the moon and the lights from outside. The bed is exactly how I left it, with the covers half on the floor. I stand here for a minute just looking at the bed, my heart beating so fast in my chest.

My feet move before my brain does, and I'm standing by the bed, my hand going to the empty glass sitting there. I pick it up, my head screaming at me to put it back down, but instead, I sit on the bed and look down at the glass with the lipstick stain. My fingertips rub over it as I remember handing her the glass in the kitchen. The memories of that night come rushing back like a wave during a storm over and over again. I can't escape it. I close my eyes, hoping to block it out, but all I see is her over me.

Her head was thrown back as she straddled me in the

middle of the bed. I look over, seeing that spot where her head was, and even after six months, it's still there. The last time I was in the house was with her. The last time I sat in this bed was the same time I told her that it was a mistake right before I packed my shit and left.

"What the fuck did you do?" I ask myself, hoping to answer my own question, but nothing comes out. The only thing I hear is the sound of the glass crashing into little pieces when it falls from my hand.

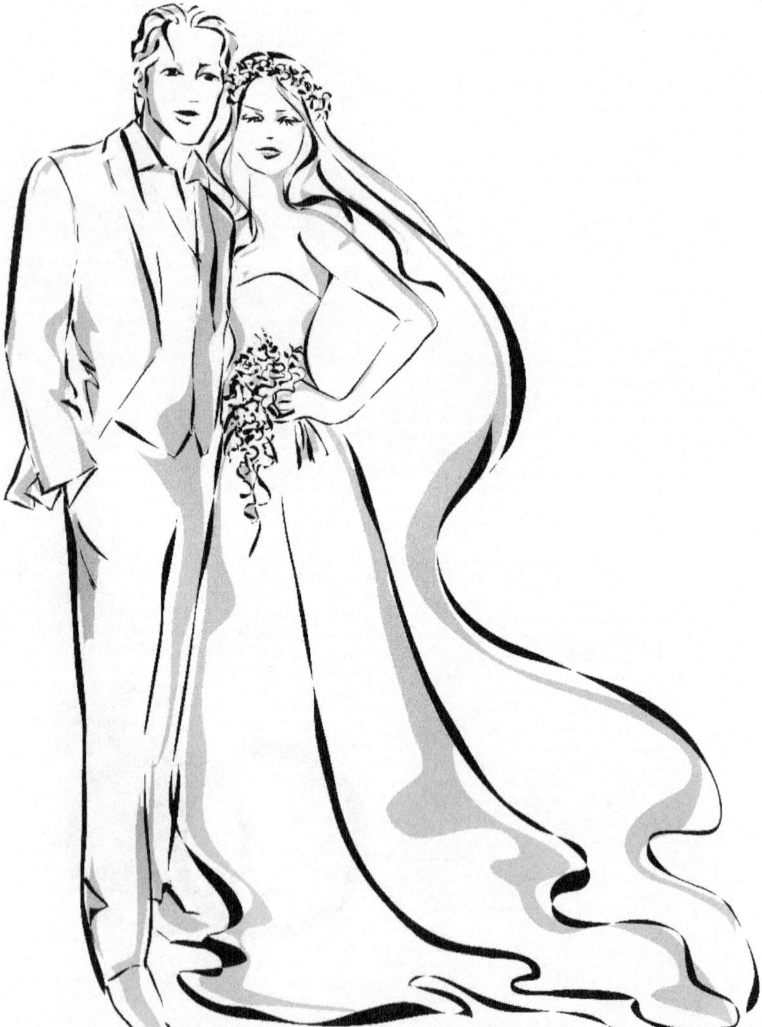

Five

Clarabella

The minute I shut the front door and hear Edward's car drive away, I walk over to the kitchen and take out the bottle of scotch that I have hidden in the back cupboard. A bottle that I said I would keep for company and never touch again. I unscrew the cap and don't even bother with a glass before taking a long pull from it. The burning hits all the way fucking down, and when I close my eyes, the memories of that fucking night come back.

"Working with you is so easy." He smiled from the other side of the counter as we both lingered. Until he asked me to have a drink with him at his house. I knew I shouldn't have gone. I knew it was a bad idea. I knew

it, yet all I could do was say, "okay." But instead, I left there with him and followed him to his house. There in his kitchen, with the lights on very low, he pulled out a bottle and poured us both a drink. Handing me my glass, he held up his. "To a great working relationship." I clinked the glass with his and stepped in a step. I took a sip of the scotch, and the next thing I knew, he was slipping his hand into mine and walking me to his bedroom. It was the best night of my life, and I literally had never felt so complete. It was everything that you see in romantic movies or read in romance novels. You have this connection with someone, and the minute you touch, it's electric. It all happened, or at least I thought it all happened until he woke up the next day and whispered four words that broke my heart.

I wipe the tear out of the corner of my eye, taking another sip of the scotch. The pain in my chest is just as much as it was that day. I ignore it all and push it far back in my head. In the little black box that I created for it. I walk over to the kitchen sink and pour the rest down the drain, tossing the bottle in the recycle bin.

The next day it's almost like I'm a zombie, or at least this is how I think a zombie would be. The black sunglasses covering my eyes which I had to spend extra time working on, to cover the fact that I tossed and turned all night long, pisses me off even more. *I bet he didn't even lose a minute of sleep, the bastard,* I think to myself as I walk up the steps to the office. I hold my coffee in one hand with my head down. I can feel a headache coming on and it's not even nine in the morning. Fine,

mine to CHERISH

the headache started last night after I left the restaurant, and I made it an excuse to stay at my place, knowing that he had to pack for an overnight trip he had to take for work. He's been going on those trips more and more, which, according to him, is a good sign.

I pull open the door and step in, looking around and smelling coffee in the air, so I know that someone is already here. I walk into my office, the sun streaming in and making it super bright. I am the only office with side-to-side windows in the corner, which is why I did a built-in bench all along the wall with huge pillows. A white table sits right in front of the bench with two plush light pink chairs on the other side. A big photo album is in front, with all the different styles of food we've done over the years. Even though I have a desk, I spend most of my time sitting at this table. I love looking outside during the day and seeing the sun.

I put my purse on the table and walk over to my desk, grabbing the files I need. "Jesus, do you own any other color but black?" I hear Shelby say when she walks into my office. She is wearing a light peach skirt with a white halter top. Her own coffee is in one hand as the other hand carries a couple of folders.

"What?" I look down at my outfit. The black leather skirt fits me like a glove and goes down to my knees. The tight black sleeveless body suit also molds onto me, paired with black patent stilettos.

"I swear, you got engaged, and boom, everything you own is now black. It's like you are in mourning." She laughs at her own joke and then stops walking as she looks at me.

"What are you guys talking about?" Presley says, coming into the room wearing cream-colored pants with a baby-blue silk top tied around her neck with a big bow.

"Do you think I wear too much black?" I turn now and ask her.

"I mean, you can definitely give Morticia a run for her money. I was thinking it was your gothic stage." She shrugs. "I'm just happy that you didn't choose a black wedding dress."

"Can you imagine Mom's face?" Shelby adds, laughing as she walks over to the white desk and puts her stuff on it as she pulls out one of the chairs.

"I haven't worn that much black," I huff.

"Okay," Shelby says, sitting down. "When was the last time you wore something other than black?"

"My thirtieth birthday party," I remind her, crossing my arms over my chest.

"And then you got proposed to and started wearing black," Presley points out. "Maybe it's your way of saying goodbye to your single life."

"That's the stupidest fucking thing I've ever heard." I sit on the bench, knowing Presley likes to sit in the chair.

"Okay, fine," Shelby says. "Tonight, I want you to go home and FaceTime me from your closet."

I glare at her. "Aren't you busy sucking your husband's dick until he chokes you?"

She throws her head back and laughs. "That was yesterday."

"Yeah, tonight it's her turn to ride his face," Presley

informs me, sitting down next to Shelby, who is just glaring at her. "Your voice carries. How is it my fault?"

"You could mind your own business." I point at Presley, who laughs.

"This from the woman who signed Shelby up on a dating site without telling her." Now it's my turn to glare at her.

"We did it together." My voice gets louder. "You think I came up with the name Shelby Wimbly by myself?" I shake my head.

"Okay, now that we got all this out of the way," Presley says, changing the subject. "What did you want to have this meeting about?"

"A couple of things," I say, grabbing my files. "The first is that we have to go over the events we have scheduled while I'm gone," I tell them, and they open their own folders. "Also, I think it's time we switch up divisions." They both stop and look at me as if I've grown a second head. "I'm tired of doing just the food," I lie to them, and I want to say they believe me, but they don't.

"You said just two weeks ago when I had to scramble for a new florist," Shelby states, "that you never want to do what I do."

"Last month, I had to get a new vendor for our crystal," Presley says. "And you walked out of the room and said, 'good luck with that.'"

"Yeah, well, I think that it's smart that we swap." I avoid their eyes, and I wait a minute, and when no one says anything, I look up at them. "What?" I ask, irritated.

"We are just waiting for the real reason." Shelby picks

up her coffee cup and brings it to her lips.

"Okay, fine." I take a deep breath. "Luke is back." I bring the cup of coffee to my lips, taking a sip and suddenly wishing it was scotch.

"What do you mean he's back?" Shelby asks, leaning back in her chair.

"I mean that I went to do my taste testing last night, and Luke is the one who cooked for us." I put my cup of coffee down and ignore the way my palms got sweaty from saying that. Or the fact that my stomach did a flip at the mention of his name, or the fact that my heart is beating so hard in my chest I'm having trouble controlling my breathing.

"Awkward," Presley says. "This explains why you look like shit." I flip her the bird. "Did you tell Edward?"

I glare at her. "What was I supposed to tell him?" I grit out through clenched teeth. "Please tell me what I was supposed to say, exactly. This is Luke. We banged once, and he took off the day after. Oh, I think we should go with the salmon."

"I'm sorry." Shelby holds up her hand. "Hold the phone. Did you just say you banged Luke?"

"Called it!" Presley leans back in her chair, and I just glare at her. "Obviously, that's beside the point. What did Luke say?"

"Nothing." I shake my head. "I mean, I think he was shocked I was the bride, and I felt him staring at me the whole time, but I didn't give him the time of day."

"Savage," Shelby says. "But I'm just going to state the obvious. It's bothering you."

"It is not," I counter so fast it would give anyone whiplash. "I'm pissed. There is a difference."

"But if you felt nothing, you wouldn't even be pissed," Presley points out, holding up her hands when I'm about to tell her to fuck off.

"I'm pissed because I was caught off guard," I say, at the same time that my subconscious laughs at me. "Also, what kind of fucking question is that?" The irritation in my voice is very apparent.

"I am not the enemy," Presley reminds me. "I'm just stating that if you feel this way—"

I stop her before she finishes the sentence because she isn't the only one who was thinking about this, and I put a quick stop to that one. "I don't feel any way," I snap.

"Okay, let me rephrase it for her." Shelby tries to defuse the bomb about to go off inside me. "If you feel that strongly about not working with him, then why don't you just switch to another vendor?"

I groan, thinking about stomping my feet like a kid having a tantrum. "Because you all know he's the best out there," I admit, and they share a look, neither of them sure what to say. "Ugh, fine, whatever. I'll just deal with it." I look at them. "I can make it work."

"What if you just ask to work with someone else?" Presley asks.

"So he can know that he gets to me?" I ask, and then I catch my words. "Even though he doesn't."

"He for sure doesn't get under your skin one little bit," Shelby says, and she rolls her lips.

"I hate you both," I say, getting up. "Is the mock-up

for my wedding day done?"

"It is," Presley confirms, standing. "Do we want to see it?"

"Can we get in a better mood before?" Shelby suggests, climbing out of her chair. "The last time you were in this mood when choosing the invitation for your wedding, it did not bode well." I might have gone off on the graphic designer just a touch, and she might have left in tears.

I stop in my tracks. "She said I didn't make her cry." I throw up my hands in frustration.

"She lied," Presley says. "Just like you are lying to yourself about—"

I hold up my hand to stop her from talking. "If you say his name, I'm going to throat punch you and make you wear a fucking hat to my wedding."

She laughs at me. "Joke's on you." She walks past me. "I look great in hats."

"You'll look even better with my foot up your ass," I mumble as she walks out of the room. I look over at Shelby. "Don't even start." I point at her. "Before I tell everyone you had sex in your office bathroom."

She gasps, "I did not."

I fold my arms over my chest. "Right there," I mimic her. "Yes, right there," I groan. "Don't stop," I moan.

"I can't get any privacy in this place," she huffs and walks past me. "Yeah, well, I bet you pictured Luke naked last night."

I roll my eyes. "Mature." I avoid looking at her eyes because I did indeed think of him naked last night, but

I also thought about him naked this morning and again right this minute. "I'm so fucked," I mumble to myself as I walk over to the venue space, ignoring the way my sister laughs at me.

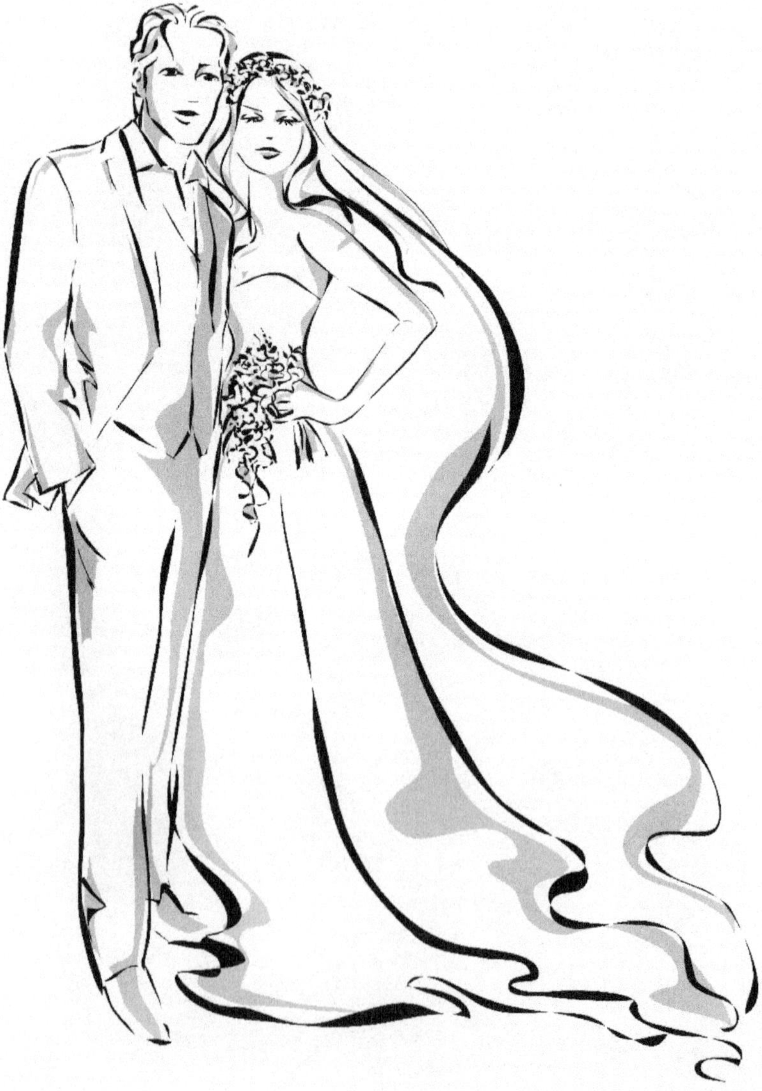

Six

Luke

My phone rings from the bedside table, and my eyes open once and then close again, ignoring it for a minute. I'm on my stomach in the middle of the bed with my face down on one of the pillows that smell exactly like her. My cock goes even harder as it presses into the bed and the images of her pushing me down and riding me. I groan in frustration. All fucking night, that is the only thing I dreamed of. It was the only thing in my dreams. Everywhere and nowhere. If I closed my eyes tight enough, I could even hear her calling my name over and over again. My arms wrapped around her waist, her head thrown back as I kissed her throat.

I turn over from the middle of my bed, opening my eyes. The room is still dark, thanks to the blackout curtains I had installed when I moved in. My hand slaps the phone on the side table to shut off the alarm. I take a second to just lie here in the bed, looking up at the ceiling. The same ceiling I spent most of the night looking at, waiting for it to tell me what the fuck to do. The same ceiling I focused on when I told her the words that broke me before they broke her. The same ceiling I looked up at while she got up and got dressed, storming out.

Throwing the covers off me, I walk over to the kitchen and start the coffee machine before going to the bathroom. I wash my face and brush my teeth, running my wet hands through my hair, then slip on some black jeans and a black T-shirt before I walk back into the kitchen and pour myself a cup of coffee to go. Grabbing my keys and phone, I head out to the garage, pressing the button, then arming the alarm before walking out. The sun hits my eyes right away, and I have to squint a bit. The heat also hits me, making me shake my head. "Nothing like May in the South."

Getting in my truck, I make my way over to the pub, knowing they should be setting up for lunchtime. The meeting is shorter than I thought it would be, and when I get in the truck, the words keep going over and over in my head. *"Clarabella has really pushed events our way."* The minute they said her name, I was all fucked up. It's like I couldn't even concentrate until I spoke to her. Not only did she keep working with my restaurants after I left but she also pushed them big-time. It just didn't make sense to me. Nothing about anything made sense. I knew coming back would be hard for me, but I didn't know it would be this hard. For my whole life, I never connected with anyone, and it was the way I liked it. Until that one night with Clarabella linked me with her on a different level, and I wasn't expecting it.

I pull up in the venue's driveway, knowing this is a bad idea. I even told myself it was a bad idea. I was heading to the restaurant, but my car drove me here. I park where I always used to park behind the venue spot, right off the kitchen. When I pull open the back door, the cold air hits me right away, and I put my aviator sunglasses on the top of my head. My palms are getting a touch sweaty when I think back to all the times I was here. Ignoring the way my heart is beating, I walk into the kitchen, and I have to stop when the memory of the first time I walked into this place comes rushing back to me.

The place had just caught on fire, and she was scrambling to get food for her brother's wedding. The two of us waited in the kitchen after the wedding got canceled, and I stood right in front of her. "So you finally caved and called me." I had to put my hands in my back pockets, or I would have been tempted to lean in and touch the curl in front of her face. It was a perfect curl, also one that you could have stuck your finger right through.

"I was at the bottom of the barrel." She didn't back down from me when I stared into her crystal blue eyes. I couldn't help but laugh. I took a step closer to her, her lips calling out to me to kiss her, but Travis walked into

the kitchen, and in that split second, the moment was over.

"Just say what you need to say and leave," I tell myself and walk into the venue space. It's usually filled with tables and decorations. But this time, it's empty except for a table in the middle of the room. I look around, seeing if anyone is here because someone is usually always walking around doing something. But for once, it's eerily quiet. All you can hear is my boots on the wooden floor.

I walk over to the round table in the middle of the room. The champagne-colored tablecloth hits all the way to the floor. The gold chairs around the table have a sheer ivory sheet over the back, and it's tied with the same color ribbon as the table. White plates fill the table with white napkins in the middle with a ribbon tied to it. It looks fancy as fuck, especially with one crystal champagne glass, a wineglass, a water glass, and another shot glass. The ivory flowers in the middle of the table complete the look. I'm so entranced by the table I don't hear the heels clicking until they are in the same room as me.

My eyes fly up when I feel eyes on me, and I see her standing there looking at me. "Sorry, I came in from the back." I point to the back of the kitchen. My heart goes crazy in my chest at her appearance. If I thought she was sexy before, fuck, she upped her game since I've been gone. Her hair is a touch shorter than it was the last time. The front is moved to the side and tucked behind her ear.

"What are you doing here?" She doesn't move from her spot, and to be honest, I'm afraid to move from my spot. Thinking that one move and she'll just be gone.

"I came by so we can talk." I put my hands in my back pockets so she doesn't see them shake.

"Nothing to talk about," she says. "You can let yourself out the same way you came in." She turns to walk out of the room.

"Clarabella." I say her name, and she stops. I can tell she's pissed just by the way her shoulders go square. She turns, and the ice-blue eyes that I once loved looking into, well, if looks could kill, I would be dead. "I really think we need to talk."

"There is not one thing in this world that I want to talk to you about, Luke," she deadpans.

"You are still using my restaurants as your primary vendor." I never move my eyes from her.

"Okay, and?" she says.

"Why?" I ask the question I've been asking myself since Mikaela told me about how much she works with her. "After everything that went down."

"Nothing went down," she retorts, making me pissed. "It was a mistake." The words cut me to the core, and it serves me right since those were the words I told her. *Nothing was a mistake*, my head screams.

"I'm back now." I wait to see if her face changes, but it doesn't. It just stays the same with the big shield up, and I fucking hate it. But then again, I put it there. It's there because of me.

"I don't see what that matters." She folds her arms over her chest. "Working with Mikaela is easy, and the two of us mesh well."

"With me back, she'll be taking a step back and focusing just on the restaurant." I watch her to see if it sinks in. "You won't be working with her anymore. You'll be working with me again."

"Again, I don't see why that would matter to me." She unfolds her arms. "My clients deserve the best, and the best is what your restaurant gives me. So until it changes, that is what I'm going to work with."

"I'm sorry that I left like that." The words come out before I can stop them, and I see right away they get to her, but she masks it.

"I don't care." She shrugs. "I don't care that you left. I don't care that you're back. What I care about is the service that you provide for my clients." Her words gut me. "Now, if you'll excuse me, I have a meeting with a client."

She turns to walk out, and I see the tattoo at the bottom of her neck. The tattoo that I traced with my tongue right before I slipped into her. "It's a beautiful table," I compliment, and she looks over her shoulder. "Very elegant."

"Thank you," she says. "I hope my wedding guests will love it." My mouth hangs open as I look at her and then back at the table. The sound of her heels clicking gets farther and farther away from me.

"She's getting married," I say the words out loud, hoping it will finally register in my brain that she is off the market and is in the "do not go there" category. "Motherfucker," I curse with all the pent-up anger I kept at bay in front of her. Having her stand there in front of me and totally brush me off killed me inside, but I don't know what I expected. I thought for sure she would rip me a new one and ask me why the fuck I did it. But I did not plan for her to brush me off. For her to stand in front of me and act like it didn't even bother her. At least that is what it looked like. Except for that one second when her guard slipped, and I saw the hurt in her eyes.

My eyes roam over the table again as I look at everything so neatly done. I want to rip everything off the fucking table and throw it to the floor.

But I don't. Instead, I turn and walk back out the door I walked into, not once looking back.

I slam the door of my truck a lot harder than I have to. Starting it and backing up, I put my glasses back on my eyes as I do what I told myself not to do. I take one look back, knowing where her office window is. I stare into it, hoping that she comes to the window, but nothing happens. Nothing happens except the roar that rips out of me and the fist that punches the steering wheel.

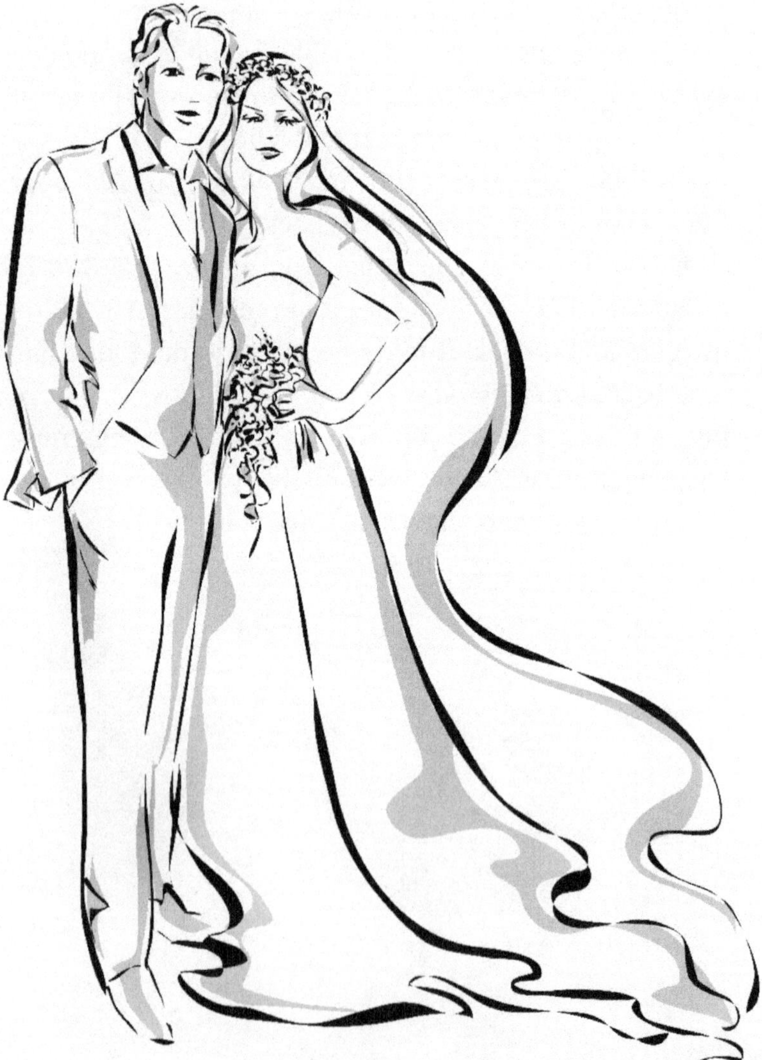

Seven

Clarabella

"Happy day before the wedding day!" Shelby enters the bridal suite while my hair is being fixed with two crystal champagne glasses in her hand. She is wearing a blush-pink tulle dress, with a beaded belt, that goes all the way to the floor. It flows when she walks, and the minute she tried it on, she bought it.

"Happy day before the wedding day," I respond back to her, smiling. That saying was something that we started to say at the beginning when we got our first couple of clients.

She comes and hands me a glass and clinks it with mine. "To the last penis you will ever have." She makes me laugh as I take a sip. The hairdresser blow-dries my hair into a perfect bob. I cut it a bit too short last time, thinking that it would grow back in time for the wedding, but it didn't, and we are just going to have to go with it. My mother tried to talk me into getting extensions, but she nixed that idea when I bought a wig with horrible bangs and showed up at her house. So they are going to go with my short hair that is layered in the front.

"To the last penis of my life," I say once I finish the whole glass.

The door opens, and Presley comes in, in her own blush-pink dress, but hers molds to her body. She went the opposite of Shelby and said since she was the only single one left, she had to be sexy for all of us. Her black hair is parted in the middle and pinned back into a ponytail. "I come bearing booze." She holds up the champagne bottle in one hand and a glass in the other. "Happy day before the wedding day."

"Fill 'er up," I invite, handing her my empty glass. "How is it going out there?"

"Well, the groom is already here," Presley says, popping the bottle of champagne. "Which is already better than Shelby's wedding." I laugh.

"And you only have the two of us as bridesmaids, so it's safe to say he hasn't fucked either of us," Shelby assures me, holding her own glass up and swallowing what was left.

"I mean, I don't know about you guys, but that's winning in my book." I clap my hands together. "Thank you for not sleeping with him." Presley hands me my glass of champagne, and I take a gulp.

"Anything for you," Presley teases. "I mean, it does help that he's the opposite of my type."

"That." Shelby points at her. "And I have my own pole to ride at home."

"I'm going to throw up if you keep calling Ace's dick a pole." I'm finishing my glass of champagne when there is another knock on the door.

"Can I join the party?" Harlow asks, poking her head in and smiling at us. "Actually, your brother is pinching my ass, so can we join the party?" I nod, and she opens the door and walks in wearing a long black dress that looks like lace. It has no sleeves, and when it gets to her knees, it's all see-through. "I wore black for you," she says. "So you feel at home."

"Happy wedding rehearsal," Travis says, holding up the drink in his hand. It's a low glass with amber liquid inside, and I hold out my hand.

"One, it's happy day before the wedding day," I declare, waiting for him to give me his glass. "And two, I just want a sip." He comes over and hands me his glass.

"I thought you gave up scotch," Presley quizzes from behind me as I bring the glass to my lips and take a sip. The burning on the way down makes me close my eyes.

"I did. I just wanted to taste it," I say, not bothering to give him back his glass. The hairdresser finishes my hair and leaves the room for me to get dressed.

"How crazy is it out there?" I ask Travis, who just smiles.

"Nothing caught on fire," he confirms, and we all

gasp.

"The universe," Shelby says. "You guys fucked around with that at my wedding, and look what happened."

"You became a legend and then had a week-long affair with your best friend," Presley reminds her. "Then married him." She finishes her glass of champagne. "I call that winning."

"I'm just going to say it," Harlow says. "If this wedding doesn't happen, your mother…" She shakes her head. "She already said she's moving."

We all laugh at her now. "My mother isn't going anywhere. You have her grandkids, and this one is going to be pregnant any day now with the amount of sex they have."

"Keep the drink." Travis grimaces as he walks over to the couch. "Why doesn't the groom's room have all this shit?" he asks, looking around the room. "There should be a comfy couch in there and a television to watch sports while we wait."

"Put that in the suggestion box right next to the 'fuck off, we don't care' box at the front door," Shelby says to him. Harlow shakes her head and walks over to him. He opens his legs for her, and she steps inside them, turning and sitting on his lap. His hand sits at the base of her back as they share a smile. My stomach flutters with the nerves I didn't know I had, and I push them aside. I also push aside the voice that asks me when was the last time I looked at Edward like that.

I inhale and take another sip of the scotch. "It's going to be fine." I speak the words out loud, and even I'm shocked they came out of me. My sisters share a look, and Harlow looks at me with wide eyes, meaning that the words actually came out of my mouth. "I mean, everything is done, right? All the things are in place."

"Everything has been checked," Shelby says.

"Double-checked," Presley fills in. "The groom is here. Nothing is going to catch on fire." She glares over at Travis. "No one slept with anyone they shouldn't sleep with." She looks at Harlow.

"Obviously, I was supposed to sleep with him." Harlow wraps her arm around Travis's shoulders and leans down to kiss him when there is another knock on the door.

"It's Grand Central Station," I mumble, taking another sip of the scotch when the door opens and Ace comes in.

"I was told that I needed to come in here and see if everything was okay," he announces, walking in and smiling at everyone until he sees Shelby, and his smile gets even bigger. "Edward is getting anxious outside waiting for you."

"At least he isn't beating down her door." Presley looks at him and raises her eyebrows. "Like a barbarian." She laughs. "Me man, you my woman," she says in a caveman's voice, making us all laugh.

"She called me and said help," Ace says, putting his arm around Shelby. "What was I supposed to do?"

"Ignore her like any proper groom does," I reply, getting up out of the chair. "Okay, time to get into my outfit."

"I'm out," Travis and Ace both say at the same time.

"I'm going to go make sure your mother is okay," Harlow states, coming to me and hugging me. "Take your time."

They walk out of the room, and I walk over to the curtain, pulling it open and seeing my outfit hanging in the middle of the room. "You going to put that glass down to get dressed?" Shelby asks from beside me, and I look down and see that my hand is gripping the glass so tight my knuckles are almost white.

"Yes," I mumble, putting it down on the table. I slip off the white satin robe that my sisters got me for the day. I'm already in my bra and panties set that they also got me for this night. "I'm nervous, I think." I look at Shelby and wait for her to tell me it's normal.

I slip into the white pants that are tight on top and then go straight down. Zipping it closed at the side. The pants reach midcalf and are tailored to me. "Like my heart is beating so fast," I say, putting my hand on my chest as I grab the beige and white top, putting my hands in the delicate sleeves that have hand-embroidered flowers that go all the way up my arm flowing to the front of it. Neither of them says anything as they watch me get dressed, which isn't helping my nerves. "I need someone to button me up," I inform them, looking over and seeing Presley wipe a tear from the corner of her eye. She comes to me and fastens the five buttons at the base of my back that lead to a train that goes down to the floor with hand-embroidered flowers scattered all over it. I put my hand to my chest and turn around, looking at them. "Is this okay?" I ask about the pantsuit I picked out to wear tonight.

"It's so you," Shelby confirms.

"Thank God it's not black." Presley walks over to the table, grabbing the glass of scotch and handing it to me. "How about you finish this, and then you can come out." I nod my head.

"That grand entrance," Shelby says. "And it's totally normal for the nerves."

"Were you nervous when you were getting married?" I ask. "Either time works."

"With Joseph, I was," she admits. "With Ace, I just wanted to get it over with." I nod at her and take a sip of the scotch. "Everyone is different."

"Put your shoes on and then come out," Presley instructs, and the two of them leave me alone in the room. I slip my feet in the nude shoes I bought to go with this outfit, then walk over to the mirror and look into it.

I look at myself from head to toe. "You are getting married," I remind myself. "Edward is perfect." I close my eyes for a minute to think back to when we met. I only said yes to his date to prove to myself that Luke meant nothing to me. I kept going out with him to spite him, if I'm honest. The first couple of dates, I made it a point to go to the restaurant, hoping to run into him, hoping to show him that he didn't break me. That was my goal, but Edward was so kind and loving. He was attentive and just everything that you want in a guy, and then it was a disservice to him to keep thinking about Luke, so a month after we started dating, I put him in a black box at the back of my mind and refused to think about him until my thirtieth birthday party.

Until Edward stood there in the middle of the venue on bended knee, asking me to marry him. I was caught off guard, and I didn't have a chance to block Luke out. Instead, while he was on his knee, the only thing I saw in my head was Luke smiling at me and laughing. I forced him back into the box and agreed to marry Edward. He was my choice. He was the right choice.

The knock on the door makes me look up, and I realize I have a tear running down my face. I use my palm to wipe my face, avoiding looking in the mirror. "We said grand entrance." Presley sticks her head in. "But this is overdoing it, even for you."

"I'm coming," I say, gulping down the rest of the scotch and putting the glass down. "Can you do me a favor?"

"No." She shakes her head and opens the door so I can walk out with her.

"Good, can you give me a glass of wine but make sure it's scotch?" I say, and she just looks at me.

"They aren't even the same color," she tells me.

"They will be if you use a black wineglass," I suggest, and she gasps at me.

"Wow, she gets married, and all of a sudden, she becomes devious." She shakes her head. "I'm on it." She squeezes my hand. "Now go in there and pretend you're happy," she says and walks away from me.

"I am happy," I mumble to myself. I take a deep breath before walking out, the whole time pretending I'm happy.

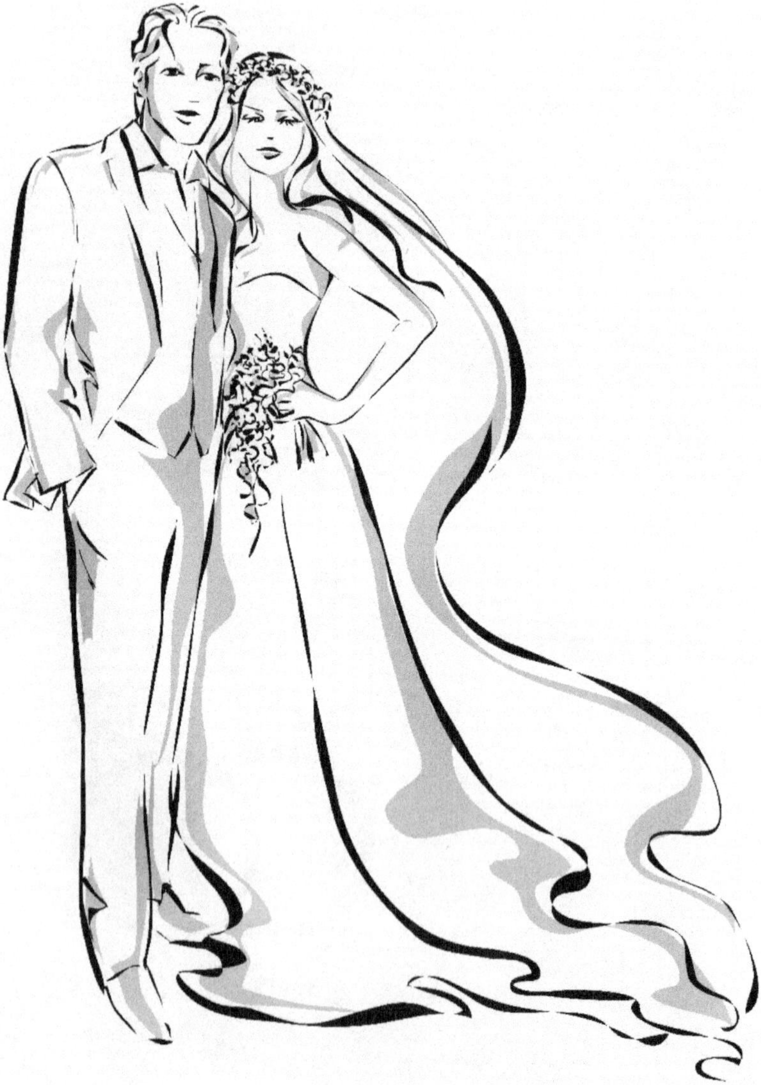

Eight

Clarabella

"Is that hammering?" I mumble with my eyes still closed. My cheek is wet from the drool that formed a puddle around my mouth. "What is that noise?" I attempt to pry my eyes open at the same time that I try to swallow, but neither of those actions is working.

"Happy wedding day," I hear my mother say as she walks into the room.

"What?" I ask, and the hammering continues.

"Oh my God," she says. "What the hell happened in here?"

"It was Shelby's fault," Presley mumbles from somewhere in the room, but then I feel movement beside me. "She was the one who stole the good juice."

"Ugh, no, it's not." I feel the cover pull off me, and then a big thud hits the floor.

"Motherfucker," Shelby curses as my mother gasps.

"Oh my God, are you okay?" I can hear her running to the bed.

"Did she fall out of the bed?" Presley gets up, sitting beside me. "Is she okay?"

"I think I broke my face," Shelby mumbles. "Mom, get off me."

"I'm not on you," my mother huffs. "I'm trying to help you up."

"Why is it so loud?" I say, trying to fall back asleep. "Can everyone be quiet?"

"Get up!" my mother shouts. "All of you get up."

"Presley," I mumble. "Tell her she's not the boss of us."

"You tell her," Presley replies. "She looks like she's about to whip our asses."

"She can't touch me. I'm getting married. If I have bruises, Child Protective Services is going to be called."

"You're thirty!" my mother yells. "Now get up. The car is going to be here in thirty minutes, and you all stink."

"I don't stink," Presley defends, and I open my eye just in time to see her raise her arm and smell her armpit. "Maybe a little. I was stuck in the middle of these two all night long." She pushes my shoulder now, and it's just the push I need to fall off the fucking bed.

I scramble to hold on, but my ass hits the floor with

a bang. "Fuck," I swear and just lie here. "I think that smell is me."

"You!" my mother shouts and points at me. "You are getting married today, and you look like you just crawled out of a dumpster." I gasp and close one of my eyes because the pounding that I thought was hammering before is my head.

"She does have raccoon eyes," Presley notes from the middle of the bed, and I laugh at her.

"Whatever, at least my hair is real." I point at her, seeing one of her extensions hanging by a thread.

Shelby sits up from the other side of the bed. "What the fuck happened?" We all gasp when we see that her lip is bleeding. "Why do I taste metal?"

"You're bleeding," my mother says, throwing her hands up in the air. "One time," she huffs as she runs out of the room to the bathroom. "All I asked for is to make one time go smoothly." She comes back in with a wet rag and hands it to Shelby, who puts it on her lip for a second and then takes it off, gasping when she sees the light pink. She gets up and storms over to the mirror, looking at her lip. "Just one time, can I be calm on the day of the wedding?"

"Relax," I say, standing up and falling on the bed. "Everything is fine." I lie back down on the pillow. "Everyone gets drunk before their wedding."

"Really?" my mother huffs. "Name one person." She puts her hands on her hips.

"Shelby," I declare, pointing over Presley toward Shelby, who turns and looks at us.

"That was because my fiancé was fucking someone else," she retorts, turning back to look in the mirror. "Oh my God, it's getting bigger." She points at her lip.

"I think I need to shower," I say, getting up. "Maybe that will help."

I stand, and the room spins again. "I might need to maybe eat something." I walk out to the bathroom.

"You have five minutes!" my mother yells from the bedroom as I close the door and start the shower. I don't even look in the mirror. Instead, I just get in the shower and let the water cascade all around me. Last night was amazing, and all the nerves went out the window the minute I walked down the aisle. He was my choice because I loved him. He treated me like a princess, and when I held his hand in mine, there was a calmness to it. He wanted me more than anything, and every single day, he has proved it to me. I am going to spend the rest of my life showing him that he chose the right woman.

"Here." Presley opens the door as soon as I turn off the water. "You need to wear this." She puts the satin set on the counter.

I look at her in her own satin set that looks like she got it from under her bed. "What happened to that one?" I point at her.

"I forgot it in my bag last night, and I wanted to steam it, but 'let's do shots,'" she mimics me, "happened. Well, it's fine. I'll steam it once we get to the bridal suite."

"Is mine like that?" I ask, picking up mine and seeing the creases from it just being taken out of the box.

"It's fine," she hisses. "Just hurry up. The car is here."

I walk out of the bathroom two minutes later and hear Presley yelling for me. "Can we get on with the program?" I walk down the stairs, looking over at Shelby, who is wearing an eye mask around her mouth.

"What the fuck is that?" I point at her and try not to laugh.

"It's the only thing that I can think of to help slow down the swelling." She throws her hands up. "Can we just get going?" She opens the door and stops, making Presley and me look over at her. "What the fuck is this?" She bends down, and I see a brown bag there. "Who the fuck ordered McDonald's?"

I gasp. "That was me." I push her aside and look down at not one but two big bags. "I forgot about this."

"When the fuck did you order this?" Presley leans down and grabs the bag.

"I asked you if you wanted to eat; you said get me a burger," I remind her. "And then the phone fell on your face when you tried to put in your order."

"Oh, yeah," she says. "But"—she gasps—"we ordered forty-seven burgers."

"No." I shake my head. "I put four burgers and seven fries." I grab the bill from her.

"Well, according to that," Presley states, "you ordered forty-seven burgers and one french fry."

"I told you that you need to wear glasses," Shelby chides from beside me, and I glare at her.

"The one looks like a seven," I huff, picking up the bag of food and grabbing a burger.

"You aren't going to eat that?" Presley asks me while

she grimaces. "It's been outside since three o'clock."

I open the wrapper and smell it. "It smells okay. Mom, can I eat a burger that's been outside since three o'clock?"

"Yes," she says, walking out of the house. "If one wants to have food poisoning."

I look at the burger and then my mother getting into the waiting limo. "We can swing by and get you something to eat," she tells me, and I look back down at the burger. "You really want to chance standing at the altar and then shitting yourself?"

"Ugh, fine," I say, tossing the burgers in the outside garbage bin. "She's such a buzzkill."

After we get into the car, I put my head back on the seat and fall asleep in a matter of five seconds. I stay asleep until the car stops, and I hear someone slam the car door. "Did we stop for food?" I ask them, and they nod their heads, holding up the brown bag.

The back door of the car opens, and my mother gets out first, thanking the driver. I get out after her and walk toward the bridal suite. Mallory is there outside holding a silver tray with four champagne glasses. "Oh my," she says when she sees me. "Happy wedding day, Clarabella."

I grab one of the glasses off the tray. "Thank you so much." I smile at her, and she looks over as Presley and Shelby climb out of the car.

"Someone had a good time," she notes, rolling her lips.

"You have no idea," I say, pulling open the door and

walking into the bridal suite.

The photographer is there to capture the first look, and she just stops. "Someone didn't clean off their makeup from last night," she observes and rubs her finger under her eye.

"I told you that you looked like a raccoon," Presley says from behind me, walking in and going over to plop down into the chairs, putting the brown bag in the middle of the table.

I walk over to the wall where four stations are set up with gold vanities and matching gold plush chairs in front of them. Mirrors with big chunky gold frames hang down in front of each chair. I look at myself and gasp. I look like I have two black eyes. The black mascara from last night plus the water from the shower is not a good look. "I went out of the house like this?" I question, looking back at Presley while Shelby walks to the mirror and takes off the eye mask that she had tied around her mouth.

"I look like I got lip injections," she whines, turning to look at us.

"Yeah, on only one side," I joke, laughing. "And then chickened out for the other side."

"Okay." The makeup artist enters the room. "How are we doing?" She claps her hands, and the hairdresser behind her just gasps.

"It's like *The Hangover* without the face tattoo." She looks at all of us.

"And the tiger in the bathroom," Presley deadpans, biting into her sausage biscuit.

"I need a shower," Shelby says. "I feel like I partied hard last night."

"You did," I point out, sitting down next to Presley and grabbing a sandwich. "You were jumping on the bed singing 'Girls Just Want to Have Fun.'" I laugh. "Mom came in and said the whole ceiling was shaking."

"And then she went into the bathroom and FaceTimed Ace," Presley shares. "And tried to have phone sex with him, and he said he was hanging up on her." Shelby gasps, putting a hand to her mouth as she remembers.

"Then she cried that he didn't love her." I can't help the laugh that comes out of me.

"I did not cry," she denies, shaking her head.

"You did, and he had to call Mom to make sure you were okay." I roll my lips, thinking of what else she did.

"Then you went into the bath," Presley says, "fully clothed and started singing nobody knows my sorrow." I can't help but spit out my food. "'Nobody Knows the Trouble I've Seen.' While the rain shower poured down on you."

"I thought that was a dream," Shelby says, sitting down on the couch in front of us. "It's all like a blur."

"If that doesn't say it was a perfect night." Presley sits up. "I don't know what does." She holds up her hand for me to give her a high five. I slap her hand, missing the first time but getting it the second. "Now, let's get this bitch married."

"Yes, let's," I agree, finishing the glass of champagne. "I'm getting married today." I clap my hands, not knowing what is to come.

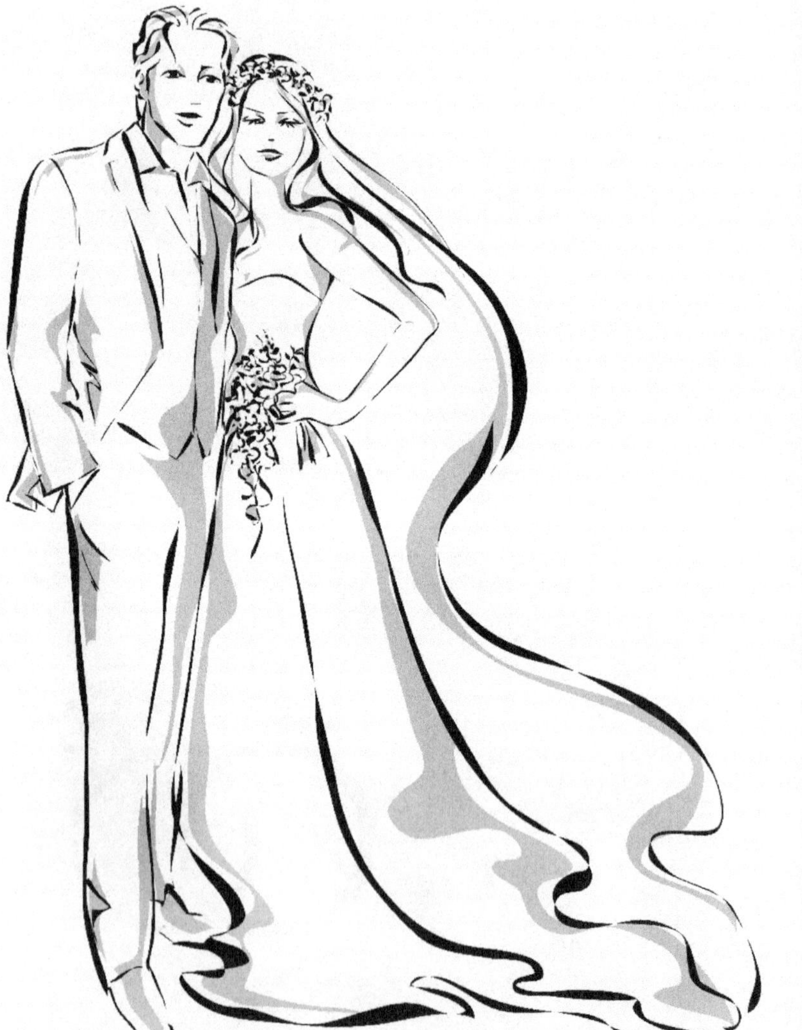

Nine

Clarabella

"How are you holding up?" Presley asks from beside me as she closes her eyes and gets her makeup done. She's in her peach satin robe with the word MOH on the back of it. I look down at my own white satin robe with the word BRIDE embroidered on the back.

"I'm feeling a million times better," I say, looking at my reflection in the mirror, which is night and day to how I started the morning. My raccoon eyes have been washed off, and my makeup is on point. My stomach even feels better, ever since I put some food into it, hopefully soaking up all the alcohol I drank last night. The flutters are there in full force, and I'm wondering if it's normal. I look over at Presley, taking a sip of my champagne. "I'm a bit nervous." I put my hand to my stomach when there is a knock on the door. I'm not going to even lie. Every single time there is a knock on the door, I expect it to be bad news. They say expect the unexpected until he slips on the wedding band, so I'm expecting the worst.

"May I enter?" Travis sticks his head in and sees all of us sitting in the chairs getting our hair and makeup done. Once he sees that everyone is dressed, he comes in wearing his black suit that we picked out for him to wear. He is the one walking me down the aisle. "I was in charge of delivering this." He pulls a box from behind his back. It's wrapped in white with a black satin bow. He hands it to me and leans down to kiss my cheek. "You look beautiful," he whispers softly in my ear, and I smile at him and look down at the gift in my hand.

"Aw, isn't that nice," Shelby says. "Open it." She claps her hands excitedly.

I put my champagne glass on the table in front of me next to the silver ice bucket holding the bottle in it. "Do I read the card first?" I look over at my sisters for an answer.

"No," Shelby says while Presley puffs out, "Absolutely not."

I laugh as I pull on the black sash, then turn over the long box, sliding my hand under the tape to rip the paper away. I open the black velour box, my hands shaking as I see the diamond tennis bracelet. "Oh my goodness." I gasp in shock as my finger trails over it. I put it down on the desk and open the card, seeing his writing.

Clarabella,
To an eternity of love.
Edward

The stinging of tears starts at my eyes, and I laugh it off as I fan my face. "I can't cry." I look at the makeup artist, who shakes her head, telling me I can't cry.

"Just remember," Presley scoffs. "You had raccoon eyes not too long ago." I can't help but laugh now, yet the nerves don't go away. Instead, they come on full force now, and I try to steady the beating of my heart.

There is another knock on the door, and this time when it opens, it's my mother, still dressed in her own satin robe with a MOB on it. We joked with her that at this point, she should just join the mob. Her eyes scan the room as she looks for Shelby and Presley. I can see the look of panic in her eyes. "What happened?"

"Nothing happened." She shakes her head. "Can't I talk to my daughters without something being wrong?" She wrings her hands in front of her nervously, so I know something is wrong.

"You can, but not with that face." I point at her. "That was the same face you had on when…" I try to think of when she did that face, and my heart starts to beat erratically as I sit up in the chair. I push away the hairdresser and stand. "What happened?" I look at my sisters, who sit up and get out of their own chairs.

"Let's calm down," Shelby tells me, holding her hands up when I glare at her. "Whatever happens, it's not as bad as you think it will be."

"Yeah," Travis says. "Look at how bad mine turned

out to be." He laughs and puts his hands in his pockets. "Everything burned down and…"

"And you never got married!" I shriek, and my mother slaps his arm.

"Idiot," she mumbles. "Everything is fine." She smiles. "But I need to speak to one of your sisters about something private."

"Private?" I yell. "Since when has anything been private with our family?"

"Never," Presley confirms. "You might as well say whatever it is you want to say. She isn't going to let you not say anything."

"Yeah, what she said." I point at Presley.

"Okay, fine. Mallory said that the caterer hasn't arrived yet," my mother says, throwing her hand in the air. "Now, will you sit back down and finish getting your hair done."

"What do you mean the caterer hasn't arrived?" The blood drains from my face and travels to the back of my neck, making it hot. The only thing going through my head is Luke doing this to spite me. Also, I'm going to murder him with my bare hands. I'm going to wrap my hands around his neck and choke him. I look at my sisters, and they both have wide eyes, but only one second passes before there is another knock on the door. I feel like I'm about to crawl out of my skin at this moment.

"Hi," Ace greets, poking his head in. He looks around and finally stops when he spots Shelby. "What happened to your mouth?" He points at her, coming in wearing the same suit as Travis since he's going to be walking my mom down the aisle.

"Presley pushed me off the bed with her big ass." She points at Presley, who laughs at her.

"Anyway, Mallory said to tell you crisis averted," Ace says, and my mother looks at me.

"See, I told you it was fine." She rolls her eyes at me. "Now sit down and finish your hair." She points at the chair, and I sit back down and grab my glass of champagne.

"Can someone please go check and see what the fuck was just going to happen?" I ask, smiling, but inside, I'm freaking out.

"I'll go," Shelby volunteers and then starts to walk past Ace, who stops her. "Oh, now you want to talk to me?" He laughs at her and grabs her hand. "No." She shakes her head, but she doesn't make any move to step away from him.

"Come here." He pulls her to him and slips his arms around her. "I missed you last night."

"You hung up on me!" she shrieks at him.

"You wanted me to show you my private area," Ace reminds her, looking at my mother. "I didn't, obviously."

"I've seen your private area," Shelby protests.

"So have we," Presley says, holding up her hand, and I just shrug.

"I turned around," I admit, finishing my drink.

"I did not," Presley says, giggling. "I'm not picking sides." She looks at Shelby and then at Travis. "But this is the best first wedding we've done."

"Mine doesn't count," Travis declares. "The fucking

place caught on fire."

"My ex was sleeping with his ex," Shelby says, pointing from her to Ace.

"Well, when you're perfect, you're perfect," I say, holding up my empty glass. "Can someone top me up?"

"How about we stop the topping up and start drinking some water," my mother suggests, and I look at her.

"It's my wedding day." I put my hand on my chest. "I'm allowed to drink."

"Just be happy it's champagne and not scotch," Shelby announces, and I wink at her.

It takes me thirty more minutes until she places the crystal headpiece at the side of my head. "There," Shelby says, and my mouth gets dry. "Now it's perfect." She makes sure everything is tucked where it should be.

"I think I'm ready to get dressed." I turn and look at everyone. Travis and Ace share a look, and after kissing Shelby goodbye, Ace follows Travis out.

"Okay, here we go." My mother walks into the room. My sisters' dresses are hanging in the middle of the room, right next to my dress that is fitted on a mannequin. "Let's get you in your dress," my mother says to me, and my stomach literally lurches into my chest, and I think I'm going to be sick. I push down the feeling, telling myself that it's just nerves. It's all just nerves.

"We'll get dressed first," Shelby states, looking over at Presley. "And then we are going to help you get into the dress." I just nod my head and look around for a glass of water.

"I need to drink some water," I mumble and avoid

that all movement has stopped as they look over at me. "I'm fine. I'm just, it's dry in here." I turn, walking back to the room and grabbing a water bottle. I take a sip, letting the cold water hit the back of my throat, blinking away the stinging of tears as I try to bring my breathing down to normal.

"Okay," my mother says, and I turn to look at her. She is wearing a forest-green dress with a sheer cape that flows to the floor.

I walk into the room, seeing my sisters wearing their blush-pink dresses that mold to them. "Okay, time to get you into this monster of a dress," Shelby informs me, and I nod, taking off my robe and stepping into the dress.

I hold the dress to my chest as my sisters button up the one hundred silk buttons all down the back. "And done," Presley says, and I turn around to face all three of them.

"You look like a fucking divine goddess," Shelby compliments, blinking away tears.

"Even though I wanted you to go with something more traditional," my mother says, "this dress is you."

I look down at my dress, and I smile. "It's very me," I agree. "Guys"—I look at them—"can I have a minute?"

"You take all the time you need," Shelby states, turning and walking out first.

"I'm going to go and make sure everything is ready," Presley says, turning to follow Shelby out.

My mother is the last one in the room. "If you need me, all you have to do is call," she reassures me, and I laugh.

"Mom, don't pretend you aren't going to be lurking

outside the door," I say, and she glares at me.

"No." She shakes her head. "I'm going to go mingle." She storms off, leaving me by myself.

I walk to the mirror and look at myself. The dress is really me. The front is a sweetheart neckline, but I had it plunge down a bit more than my mother liked. It's tight until my knees, and then it ruffles out in hundreds and hundreds of layers, something else I added. It's simple and clean and perfect. When I meet my gaze in the mirror, I try to calm myself down. "This is really happening." I put my hand to my stomach and wonder if maybe I did the dress too tight since breathing is starting to be hard. "You are going to be fine." I try to encourage myself. "It's all going to be fine."

I put my head back and close my eyes when a soft knock fills the room. I shake my head, turning and picking up the bottom of the dress as I walk to the door. My hand turns the handle, the sun hitting the bracelet that Edward gave me, not knowing that once I open this door, everything in my life is going to change.

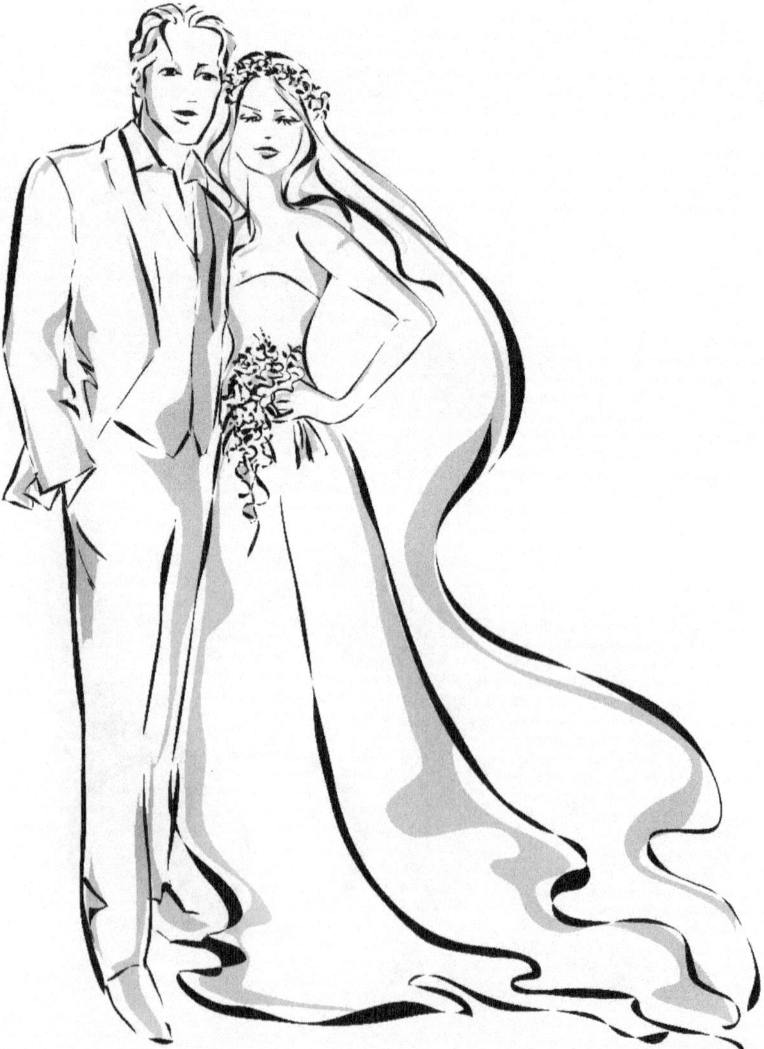

Ten

Luke

I walk out of the house toward my truck, tossing my bag in the back seat before starting the truck. The sun is high in the sky, shining so bright, making it a perfect day for a wedding. I swallow down the lump in my throat and shake my head.

My head goes back to the last conversation I had with her over two weeks ago. When I came back to the restaurant, I went straight behind the bar and poured myself two shots of scotch before I said a word to anyone. Mikaela came in and took one look at me and just waited. "If it's okay with you," I said, "I will take over the whole catering thing, but it'll be after Clarabella's wedding."

She didn't ask any questions. She just nodded and went back into the kitchen. Only after my fourth shot did I agree to do all the prep work for her, which she gladly accepted.

So I got up at four o'clock this morning and went in. I made sure that everything was done before turning and walking out, not looking back. The minute I saw we were doing the rehearsal dinner and the wedding, I knew there was no way I could be there. Not a chance in hell. I would rather walk over burning coals than be in the same building as her and her family as they celebrate her getting married. So I'm leaving town. My goal is to go up to my secluded cabin where I get no Wi-Fi, no cell service, no nothing, and get totally shit-faced.

I start the drive out of town, my hands gripping the steering wheel as I make one stop on the way out. The restaurant. My plan is to drink until I pass out, but I have to have some kind of food first.

I go out of my way to make sure I don't pass the venue, making the drive in forty minutes instead of fifteen.

Pulling up to the restaurant, I see that the van is gone, so I know that Mikaela is gone. I park my truck, then get out and walk in. I nod to the chefs setting up for the day. "I thought you were leaving town?" one of them asks while I walk over to the fridge.

"Just stopped for provisions," I inform him, grabbing stuff in my arms, then walking over to the wooden table where I spent the morning prepping everything. Putting the things down, I walk to my office in the front and grab a bag. Walking back into the kitchen, I fill it up with enough food to last me at least four days. "Okay, I'm out. See you guys next week," I say, not knowing exactly which day I'm going to be coming back.

I place the food bag next to my bag and get back into the truck. "Next stop, cabin."

I'm almost out of the state when the phone rings, and I see it's Mikaela. "Hey," I greet, pressing the green button on the phone.

"Luke," she says, huffing. "Where are you?"

"Almost at the state line," I reply, looking at the phone.

"We have a problem," she says, and I don't know why but my heart freezes in my chest. "Van broke down." The words no caterer wants to hear. "I'm trying to get the food transferred, but you are the only one with a big truck."

"Fuck," I curse, knowing there is no choice. If I don't go, the food goes bad, and Clarabella ends up hating me for the rest of her life. "Send me your location," I say, turning the truck around and then pressing in her location and finding that I'm about thirty minutes out.

"It's fine," I tell myself. "I'll get there, grab the food, and bring it to the back of the kitchen." My finger drums the steering wheel as I drive back toward Clarabella. My heart pounds so hard in my chest I open the windows to get my breathing under control. "She'll be getting married, so there is no way you even have to see her." I try to talk myself off a ledge, but nothing and no words can calm me down. "I guess this is what I deserve after everything that I did. My penance." I laugh. "My fucking penance." I roll up the window and blast the air-conditioning, knowing that I'm going to have to transfer the food from the van to mine.

I make the drive in under twenty-five minutes, spotting Mikaela walking back and forth on the side of the road. "Thank God you weren't that far away. It's hotter than a whore in church," she huffs. "Luckily, the fridge has its own compartment." She opens the back of the cab, and the cold air rushes out. The tow truck shows up at the same time as I'm about to unload the van.

"Can you tow us to the venue?" I ask. "We can unload, and then you can take the van."

"It'll be an extra charge." He looks at me, and I just nod, turning to Mikaela. We get back in my truck, neither of us saying anything.

"I'm behind." She looks over at me, and I know what is coming next. "You are going to have to stay a bit and help me out." I don't say anything. Instead, I just nod my head because all the words are stuck in my throat. I definitely am paying my penance.

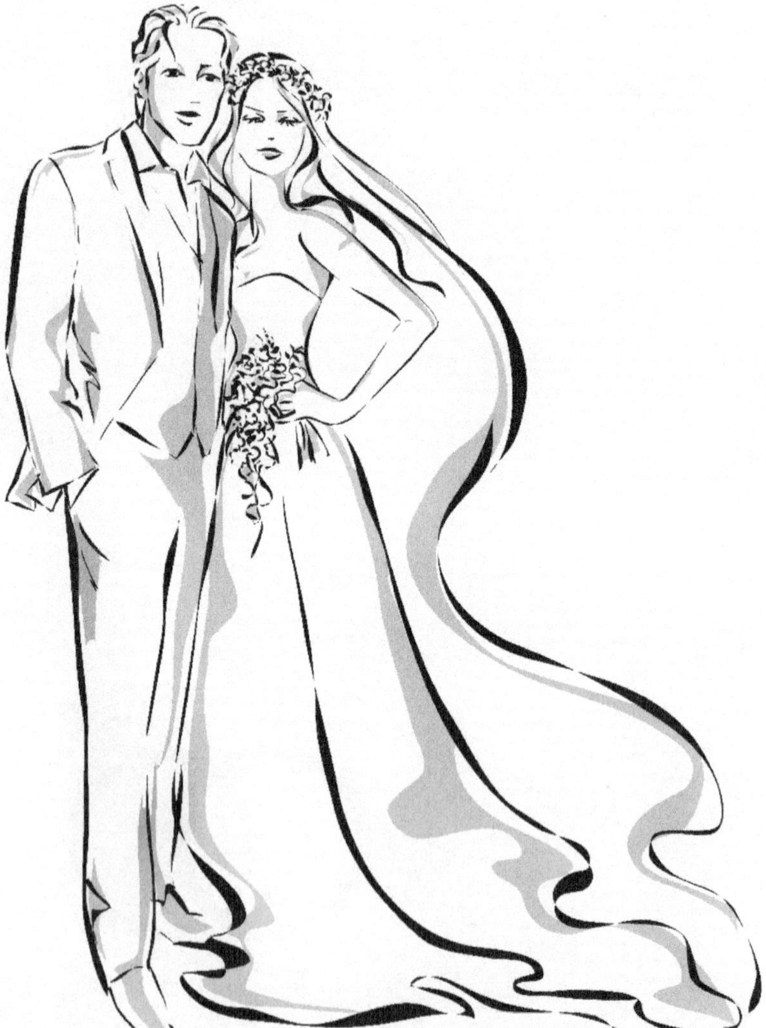

Eleven

Clarabella

The soft knock has me looking away from the mirror to the door. I pick up the bottom of my dress to turn and start walking to the door. All I wanted was a couple of minutes to push down the nerves, the jitters, but all I got were a couple of seconds. I guess I should be happy that they gave me at least that. "You've been gone for one minute," I say, pulling open the door, expecting it to be one of my sisters, but it isn't. It's a woman standing there, holding a baby in her arms. She has long black hair in a braid, the tail over her shoulder. Her brown eyes look very tired and are bloodshot to show that she has been crying. "I'm sorry," I say, confused as to why she is here. "Are you lost?" I look around the empty hallway, wondering if she is stuck, but it's empty, the side door still closed.

"No," she says, her voice coming out soft, and the baby squirms in her arms. She looks down at the baby wrapped in a blue blanket. I don't know much about babies, but I don't think this baby is very old. "You must be Clarabella." She says my name, and the hand that is still holding the door handle is now in a death grip. My heart starts to speed up a touch as the blood feels like it's draining through my body. I can't explain how I know this will be a moment I remember forever, but I do.

"I am," I confirm to her, my arm dropping from the handle of the door. My body feels as if it's slowly detaching, and I'm watching a movie. A movie that I don't want to be a part of. Like a horror film, when you scream, "don't go in the building," but they go in there anyway. That is exactly how I'm feeling now. My mouth suddenly goes dry when I ask the question my head has been screaming since I opened the door and saw her. "And you are?"

"I'm Louise," she replies softly. "May I come in?" she asks, and my head screams no, but my mouth doesn't catch up with my head.

"Sure," I say, moving my dress out of the way to give her some space to walk in. "Are you a friend of Edward's?" I ask, thinking that maybe she is here for the wedding, but her attire of black leggings and a white T-shirt tells me otherwise.

"You can say that," she responds and stops in the

middle of the room. Her head moves around, taking in everything before she says, "I need a minute of your time, and then I'll be gone." She turns to look at me. The tears run down her face freely as she holds the baby close to her chest.

"Are you okay?" I ask, suddenly worried for her. "Do you need water or something?"

She shakes her head. "This would be a lot easier if you weren't so nice to me," she admits, her voice cracking as she looks down at the baby in her arms. The love is written all over her face.

My hands start to shake now, my head putting the pieces together, but my heart does not believe it. "Listen, I don't know what is going on," I say. The sound of my heart beating fills my ears. "But as you can see, I'm about to walk down the aisle."

Her eyes roam from my head to the bottom of my dress. "Oh, I know," she says, smiling. "Trust me, I know."

My head is spinning right now, and I'm two seconds away from telling her to fuck off, but there is something inside me that stops. "My name is Louise." She repeats her name, and she just looks at me. I say her name in my head, trying to place her, but come up empty. "Well, from what I see on your face, I'm assuming you don't know about me." I can't answer her, nothing comes out, but my head shakes from side to side. "This is Edward," she announces, looking down at the baby, and everything stops in time. I feel the air in the room stand still. Time literally stands still. The only thing that doesn't stand still is the beating of my heart. "He's a month old today," she says, her voice filling with pride.

The feeling I had before comes back tenfold. My hand goes to my stomach now as it dips and rises. Almost as if the storm is coming, and my stomach is the waves picking up. I think I'm going to throw up. Louise doesn't wait for me to talk. Instead, she just goes ahead and continues her story.

"I met Edward four years ago," she starts. "I fell in love with him after the first date." She wipes the tear rolling down her face. "I never had anyone treat me with so much love and affection before. He was the Prince Charming that they talked about in Disney movies." I try to swallow, but my mouth is dry, and the lump in my throat grows bigger and bigger. My dress feels like it is squeezing my chest, making it hard for me to breathe. "He took me home to meet his parents, and they didn't exactly approve of me. I didn't have an education like they thought I should. My parents were in and out of my life, and I was a server." I swear my breathing comes out in pants now, or at least that is what it feels like.

"So he decided to hide our relationship, and I agreed with him at the beginning. It made it better, to be honest, there were no disapproving phone calls when we were together. No one to tell me exactly why we couldn't be together. We were living with each other, and his family had no idea." I close my eyes for a minute, each and every single word that she is saying is like a stab to my heart. Every single word sinking in more and more, and the only thing I think is that it's all been a lie. "But then *mine to* CHERISH

they found out, and they gave him an ultimatum. It was them or me." She takes a big breath.

"So he chose them. Even though I hoped he would choose me and stand up to them. I knew that the choice would be them. After all, Edward was living off them. They supported him; they still support him. They would cut him off if he didn't break it off with me." My head spins around as I think back to the conversation I had with him about his family, especially his parents. I met his parents only a handful of times because they traveled so much. His father was a retired stockbroker, and his mother was a stay-at-home mom. "So, he moved me into a little apartment an hour away from them, and every single Thursday night, he would show up and stay until Monday." I swear the room is spinning, but it's just the beginning of the tip of the iceberg.

"When I told him I was pregnant, he was happy, so happy." She smiles through the tears at the memory she has of them. She leans forward and kisses the baby on his head. "I don't know why but I thought having his baby would change things. But one week turned into another week. Every single time he promised he would tell his parents about the baby, he came back and said it wasn't the right time. There was never a good time. But then, six months ago, he started acting strange." My knees start to shake, knowing that this is when we met. "And standoffish, I thought it was because he was nervous about the baby. But then the weekend trips would be canceled at the last minute, and instead, he would come by during the week. I knew in my bones that something was going on. So a month ago, I followed him one day and saw you walking out of your house. He ran up the stairs to greet you and handed you a bouquet of sunflowers." The memory of that day comes back, he was gone all week and was supposed to come back on Wednesday, but his trip got extended. The sunflower bouquet was in his hand as he apologized over and over again. "I drove back home that day. My heart broke that he was lying to me. Broken that I put all this faith in him, and every single time he just broke my heart. Broken that the family I envisioned giving our son was over. I think all the stress and the nerves pushed me into labor. I called him as soon as I was admitted to the hospital. It went straight to voice mail, and when he finally called me back, I was almost five centimeters. He made it there in time to see Edward being born." She looks down at her son, who sleeps in her arms as she sobs.

The memory of that day again, piecing all together; he walked out of the room two hours after he got home, and when he walked back into the room, he was as white as a ghost. An emergency had come up, and he had no choice but to go. I never even questioned him, never even thought anything of it. I was a fool. "I tried to keep my calm, but with all the hormones in me, I confronted him about you, but he said it was just a fling. He would end it with you, and then the three of us would be a family. I was stupid and naïve to think he was telling me the truth. But he started coming around more and more, spending all week with me. A couple of weeks ago, he was in the shower, and his phone beeped." I can't even imagine what she saw. "There in the middle of my living room while I was nursing our son, you sent him a message informing him that he needed to go for his suit fitting so it would be ready for the wedding."

"Oh my God." That's the only thing I hear, and it's from Shelby and Presley, who are now standing in the doorway. Louise looks over at them, and the fear fills her face, and I can tell she wants to run.

"These are my sisters." Those are the only words that come out of my mouth. "Come in and close the door, please." My voice is almost robotic as Shelby and Presley come in, closing the door behind them. Shelby's eyes never leave me as Presley walks over to the table and grabs a water bottle. "How much did you hear?" I ask them, not sure I can see them through the tears filling my eyes.

"Enough to get the whole picture," Presley confirms, handing me the water bottle, and my hand comes up, but it's shaking like a leaf. I can't even hold the bottle, so I shoo it away.

"I'm sorry," Louise whispers as her shoulders start to shake. "He doesn't know I'm here, and to be honest, I don't know what he will say, but I figured that if it were me and I was marrying Edward, I would want to know."

Shelby looks at her. "Do you want something to drink?" she asks her, and Louise just shakes her head.

Louise reaches around her and grabs a white envelope out of her back pocket. "I didn't know if you would believe me"—she holds the envelope for me—"so I had these printed so you would see."

My hand moves on its own accord, reaching out for the envelope. It's almost similar to the one that I opened not too long ago with the diamond bracelet. I pull open the flap in the back and take out the stack of pictures. The first one is of Louise and Edward with the baby in her arms. It was when she gave birth to him. Edward with his arm around her shoulders as she holds the baby to her chest. The tears stream down her face. I take a minute to look into his eyes, wondering if I would see anything, but nothing is there. I slip to the next picture, and it's Edward wearing shorts, sitting on a couch with the baby on his chest as he bends to kiss the child's head.

The last picture is of their gender reveal, both of them holding something in their hand as blue confetti falls down on them. Her face is filled with happiness as well as his, and when my eyes find the date, I almost drop the picture because he proposed two days later.

"My number is on the back of the picture," she says. "I know you must be in shock, and it's a lot to take in. I don't know if you'll marry him or not." She shrugs. "All I know is that you deserve to know." She moves the baby, placing him up higher. "I'm going to go." She looks at my sisters and then at me. "Thank you for not kicking me out," she tells them, and they just smile sadly at her. "I've been the second choice for a long time." She smiles through tears. "I won't be that anymore. I deserve better." She kisses her son's head. "He deserves better." She takes one more look at me and then turns to walk out of the room. The door closes behind her at the same time that the pictures fall from my hands.

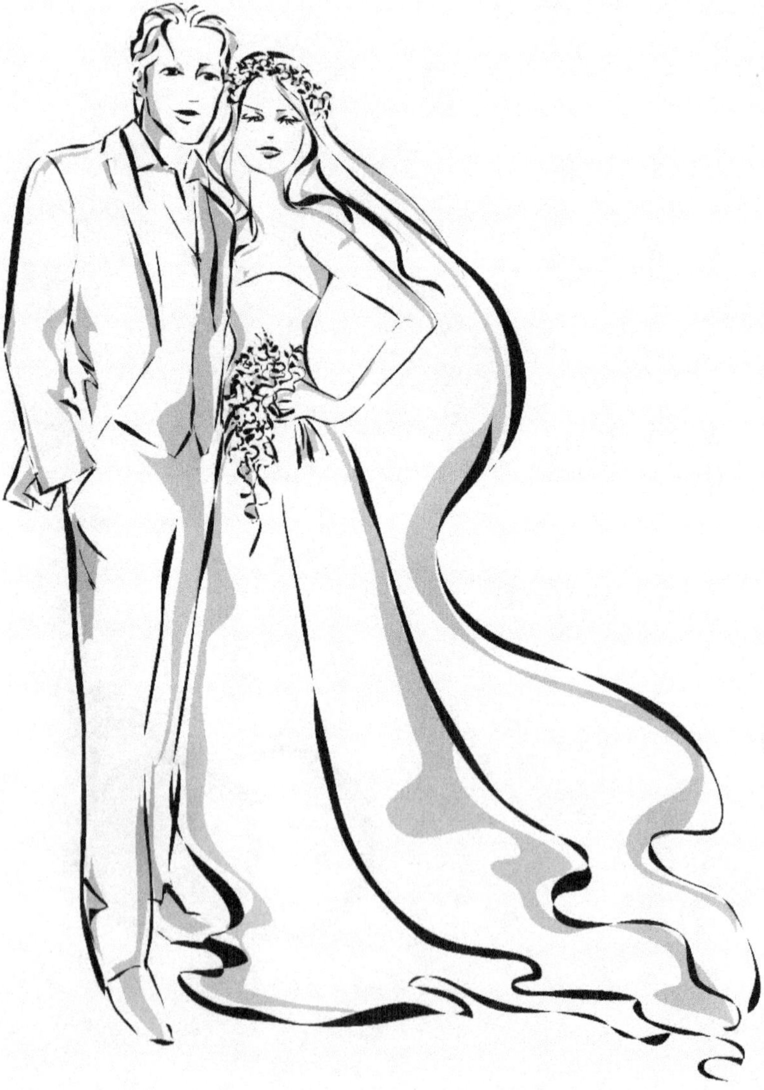

Twelve

Clarabella

The photos fall from my hand, and my knees finally give out. I'm about to hit the floor when Presley wraps her arm around my waist and tries to hold me up. Shelby grabs the other side, and the two of them help carry me to a chair. I sit in the chair and don't even notice that tears are running down my face. Were they there the whole time? Did she see me cry? "This isn't happening?" I say, wiping away the tears from my cheeks angrily. "Like, this is a dream." I look at Shelby and then at Presley. "I mean, it's more like it's a nightmare." I nod at them. "It's a nightmare, and any minute I'm going to wake up, and we are all going to laugh about it." I laugh nervously when Shelby gets up from beside me and walks over to the bar area that she set up.

"I didn't think we would need this." She squats down and moves bottles aside as she pulls out a bottle of scotch. "I only had it here in case you got jittery and nervous." She opens the bottle and pours three shots and then comes over.

"I don't know about you," Presley says. "But this was the best idea you've had in a while." She hands us each a shot. The minute my hand grips the glass, I just swallow the shot without waiting. I then look over at Presley, giving her my empty glass while I take hers. "Well then," she notes, looking down at the empty glass in her hand. "I guess you need it more than I do." I don't say anything as I breathe through the burning that is now spreading from the top of my throat to the bottom of my stomach. Shelby doesn't even try to take her shot; instead, she just holds it up for me. Grabbing the empty one from my hand, she transfers me the full one. Only when I swallow the third shot do I say something.

"Did that just happen?" I ask, then my eyes focus on one of the pictures that is lying on the floor, the one of him with Edward on his chest.

"It happened," Presley confirms, getting up and walking over to the bottle of scotch that Shelby left at the bar. "I'm not even going to lie about it." She walks back to the couch, pouring another shot in my empty glass. "I would have bet my life that this wedding was going to be perfect."

"Oh my God." Shelby gasps. "It can still happen." I

turn my head and my eyebrows pinch together. "What?" she shrieks out. "I don't know what you're thinking."

"What she's thinking is that motherfucker," Presley says, drinking a shot from the bottle. "That is what she is thinking."

"Okay, can we all take a minute," Shelby suggests, getting up now and looking at us. "What are you thinking?" she asks me.

"I'm numb," I admit honestly. "Totally and completely numb."

"That's a start," Shelby says. "But what else?"

"I need to talk to him." I swallow now and turn to look at Presley. "Someone needs to go get him."

"Um..." Presley gets up. "What are we going to say?"

"I don't care what you say." I get up now, and my knees give out again, and I sit back down. "I don't give a shit if you have to drag him here." My legs start to shake nervously.

"I'm going to distract Mom," Shelby states. "You"—she points at Presley—"you go get him."

Presley doesn't say anything; instead, she just nods her head. "And you..." She points at me. "You just..." She shakes her finger at Presley to see if she is going to give her some sort of encouragement, but all Presley does is shake her head. "You sit there and try to calm down."

"Oh, surprising." I look at both of them. "I'm fucking calm. Calm as a fucking cucumber."

"This is going to be very, very bad," Presley says, walking toward the door. "I'd prefer it if you were trashing the place and throwing things around." She opens the door. "This is almost like premeditated murder status."

"Can you not," Shelby grits with clenched teeth, "give her ideas." She huffs and walks over to the door, pushing Presley out. The sound of them bickering as they walk away from the room. I get up slowly, walking over to the pictures in the middle of the room. I pick them up and then walk back to the couch, sitting down to wait for him. I go through the pictures again, once, twice, three times. Each and every single time, the pain in my chest dulls as the anger starts to set in.

There is a soft knock on the door, and I take a deep breath as the door opens, and Edward sticks his head in. "Oh my God, Clarabella," he says, walking inside of the room. He's wearing his black tux, and his hair is perfectly styled. "Presley said you were hurt." I hold up my hand to stop him from taking another step toward me. He stops in his tracks as a look of worry and confusion fills his face. "Are you okay?"

My eyes look straight into his as I say the words. "I know about Louise," I declare, and the color drains from his face. "And about Edward."

He opens his mouth and whispers, "I can explain."

"This I would love to hear," I say, my heart beating fast in my chest, and I hold the pictures in my hands. "Please explain to me how you had a child with a woman while engaged to me?"

"It's not what it seems," he starts to say, and if this wasn't happening to me, I would laugh out loud and scream bullshit.

"It never is what it seems," I reply, my voice a lot calmer than I thought it would be. "Please enlighten me."

"Louise and I," he starts to say, and as I look at him, everything in me wants to just walk out of this room and not give him the time of day, but when I do walk out of this room, it's going to be with everything on the table. "I dated her a while ago."

"So you weren't at her house last week?" I ask, and he just stares at me. "Okay, well, since you aren't going to tell me the truth…" The anger starts to seep out of me now, the hurt being pushed down. "Because well, you probably don't know how. I'm just going to lay out the facts that I know," I state. He puts one hand in his pocket, and the other holds the back of his neck.

"Clarabella," he pleads.

"Did you or did you not have a baby one month ago?" I hold up the picture of him and Louise in the hospital. He doesn't say anything, and I almost laugh, but instead, I just continue. "Did you or did you not lie to me about going away on a business trip, but instead, you were helping care for your son?" I hold up the second picture. "I mean, I don't even know how you can even spin this." I shake my head.

"Louise and I go way back," he starts again. "And yes, at one point, we were a couple."

"At which point exactly were you two not a couple?" I ask. "Because if you are going to stand there in front of me and tell me you didn't sleep with her in the last six months." I glare at him. "You're a bigger liar than I think you are."

"It's over," he says, and now I can't help the laughter that escapes me.

"Let me guess. After today, you were never going to see her again?" I fold my arms over my chest. "What about your child?" I stare at him as I see him trying to find the words. "You lied to me about having a child. A fucking child. A son." My voice goes higher and higher.

"I was going to tell you," he defends and takes a step toward me but then stops when I take a step back.

"When were you going to tell me?" I ask.

"I'm not even sure he's mine," he says, and whatever I felt for him before is gone. "I was going to wait for the DNA testing before I said anything."

"You are actually going to throw your son under a bus to save yourself?" I ask, shocked. "Even after everything, I expected you to be a stand-up guy and take responsibility."

"When I met you, everything changed," he says, and I throw my head back and laugh. "I know it's cliché." He holds up his hands. "But it's just I knew you were the one."

"Really?" I ask, and his head tilts to the side. "When did you know I was the one?" I look at him, and all he does is look back at me. "Now this is the million-dollar question, isn't it?"

"The first night I met you, I knew," he declares, and I glare at him.

"When did you pick out my ring?" I ask, and there is a reason for this. It's what I call my ace in the hole. "I'm waiting."

"The day before I proposed to you," he says, and now I take a step forward.

"So, the day before you proposed to me, you went out and bought this ring?" I hold up my hand. "The day after you had a gender reveal party and celebrated that you decided I'm going to ask Clarabella, who isn't the mother of my child, to marry me." He looks at me, shocked that I know this. "This picture speaks for itself." I hold up the last one. "I'm just." I shrug. "You are a liar!" I shout at the top of my lungs. "A fucking coward." I shake my head. "Now the question is why. Why the fuck did you do it?" I ask, and then it hits me, and I take a step back. "Was it because you loved me, or was it because I had a better social status?" He just swallows. "Oh my God." I clap my hands together. "Wow, was I a fucking idiot."

"It's not that," he says, trying to cover it up. "It's you and me; we just fit."

"We fit?" I scoff, disgusted. "We"—I point at him and then to me—"fit?" I shake my head, smiling. "We don't fit because I hate cowards." I point at him. "And liars." I point again. "And weasels." I point at him again. "Which you are all of the above. You have a child, who has your blood, with someone else and you…" I close my eyes. "Pathetic." I take one more look at him and then start to walk out of the room.

I walk past him, and his hand grabs my arm, stopping me from walking out. "Please, Clarabella, I was going to tell you. I was just waiting for the right time."

I yank my arm out of his touch, and his hand falls to

the side. "The right time would have been the first night you took me out." I put my shoulders back. "Like this is the perfect time to tell you one, go fuck yourself, and two, the wedding is off."

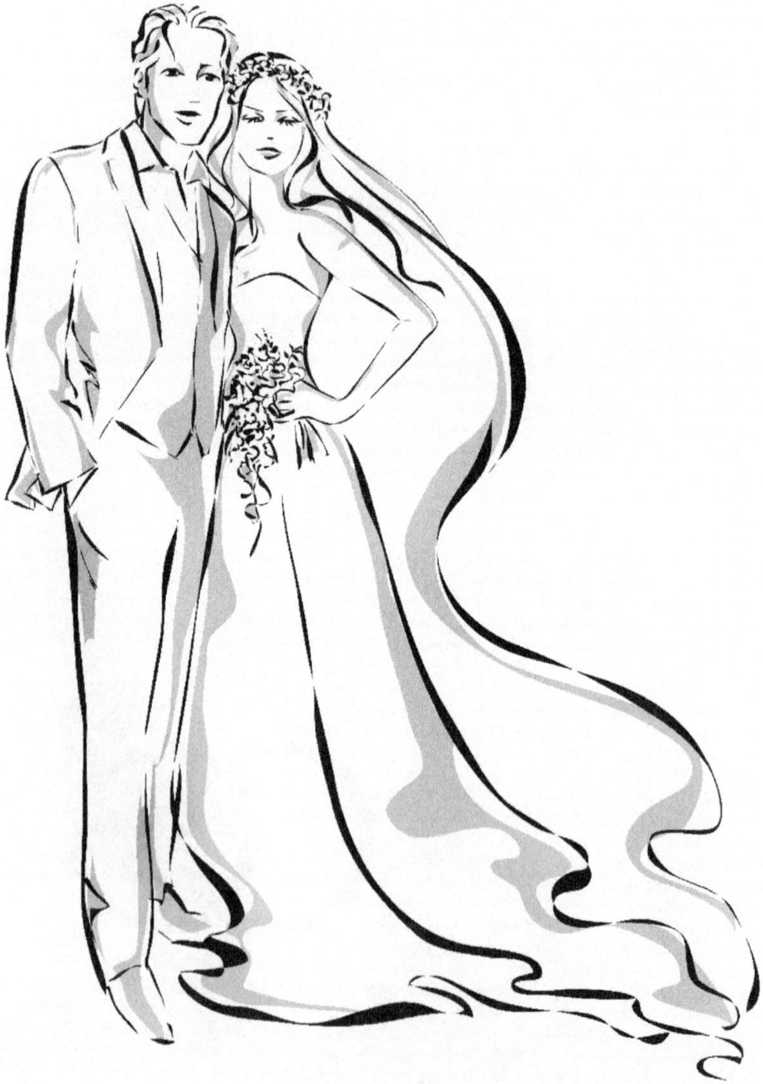

Thirteen

Luke

"Are you okay?" Mikaela asks me from the passenger seat as soon as I start driving behind the tow truck.

No, my head screams at me. "Yeah, I'll be fine," I lie to her, but my hands are getting sweaty, and my heartbeat is going so fast it's all I hear echoing in my ears. My stomach feels like there is a hurricane in the middle of it just spinning shit around. I pull up to the back of the venue, and I can see that the parking lot is full of cars. I make my way away from the cars as I head toward the kitchen area.

"I called ahead," Mikaela says once I park the truck. The back door opens where the kitchen is, and Mallory comes out. She's wearing her black pants with a white shirt and a black jacket. Mikaela jumps out of the truck, giving me a second to get my head together, but to be honest, nothing can prepare me for this. Nothing. Just the thought of being here has me all shaky.

I take a deep breath before jumping out of the truck and going over to the van. "Good news," Mallory says, coming down the stairs toward the van. "We are running a bit behind schedule," I hear her saying to Mikaela. My head's spinning at this news. Now that it's running behind schedule, does that mean I'll have a better chance of seeing her?

"Thank you, Jesus," Mikaela breathes out, looking at me as she opens the back of the van. "Do you want to go in and start preparing stuff while I unload and bring things in?"

"No." I shake my head. "I'm only helping set up. You should get into the groove," I reply, avoiding everyone's eyes.

Mallory takes the tray that Mikaela hands her before the two of them rush inside. I unload the van with my head down the whole time. I walk into the kitchen, hoping I don't see her sisters, just in case they know that I fucked their sister over.

"I don't know what's going on," I hear Mallory say while I bring in the second tray and put it on the counter. "Usually, they are on time to the second." She looks over at the kitchen door. "I just hope she's okay," she says under her breath, and just the thought of her not being okay makes my stomach even more upset. I need to get the fuck out of here now.

"Well, whatever it is," Mikaela says, putting a tray down on the wooden counter, "I'm thankful." She looks up at me. "It would get me up to speed if you start doing the grilling." I don't know if she is asking me or telling me. I know that she's just freaking out because she's behind. I also know she'll get it done regardless of whether I'm here or not. But I know that if I leave now, I'm an asshole. I also know that if I stay longer and risk the chance of seeing Clarabella in a wedding dress, it might just push me over the edge.

"Sure," I reply, my head telling me this is a bad idea. I walk over to the sink to wash my hands before I start anything. I walk to the side where I know an apron is hanging, slipping it over my head before heading over to the grill. I block it all out, or at least I try to. I start the grill and then walk over to the veggies to grab them. But every single time the door opens and someone else comes in, my head whips around. Pretty soon, I'm going to give myself whiplash.

"Don't fuck things up," Mikaela warns as she rushes around, trying to get everything set up. I hear pots and pans start smashing together as she puts her things on the stove. The kitchen starts to fill up with more and more people. I look over and see the waitstaff waiting in the corner for things to start. I can hear whispers coming from every direction, but I don't pay them any attention. If I stay in my little corner, no one will take notice of me. I also stay in the corner, hoping that this goes fast. I finish grilling the veggies just in time to see Mallory, who comes back into the kitchen with a worried look on her face. "We are really behind." She looks around now, but I can tell from her face she's about to freak out. Running behind at a wedding can happen, but when it does, it's a snowball effect.

"Is everything okay?" Mikaela looks at Mallory as she wipes her hands on her apron.

"We have no idea," Mallory says. "They aren't telling us anything. Her sisters just came in and said that there was a dress emergency." She looks around. "Is there anything ready I can take out there?"

"Give me five minutes," Mikaela responds, going to get trays set up. "I'm good to go." Mikaela looks over at me. "I can catch up now that things are a bit behind." She looks over at Mallory, who is now talking to the waitstaff as they get ready to go and offer drinks to the guests.

"You sure?" I ask, even though my head tells me to run. She nods her head at me as she prepares a couple of trays. "Okay," I say, walking back to the side and taking off my apron. I walk to wash my hands. "I'll see you sometime next week."

Mikaela smirks at me. "Have fun."

I laugh. "I'm planning on having a ball," I throw back but then just turn around knowing that as soon as I park my truck, I'm having a drink in the truck. I look around, seeing people scrambling, and just turn to walk out. "Call me if you need anything," I say, even though I know I won't have service, and I can hear her laugh out loud as I walk out of the kitchen. "Almost there."

I open the truck door and stop when the side door

opens, and I see her. Everything stops. And I mean everything. My heart, my breathing, time stops when I take one look at her. I knew she would be beautiful, and I knew that she would take my breath away, but whatever I imagined doesn't come close to how she actually looks. Her head is down, and I see her hair falling into her face from one side, and when she looks at the other side, I see the sparkle. Her shoulders are bare and just beg to be kissed. She holds the right side of her dress as she walks forward. While the other hand wipes away what looks like a tear. Is she crying because of her dress emergency? Her eyes look up and land on mine. "Of course." She throws up her hand in the air and shakes her head. "Of course, out of every single person that I could run into." She picks up her dress again and starts to walk toward me, my eyes do a once-over, and I see that her dress fits her like a glove.

"Are you okay?" I ask as soon as she gets close enough to me, and I see the tears in her eyes. My hands itch to lean up and wipe a tear away from her eye, but instead, I put them in my back pockets where they'll be safer.

"I will be as soon as I can get out of here," she says, looking around, and I'm wondering if she's waiting for her husband to come and get her. "I need to get out of here." Her lower lip quivers. "Like now." All I can do is open the passenger door for her. Her eyes fill with tears, and I have no idea what to say. None.

Instead, I look at her and put one arm around her waist while I pick her up and put the other under her legs. "Oh my God," she huffs when I turn her around and place her in the truck. "What the hell?" she says once I let go of her.

"I figured it was easier than you trying to jump up into the truck," I explain, making sure all the dress is in the cab of the truck before slamming the door. I walk over to the driver's side, getting in and turning to look at her. "Are you sure about this?"

"I need to get the fuck out of here." She looks at me and then looks over at the door where she walked out of less than two minutes ago. Then turns to look back at me. "I need to get away from here. Far, far away from here."

"I know just the place." I put the truck in drive and start moving away from the venue. "Do you want to tell me what's going on?" I ask as we pull out of the parking lot. I look in the rearview mirror to see if maybe the groom is going to come flying out the door running after the truck. But the doors stay closed, and not even a shadow appears in the window.

"No," she says, looking out the window and trying to wipe away her tears. I lean over her, and she goes stiff as I open the glove box and hand her the tissue box. "Thanks," she mumbles, grabbing the box from me. She puts the box on her lap as she takes a tissue out and dabs the corner of her eyes. "Isn't this poetic?" she says and looks at me.

I don't say anything to her. I can't say anything to her because the lump in my throat is so big it feels like a boulder. Her blue eyes are even clearer when she cries, and all I want to do is hold her and tell her that it's okay. "That of all people in the world for me to bump into on the worst day of my life, it would be you." She laughs as she dabs her eyes again. "I mean, seriously, why?" She turns to look at me, and the way she is breathing, my eyes go to the middle of her chest that I didn't even notice was bare. "Why, out of everyone in the whole universe, or I don't know, four hundred million people, were you the only one there?" Her hands fly up. "How? Why?"

"Well, I wasn't waiting for you to come out that door if that is what you were asking." Those are the only words that come out of me.

"Okay," she says, sounding like she doesn't believe a word of it.

"I was headed out of town when Mikaela's van died on the side of the road," I share. "And then I stayed to help her out so she wouldn't fall behind."

"You were leaving town?" She raises her eyebrows at me. "Isn't that a shocking development?"

"Do you want me to drop you off at your house?" I don't bother looking at her.

"Where were you going?" she asks me, and I just side-eye her.

"I was going to my cabin in the woods," I reply, slowing down and waiting for her to tell me where she wants to go.

"How far is this cabin?" she asks.

"About two hours, give or take," I answer, and she just nods her head.

"That sounds good to me," she says, and now I'm the one who gasps.

"You want to come with me?" I look over at her as she

avoids looking at me, her eyes on the road in front of her.

"I have two choices at this point." She wipes her eyes, turning to look at me. "I can stay here and deal with that situation, which is the last thing I want to do, by the way." She points behind her with her thumbs. "Or take off far away from here with you, which is the second to last thing I want to do, for a bit and wait for the dust to settle. So I have no other options. Going with you is the lesser of two evils." I don't say anything to her. Instead, I just put my foot on the gas and drive her and myself out of town, knowing full well that I'm in way over my head.

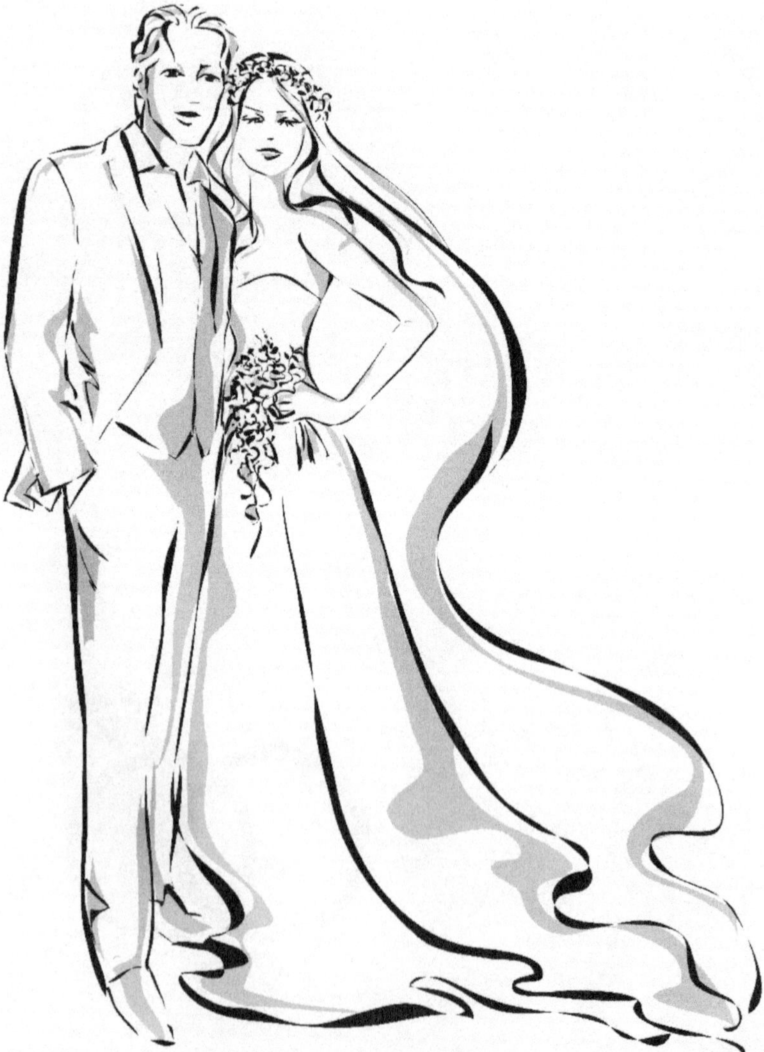

Fourteen

Clarabella

"You want to come with me?" His tone goes even higher when he looks at me, and I avoid looking over at him. My eyes focus on the road even though the tears make my vision blurry.

"I have two choices at this point." I wipe the corner of my eye with the tissue, turning to look at him. "I can stay here and deal with that situation, which is the last thing I want to do, by the way." Pointing behind me, I know if I would go back there, people would see me break. "Or take off far away from here with you, which is the second to last thing I want to do, for a bit and wait for the dust to settle. So I have no other options. Going with you is the lesser of two evils." I turn away from him and look at the road, dabbing my eyes. The pain and sadness are starting to build, but I don't think the anger will make it come up.

I'm angry. I'm so fucking angry that he lied to me, and I was a fool. I shake my head as the tears come. My phone buzzes in my hand, and I look down to see that the notifications are going up by the second. I walked out of the bridal suite thinking that I just needed a second to think, knowing that in five minutes, I would have to tell my family that the wedding was off. Knowing that there were going to be a million and one questions that I would have to answer. Knowing that at the end of the day, I would stand there, and people would look at me with pity in their eyes. The whispers would start and then even some finger-pointing, and to be honest, I just needed a minute to think.

Then I looked up, and he was there, even though the last person on earth I wanted to see was Luke. Standing there just looking at me like he was waiting for the doors to open. I put my head back on the seat and close my eyes, if only for a minute. While the phone goes nuts in my lap and I know that I have to answer them. They must be worried sick looking for me. "Do they know you left?" I hear Luke ask from beside me, and with my eyes focused on the road, all I do is shake my head. "Do you want me to call and just let them know you're safe?"

"It's not your concern," I scoff, my heart speeding up in my chest. I swear this dress is getting tighter and tighter as the drive goes on.

"My concern is that you're sitting in my truck, and

they can call the cops and say I kidnapped you." My head whips to him, and I see him smirk.

"Don't flatter yourself," I say, and all he does is roll his lips. I pick up the phone, seeing the red notification beside the text bubble.

Opening it up, I take a big deep breath before clicking on the top message that is a family group chat.

Shelby: We lost Clarabella!!!

Presley: What do you mean we lost Clarabella?

Travis: Define lost?

Shelby: I went back to check on her, and she's gone. Vanished.

Presley: She's wearing a ten-pound dress. How far could she have gone? She has to be somewhere.

Travis: I'll check the bar area.

Shelby: She isn't there.

Travis: Well, she isn't in the chapel.

Presley: Where is Edward?

Shelby: No idea.

Travis: You guys left her alone with him. WHAT THE HELL WERE YOU THINKING?

Shelby: NOT NOW, TRAVIS!

Travis: Does the phrase accessory to murder mean anything to you?

Presley: I do not look good in orange.

Presley: Can you imagine me in jail? I'm going to be someone's bitch.

Shelby: Get over yourself for a minute and focus.

Travis: You guys had one job. ONE.

Shelby: How do I remove someone from this chat?

Me: I'm fine. I left, and he was alive.

The phone rings in my hand, and I see it's Shelby, but I press decline.

Shelby: Did you seriously just fucking decline me? Well, if that doesn't scream fuck off, I don't know what does.

Me: I need some time to think.

Presley: You have two hundred people waiting for you to walk down the aisle.

Me: The wedding is off.

Travis: Shocker.

Me: Can you handle it?

Shelby: What choice do we have?

Travis: I'm not telling Mom.

Presley: Are you okay?

Travis: I'm fine. I'm just not telling Mom.

Presley: I wasn't asking you, idiot. I was asking Clarabella!

Me: I'm the least bit fine, but I'll be okay. FYI, WE HATE HIM, AND HE'S A FUCKING LIAR!

Travis: It's like the family is cursed for weddings. Presley, I'm not coming to your first wedding.

Presley: AS IF AFTER WATCHING THE TRAIN WRECK OF MY FAMILY TRYING TO GET MARRIED, I WOULD EVEN ATTEMPT IT! FUCK THAT SHIT. SINGLE WOLF FOR LIFE.

Travis: You really think you are wolf status?

Shelby: Meeting in the bridal suite now.

Presley: Shit, Edward just walked into the chapel and told everyone the wedding is off.

Travis: Well, the good news, he's alive. Bad news, I think I hear Mom screaming.

I put my phone down and put my head back. "Do you want to tell me what happened?"

I look over at him. "I need a drink," I tell the truth. "Not just a small shot, like the whole bottle."

"I don't think I have any white wine with me." He smirks at me, and I want to throat punch him, but instead, I flip him the bird and turn to look out the window, the sound of him laughing irritating me. The last thing I need is for him to pull over and dump me in the middle of nowhere. My head spins around and around as the trees pass by faster and faster while the phone vibrates in my lap.

Presley: Well, that was fun.

Shelby: If that was fun, I would hate to know what you find is really fun.

Me: How did it go?

Travis: Mom freaked out.

Me: Is she okay?

Travis: She will be okay. Harlow is with her, and I saw her take a shot of some sweet tea.

Shelby: FYI, he called you a runaway bride.

Me: Well, once a pencil dick, always a pencil dick.

Travis: I just threw up in my mouth.

Presley: It could be worse. People were comparing you to Julia Roberts.

Shelby: I love her.

Me: Could be so much worse. What happened with Mom?

Travis: She was in shock. I have to say, after the first two, I don't know why she's surprised.

Shelby: Edward's parents told her that they are going to sue you for emotional distress.

Me: WHAT THE ACTUAL FUCK?

Presley: Oh, wait, it gets better.

Shelby: Mom told them to fuck off and that they weren't leaving until they settled their tab.

Me: WHAT?

Travis: Then she looked at me and told me to tell them to suck my dick since she didn't have one.

Presley: SHE IS MY HERO.

Me: Is she okay?

Shelby: Yes.

Presley: Yes.

Travis: Absolutely not.

Shelby: TRAVIS, WHAT THE FUCK? CAN SOMEONE KICK HIM OUT?

Travis: Hey, you try talking Mom down off the ledge for the second time. Do you know what she said? She has to wear black for the rest of her life to sacrifice herself for her daughters. She even mentioned a hat and veil.

Presley: It wasn't that bad.

Shelby: I hear glass smashing.

Travis: Oh, fuck, code black.

Me: What the hell is going on? What the hell is code black?

I look down at the phone, waiting to see if they answer. My body shakes with nerves now. Maybe walking away wasn't the best thing to do. Maybe I should have stayed and faced the music. At least told them the truth as to why I left instead of taking all the shit that was going to come my way.

Me: Hello?

Presley: Edward wanted to talk to Mom and explain himself.

Me: Why did glass break?

Travis: HE HAS A CHILD?????? WTF? WHY WOULD YOU NOT TELL ME THIS DETAIL?

Shelby: I was busy.

Presley: It was a secret.

Travis: HARLOW STEPPED IN FRONT OF MOM AND USED HER PREGNANT BODY AS A SHEILD.

Presley: OH MY GOD, SHE'S PREGNANT? WHY DIDN'T YOU TELL US?

Travis: I was busy. It was a secret.

Shelby: Petty much?

Only my family would come in and make this whole thing about them. Forget that I ran away from my wedding. Forget that now I'll probably be labeled as the runaway bride. Forget everything except their drama. I look down at the phone, waiting to see the three dots. "Not to interrupt you," Luke says, "but you have about ten minutes until you lose service."

I look over at him, confused. "What do you mean?" I look down at my phone and see the three bars at the top go down to two.

"It's a secluded cabin," he explains, and still, it's like

he's talking a different language. I literally don't get what he's trying to say.

"There is no Wi-Fi?" I ask, shocked. "How can that be? There are signals everywhere." I look around at the denseness of the trees. The sun has gone down, and the only lights are the headlights.

"The only thing the cabin has is running water and electricity," he informs me.

"Is this *The Hunger Games*?" I ask, looking down at my phone, seeing that the two bars have gone down to one. "Fuck," I swear and just dial Shelby.

"Oh, now she calls," she says, answering the phone after one ring.

"Listen, I don't have a lot of time to talk," I start to say. "Apparently, there is no signal where I'm going."

"Oh my God. It's *Squid Game*," she says, and I close my eyes and put my hand to my head. "Where the hell are you even going?" she asks, and I look over at Luke.

"Where are we going?"

"Who are you with?" Shelby asks me as soon as I finish asking Luke the question. "What color is the brown bear?" she asks me, and I laugh. It was a secret code that we had when we were younger in case we were ever in trouble.

"Purple," I reply, laughing. "I'm with Luke."

"Um, excuse me," she says. "I'm sorry. You really are in a bad part of town if I just heard you say you are with Luke."

I turn my head, not wanting him to hear my conversation, but I'm in the middle of nowhere in his truck where no music is playing. "I walked out of the door, and he was standing there."

"Not waiting for her!" he shouts from his side of the truck, and I turn and glare at him.

"I'm having a private conversation," I grumble between clenched teeth.

"You aren't even whispering," he says. "You have two minutes," he points out as we get off at a dirt road.

"I'm sharing my location with you right now," I tell Shelby. "How bad is it?"

"On a scale of one to ten," she says. "It ranged about fifteen."

I close my eyes. "How can this be a fifteen when you walked down the aisle and left him there?"

"I walked down the aisle." She laughs. "You ran."

"I didn't run. I needed a break. I'm going to call you as soon as I get a signal," I say, and then the call drops. I look over at Luke. "I didn't even share my location with her!"

"I warned you," he reminds me as he turns down another road.

This one is definitely deserted, and we bounce up and down as he makes his way down the road to the little house that sits in pitch black. The lights from the car light it up. "Is this it?" I ask, not sure what else to say.

"Welcome to my cabin, Clarabella," he says softly,

getting out of the truck and leaving me with my thoughts for one second before he walks over and opens the door for me. He holds out his hand for me. "Let me help you." His words make my whole body shiver. I don't move a muscle as he looks at me. "I won't bite," he says, smirking at me. "At least not unless you want me to."

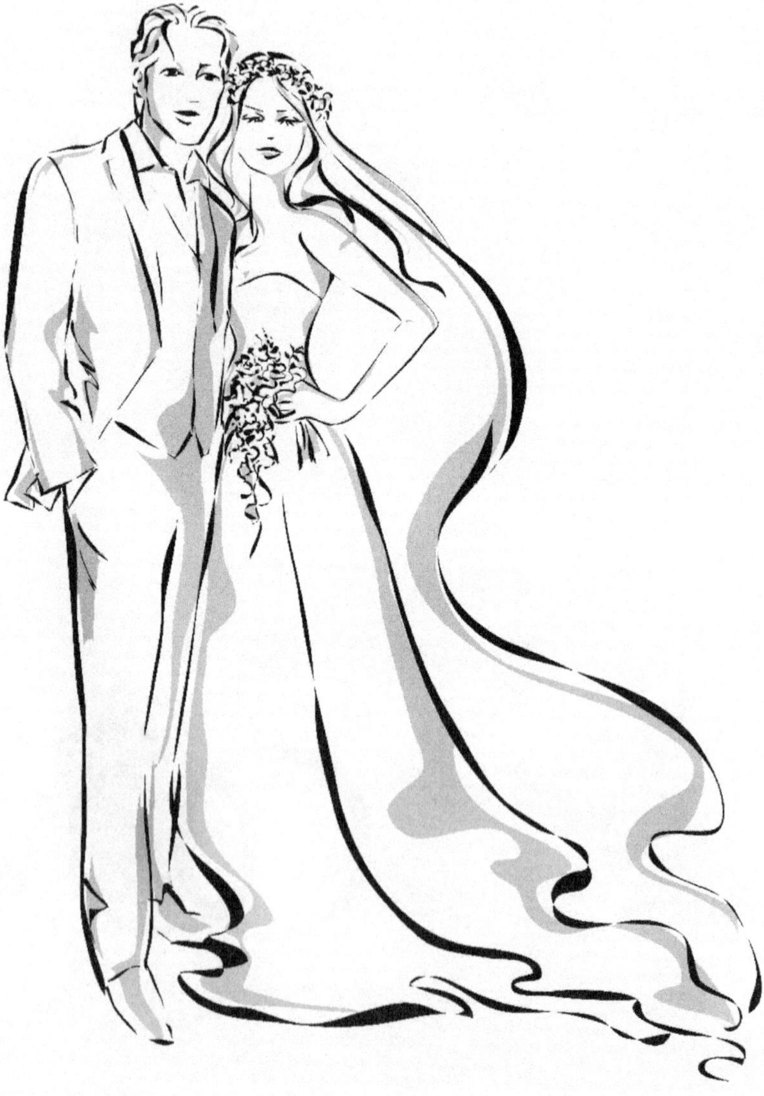

Fifteen

Luke

"Welcome to my cabin, Clarabella," I say softly to her as my hand reaches out and grabs the handle of the door. I get out of the truck, keeping the lights on to give me a pathway to the house. If she wasn't here, I would have no problem, but with her dress, I don't want her to trip over anything. I walk around the truck and open the side door. She looks at me in shock with her phone still in her hand. I hold my hand out for her. "Let me help you." All she does is stare at me, the grip on her phone getting tighter and tighter as her fingers get white. "I won't bite." I smirk at her. "At least not unless you want me to."

She rolls her eyes. "Simmer down there, cowboy."

She finally puts her hand in mine while she deals with the bottom of her dress. "I can't see my feet," she tells me, and I look at her.

I let go of her hand and move in to scoop her out. "Oh my God," she huffs, putting her hand to her chest as I turn to walk to the cabin. "If you carry me into your cabin, I'm going to stab you in your sleep," she warns me, and I can't help but laugh. She is the only woman who turns hot and cold in a matter of seconds. She is also the only woman who can make me want to rip the hair out of my head. I turn around, and all I can do is talk calmly to her.

"I wouldn't think of it," I say as I walk up the five steps to the front door. "I'm going to put you down." I gently put her on her feet before standing up and fishing the keys out of my jeans pocket. I unlock the door before walking in and turning on the one light that lights up the whole place. "I'm going to go and make sure there aren't any guests around." The living room to the left side of me has an L-shaped couch facing the fireplace. It leads to the kitchen area. I spent the most money in the kitchen since I got most of my inspiration from there.

She looks at me with wide eyes. "What does that even mean?"

"There may have been once." I hold up a finger. "I forgot to close the door, and well, a family of raccoons decided that they would live here."

"Oh my God." She puts her hands to her mouth. "It is like *The Hunger Games*." She looks around as sounds start to come out of the forest. The sound of leaves rustling has her walking into the house with me.

"It's fine. It's just a squirrel," I joke, and I can see her gritting her teeth.

"I need a drink," she says, looking around but not moving from her spot. "Maybe more than a drink. I need several," she adds. "Bottles of drinks."

"Okay, let me check, and then I'll get the booze from the truck," I walk toward the kitchen and open the cupboards under the sink, seeing that no one is there. The cabin isn't much, but it's someplace that I can take off to and totally leave the outside world behind.

"I think we're good."

"You think?" she questions, looking around. "That sounds great." She throws her hands up in the air. "I mean, what's the worst than can happen to me?"

"Rabies," I deadpan, putting my hands on my hips and trying not to laugh at her. Even after crying half the time in my truck, she still looks beautiful.

"Go get the booze, Luke," she orders with her teeth clenched together as her eyes dart around the room to see if there are any movements.

"Don't run off," I joke and then roll my lips after she glares at me. "Too soon?"

"I don't see booze, Luke?" She puts her hands on her hips and then tucks her hair behind her ear. "And as the seconds go by, I become more and more unhinged."

"Duly noted," I say, turning and walking out of the cabin, going to the truck. I grab my backpack with the food bag and then the three bottles of scotch I thought I was going to drink the whole weekend by myself.

When I walk into the cabin, she sits on one of the stools against the kitchen island. With her dress all around her, she looks like a motherfucking princess. She looks at me, and I see that she has a wooden spoon in her hand. "What's with the weapon?" I ask, lifting my chin toward her.

"If there was a raccoon, I was going to hit it with this." She holds up the spoon. "Right before I kick it with the heel on my shoe."

"Your brother is a vet." I laugh, walking into the kitchen and putting the food and booze on the counter. Then I walk to the bedroom and throw the bag on the bed.

"If it's me or the raccoon." She points the spoon to her chest. "I win each and every single time."

She leans over the counter, grabbing one of the bottles of scotch. "Do you want a glass?" I ask as she unscrews the top and brings the bottle to her lips.

"Nope," she replies, right before she takes a big gulp and closes her eyes and tries not to cough.

I walk into the kitchen and lean on the counter, facing her as she takes another gulp. "What are you looking at?"

At the most beautiful woman in the world, but I know that she'll tell me to fuck off as fast as the words leave my mouth. "I thought you gave up scotch." Those are the only words I can come up with.

"Things change," she answers, taking another pull of the scotch, and this time, she closes her eyes when she puts down the bottle in front of her.

"Apparently, they do," I agree, crossing my arms over

my chest.

"I bet you're wondering what I'm doing here," she says, laughing as she picks up the bottle and takes another gulp, then wipes her mouth with the back of her hand. "Especially in a wedding dress on my non-wedding day."

"I was wondering, but I was also wondering how you can walk out of that building with no one chasing you."

"Well," she starts. "I got dressed, and well, I was a bit nervous." She takes another shot of the scotch, and I don't interrupt her. My heart starts to speed up faster for her, and my stomach sinks, knowing that whatever pissed her off or happened made her end up running away from her own wedding. "I asked my sisters to give me a couple of minutes." She laughs as she looks at the bottle, and her eyes fill with tears, making my gut twist. "There was a knock on the door, and well." She looks at me, and a tear escapes her eyes. "You know in the movies, when you yell, don't open the door?" she asks me and laughs through her tears. But when she lifts her hand to wipe the tear away, I see her hand shaking. "Well, I should not have answered the door."

"You don't have to continue," I say, not needing to know the rest. Just seeing her like this, reliving it, makes me want to throw something against the wall.

"You deserve it," she says. "Never thought I would say those words." She takes a shot of the scotch. "A woman was standing there. She was beautiful, and she was holding a baby in her arms." I stand up straight, my heart beating so fast I think it's going to come out of my chest. "Yeah, you guessed it," she continues, pointing at me as the tears run down her face like a stream going downriver. "Her name is Louise." I swallow, and I can't even fathom what she felt. "And her son is named Edward." She tilts her head to the side. "I guess you can say he's a junior. But I'm not sure how it works."

"He has a child?" I ask, my voice so low I'm surprised she heard it.

"He does," she admits to me. "They were together for four years."

"Did you know?" I ask, and she just looks at me. "Not about the baby but about her."

"No." She shakes her head. "When I confronted him about it, he said he was waiting for the DNA results."

"Asshole." I shake my head. "Listen, my parents are far from being parents of the year," I offer, and for the first time ever, I talk about my parents. "They really didn't give me much. Not sure they even loved each other, but they stayed with each other. I don't know if they did that because they wanted to or neither of them had something better. But at least they acknowledged that I was their kid. I mean, they sucked at it." I look at her and see that her tears have stopped.

"I don't think I've ever heard you talk about your parents," she says. "Like, not even in college."

"Nothing to talk about. They gave me a roof until I was sixteen, then I had to pay my way and decided that it was cheaper living with other people," I admit to her and only her.

"When was the last time you saw them?" she asks, and the only reason I'm still talking about this is because she stopped crying. That is the only fucking reason.

"Maybe seven years ago. Not sure."

"Wow," she responds, looking down at her hands. "I can't imagine going a day without talking to my mom, no matter how crazy she makes me." She looks at me. "Anyway, I told him he was a liar and that the wedding was off." She leans back. "Grabbed my phone and then walked out of the door. He tried to call my name, but I turned around and said if he called my name one more time, I would go and tell his parents they were grandparents." She picks up the bottle, bringing it to her lips. She smiles right before taking another sip, and I was wrong before. Here right now, sitting at the island of my cabin in the middle of nowhere with her face streaked with tears and red eyes, she looks more beautiful than she has ever looked before. "And then I became a runaway bride."

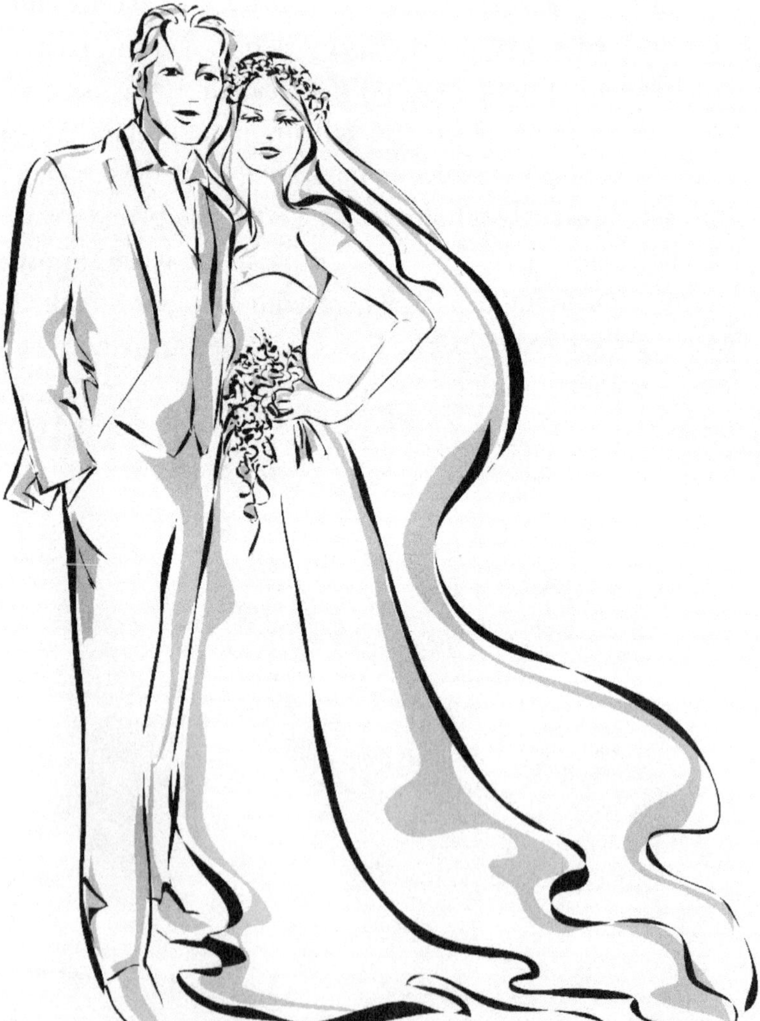

Sixteen

Clarabella

"Wow." I look down at my hands, not sure what to say to his story. "I can't imagine going a day without talking to my mom, no matter how crazy she makes me." I look up at him. "Anyway, I told him he was a liar and that the wedding was off." I lean back in the chair, not willing to let my shoulders slump. "Grabbed my phone and then walked out of the door. He tried to call my name, but I turned around and threatened him that if he called my name one more time, I would go and tell his parents they were grandparents." The words are bitter in my mouth, so I pick up the scotch bottle and bring it to my lips. The smile fills my face right before taking another sip, and I know it's the scotch hitting me already. "And then I became a runaway bride." I take one more swig of the bottle before putting it down and looking at Luke straight in his eyes. I laugh out loud. "Of all people to rescue me, it had to be you." This is the universe kicking me in the vagina without even batting an eye.

He laughs. "I didn't come to rescue you." He stands and walks over to the bag, taking the food out of it. "I was there to help Mikaela."

"Well, you were there at the right time and place, then," I say, looking around. "I mean, at this point, that should have been a sign."

"What do you mean?" he asks, and I laugh.

My hand spins the bottle in it. "Well, for Travis's wedding, there were signs that it was doomed." I laugh. "One, the fire in the kitchen." I hold up a finger. "Two, the wrong flowers coming." I put up one more finger. "Three, the bride being rushed to the hospital."

"Three strikes and you're out, I guess," he says, putting one hand on the counter beside him.

"Then with Shelby, the groom was late." I hold up a finger. "Then, well, I think that was the only sign, but I mean, it was a huge one before she got a love letter that was for someone else."

"But she ended up with Ace," Luke points out, "which was always the obvious choice."

"I never thought of it like that. I mean, I knew they were best friends, but I don't think I ever saw them as lobsters."

"Oh, here we go." He laughs, shaking his head and

putting his hand on his forehead. "The minute you saw that episode of *Friends*."

I can't help but clap my hands and laugh, picking up my fingers and trying to get it like Phoebe, but with the scotch I drank, it doesn't work out that way. "She's his lobster."

"You kept saying that for a whole month," he reminds me, and I'm wondering why he even remembers since it seems like a lifetime ago.

"It's poetic," I defend. "A masterpiece."

"Oh, God." He shakes his head. "A masterpiece, really?"

"Anyway." I ignore him. "There were signs that Edward wasn't the one for me."

"Like what?" he asks, and I just look at him.

"Um, one." I hold up my hand. "I was a bunch of nerves."

"I think everyone who gets married has some sort of nerves." He looks at me, and I just tilt my head to the side, waiting for him to finish what he started. "It's a big commitment."

I chuckle. "That it is." I bring the bottle to my lips, taking a sip. "Some would say it's forever."

"Exactly." He takes a deep breath. "Forever is a long time, and you have to be one hundred percent sure of the person." He's got a point there, as I bring the bottle back to my lips just to keep from saying something that I'll regret. All I can do is look at his face. His scruff is a bit longer than it was the last time I saw him. I'm going to be really honest. I've avoided going out since I knew he was back. I would go to work and then go home. I never ventured out, making the excuses that I was busy, but the truth was I didn't want to run into him. His blue eyes almost look green in this light. I could get lost in them. The minute the thought runs into my head, I look down at the bottle and think maybe I should stop drinking now.

"Well, whatever it was, the woman showing up with his child was all I needed to see. The fact that he kept a child from me. His flesh and blood." There is no excuse, none, not one that would make it okay. "By any chance…" I look down at my wedding dress. "Do you have a change of clothes?"

He turns and walks into the room that I'm assuming is the bedroom, coming back with the backpack that looks empty. "I have T-shirts and a pair of boxers."

I look at him with my mouth open. "How do you go away for the weekend and pack just T-shirts?"

He laughs at me. "I was planning on getting trashed all weekend long. I was going to change my shirt and boxers," he says, and the minute he says boxers, the memory of me taking his off comes to me, but just like all the other times, I push it away.

"Don't you leave clothes here for the next time?" I ask, still trying to wrap my head around the fact that he went away for the weekend with no clothes.

"Not really. I bring what I need." He shrugs and tries not to laugh while he looks at my face.

"I guess I have no choice," I say, getting off the stool and wobbling back and forth. My hand holds the island so I don't fall. "Do not drink and then stand suddenly." I laugh at my own inside joke. "Can you imagine if I fell and busted my face? Now that would be funny."

He shakes his head. "That would not be funny at all." He hands me the bag and puts his hand on my elbow. "Especially since the closest hospital is an hour from here."

"What are you doing?" I ask as he starts to walk with me.

"I'm helping you to the bedroom so you can change," he replies, and I gasp.

"You want to see me naked?" I turn to see his face and the smirk comes out. I want to hate it, but let's be real; there is nothing I hate about Luke. I mean, I'm sure once my head isn't cloudy the way it is right now, I will come up with things to hate about him. Like having the best sex of my life and then leaving me. Yeah, hate that about him.

"I'm walking you to the bedroom and closing the door with me on the outside of it," he mumbles, avoiding looking at me. Maybe I was the only one who had the best sex of their life that night. God, maybe I wasn't as good as I thought I was. Maybe it wasn't even good, and I'm imagining it was.

"Whatever," I say, turning to walk into the room and stopping when I can't see anything. I reach out, flipping the switch, but when the light turns on, it's very dim. The room has a soft yellow glow as I look around, seeing just a king-sized bed in the room and nothing else.

"Call me if you need me," he says, then closes the door, leaving me by myself.

I kick the bottom of my dress as I walk toward the bed and sit down for a second. My hand comes out to take the headpiece out of my hair. My fingers trace the jewels as I think back to five minutes ago when I told him my story. I didn't know if I would be able to do it.

I know that when I get back to reality, I'm going to have to sit down with my mother and explain everything. Regardless if she hears the story from Edward or my sisters, she deserves to have the whole story, and she deserves to hear it from me.

Repeating the story again, I was wondering if the pain would hurt less. But the pain was just anger. Angry that I got played. Angry that I didn't see it right in front of my eyes. Angry that I let it happen. Angry that I fell for all the fucking charm he dished out. Angry that I knew I should have taken my time and not rushed into it.

I put the headpiece down, then stand to take the dress off. I look over and try to get to the buttons, but my fingers keep slipping. "Great," I mumble and walk to the door, pulling it open. He's standing with his arms stretched and hands propped on the island. His head hangs down, and the bottle of scotch sits in front of him.

His head moves up when I clear my throat. "You have to unbutton me."

"Um," he stutters, not sure what to say.

"I've tried, but I can't reach them." I turn, showing him that I can't get to them. I don't wait for him to come to me. Instead, I kick off my shoes and pick up the bottom of the dress with both hands as I walk to him. Once I get beside him, I turn and wait for him to unbutton me.

"Don't worry," I say over my shoulder. "I won't bite." I roll my lips as I feel his hands touch the first button. "Unless you want me to."

He groans, and I can't help but throw back my head and laugh. My body shivers when I feel his fingers against my back. I close my eyes and count to ten to try to distract myself from his touch. "I need a drink," he says.

"You can't. I'm the only one who is drinking tonight," I inform him and hold the dress to the front of my chest when I feel it start to slip down.

"Why is that?" he asks, and I can see his eyes are concentrated on the buttons.

"Because I'm the runaway bride." I giggle. "I wonder if I am going to have to add that to my business card."

"You are all done," he announces, turning and walking as fast as he can away from me.

I hold the dress to my chest as I walk back to the bedroom. I can feel his eyes on me, but I avoid looking back at him.

As soon as I close the door to the bedroom, my back falls against it, and I shimmy my hips so the dress falls straight down. I step out of it, and it still keeps its shape and doesn't fall over. I take a second to pick up my dress and put it in the corner. It's not like I'm going to be wearing it anytime soon. I giggle, opening the backpack as I stand here in the middle of the room with my barely there white thong on. His smell hits me right away, making my stomach have little butterflies. "I'm just hungry," I mumble to myself to make an excuse for why I'm getting all my feathers ruffled because of him. It's stupid. He made it clear that he isn't interested in me like that. I pull out one of his T-shirts and opt for the black one since I don't have a bra to wear. Even though he's seen all that I have to offer, I shouldn't just flaunt it. Slipping the shirt over my head, I see it lands just in the middle of my thighs, and I don't even bother putting the boxers on. It is one thing to wear his T-shirt but another to put on his boxers. There is a line that shouldn't be crossed, and this is one of them.

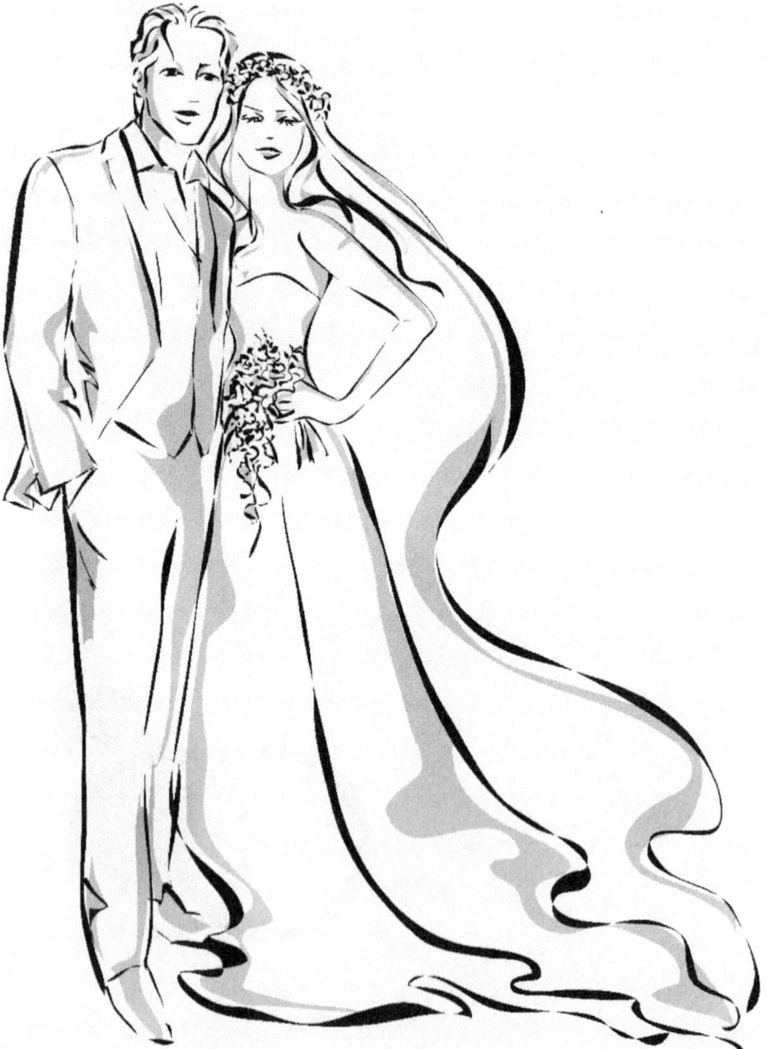

Seventeen

Luke

My hands shake as I hold the bottle and take a swig of the scotch. I close my eyes as I try to steady my breathing, the smell of her still around me. Fuck, she smells like heaven, the smell of a ripe lemon on a sunny day. All I wanted to do was lean into her and smell her one more time.

The minute she turned and asked me to unbutton her, everything in my body came alive. My fingers worked one button after another, and when I finally unzipped her, I looked up and saw that little freckle on her back. The same freckle that I kissed when we were together. My eyes go back to the closed door as I picture her getting out of her dress and standing in the middle of my bedroom almost naked. My cock springs to action, and I bring the bottle back to my lips to calm myself down. The burning hits the back of my throat right away as I swallow the amber liquid. "This is not how I planned to spend the night." I look up at the ceiling, trying to talk myself off the ledge when the door opens, and I don't know why, but I stand up straight.

"That's better," she says, walking toward me wearing just my black T-shirt. The way she swings her hips, I see the shirt sway against her upper thighs.

"That is most definitely not better," I mumble to myself as she walks toward me, and I really fucking hope she is wearing boxers under that shirt. Her long legs look sensational, and all I can do is watch her. She makes her way to the stool and climbs back up on it again, and I'm thankful that the island is covering the fact that I'm sure the shirt has risen, giving me an even better view of her legs.

"I didn't realize how heavy that dress was." She laughs as she sits down.

"I should go," I say at the same time that my head yells this is a bad, bad idea. She looks at me, confused. "I'm going to go and call your sisters and tell them where you are." The pressure in my chest suddenly makes it hard to breathe as my breathing now comes in pants.

"Why?" She gets up on the stool, leaning forward, and grabbing the scotch from me.

"There are a bunch of reasons," I reply. She brings the bottle to her lips, and I don't know why but they seem plumper.

"Which are?" She puts the bottle down after she finishes taking a sip. I should be happy that the gulps have now switched to sips.

"A whole bunch of reasons," I repeat, making her laugh.

"So you said, yet you can't come up with them." She tilts her head to the side. Enjoying that I'm fumbling.

"Well, for one, you just ran away from your wedding." I try to make sure that my words make sense.

"I don't know why that would matter that we are both here." She grabs the bottle again and sips it.

"And here we are, the two of us are alone." I stare at her as she tucks her hair behind her ear. "Alone in a cabin. With no one else. Alone."

"I don't think you said the word alone enough." She shrugs. "Not a big deal. What's your next one?" I just stare at her now, all the words are lost from my vocabulary. "You said there are a bunch of reasons, but you've only given me one."

"Two, it's a bad idea." My head spins as I think of reasons I shouldn't stay. Why I can't stay. Every single time she talks to me, my mind goes to fucking mush.

"Right." She giggles. "So far we have that I was getting married and it's a bad idea." She holds up two fingers.

"We are alone in a secluded cabin." My head starts to throb. I reach my hands out, putting them on the counter on each side. "I just don't want people to talk."

"Well, considering I ran from my wedding." She

crosses her hands in front of her. "People are still talking."

"But I don't want them to talk about us being here." The look of hurt fills her face, and I don't know why. Then it hits me that my words make it sound like I don't want to be here with her. "I don't want you to have a reputation because of me. Someone could have been outside and saw me carry you to my truck and take off." She rolls her lips. "What if they think I kidnapped you?"

"Relax, no one is grabbing their pitchforks and coming to kill the beast." She claps her hands together. "Get it? Beauty, which is me." She points at herself. "And the Beast." She points at me. "Which is you."

"Yeah, I got it," I say, and I seriously think I'm going to have a panic attack. "You're hilarious."

"It's one of my many talents," she says, and I miss this side of her. The side where we used to sit down and just talk after we would take care of whatever business we were dealing with. The funny Clarabella who used to just shoot the shit with me and make me laugh every single time she opened her mouth.

"Oh, trust me, I know," I respond, not telling her she has other talents I loved more. "But seriously. I'm going to leave and call your sisters and tell them where you are."

"I just don't know what the big deal is." She grabs the bottle and takes a sip.

I close my eyes as the thumping of my head comes on. "Are there any other reasons you shouldn't stay here?" She waits for me. "You really should know that when you say a bunch, it's not two. Two is a couple." She holds up her two fingers. "A bunch is more than five."

"Says who?" I put my hands on my hips.

"Google," she says, rolling her eyes and then taking another sip.

I want to reach for the bottle, but I know that if I'm going to drive, I shouldn't touch another sip. "We shared something," I finally say out loud, and the funny Clarabella is gone, and in its place is the Clarabella you don't want to fuck with. Her whole demeanor changes, and all she does is glare at me. *Idiot*, my head yells at me. At the same time, I want to tell her to forget it, but now that it's out there, I can't put it back in the box.

"Did we?" She folds her arms over her chest, and I regret even saying a word. "You don't say." I'm about to say something when she holds up her hand. "Wait a second. I believe what you said is 'this was a mistake.'" She looks at the ceiling. "Yeah, from my memory, which is foggy right now, but I'm pretty certain you looked at me and said 'this was a mistake.'"

"Clarabella," I say her name through clenched teeth, but it doesn't seem she is done speaking.

"Yes." She nods her head, putting her finger to her chin and tapping it to pretend she is thinking, but you know she doesn't have to think about this. "That is exactly what you said to me." She slams the hand that was tapping her chin on the island. "One minute, we were in bed together. You were all up in me." My teeth clench when she says that. "And then the next, you are sitting on the side of the bed while I lay there naked, telling me that it was a mistake." I'm about to speak, but she just glares at me. "I would choose your words very carefully, Luke."

"I have no excuse for that but to say I was scared." I swallow the lump in my throat.

She laughs, and I know she's not really laughing. Actually, come to think of it, it's the sound one makes before lunging for a person to choke them. "Okay, maybe that word isn't right." I hold up my hands. "I just didn't want anything between us to change." She just shakes her head. "What we shared was more than just a one-night stand." I run my hands through my hair, wanting to rip it out for her. "I'm not explaining myself well."

"Oh, you're definitely fucking this up to the tenth degree," she admits. "One minute, we were a mistake, and the next, you were gone." She laughs bitterly at me. "Fun. Good times." She takes a sip. "Also would not fucking recommend."

"Are you done?" I ask. And if I thought she was glaring at me before, I was wrong. I've always heard the saying if looks could kill, but for the first time in my life, I'm given that look. "I had no choice but to go. It was an opportunity of a lifetime. When Francois called me about the place in New York, I had no choice. It was my dream to have a restaurant in New York City. Not only was it my only chance but he also gave me six hours to get to him. I didn't know what to do."

"And you couldn't pick up the fucking phone to call and tell me?" she shouts and then throws up her hands. "Imagine that, picking up a telephone and calling." She brings her hand up to her ear with her thumb and pinky out, putting it to her ear. "It's barbaric, I know, but that's the way people communicate."

"What was I supposed to say?" I put my hands on my hips, my whole body now filled with nervous energies as we throw words at each other from each side of the island.

"I wanted you to say anything!" she yells. "Anything would have been better than nothing."

"What did you want me to say to you, Clarabella?" I look at her, and this time, I'm the one who doesn't give her a chance to say anything. "You wanted me to call you after you stormed out of the house and be like 'last night was amazing.'" My voice goes louder. "Best night of my life, but I'm leaving, so catch you on the flip side." I stare into her eyes. "Is that what you wanted?"

"It doesn't matter what I wanted," she says, and I can hear the hurt in her voice.

"Clarabella," I say her name again, this time soft, this time with a plea for her to look at me, but she doesn't. Instead, she looks to the side, and I see her blinking away tears. The fact that I made her have tears after everything she's been through today just pushes me over the edge. She deserves so much better than whatever it is that I have to offer. The fact that I brought her to tears breaks me, and I don't think I've ever felt this broken inside. The pain in my chest and the need to want to pull her to me is one that I will never be able to explain.

"You made your choice," she says, her voice low. "And I wasn't worth a thirty-second phone call. Instead, I had to find out from Mikaela."

I was wrong before. This right here shatters me. That she would think that she wasn't worth a thirty-second phone call is the dumbest thing she's ever said. "You are worth more than that."

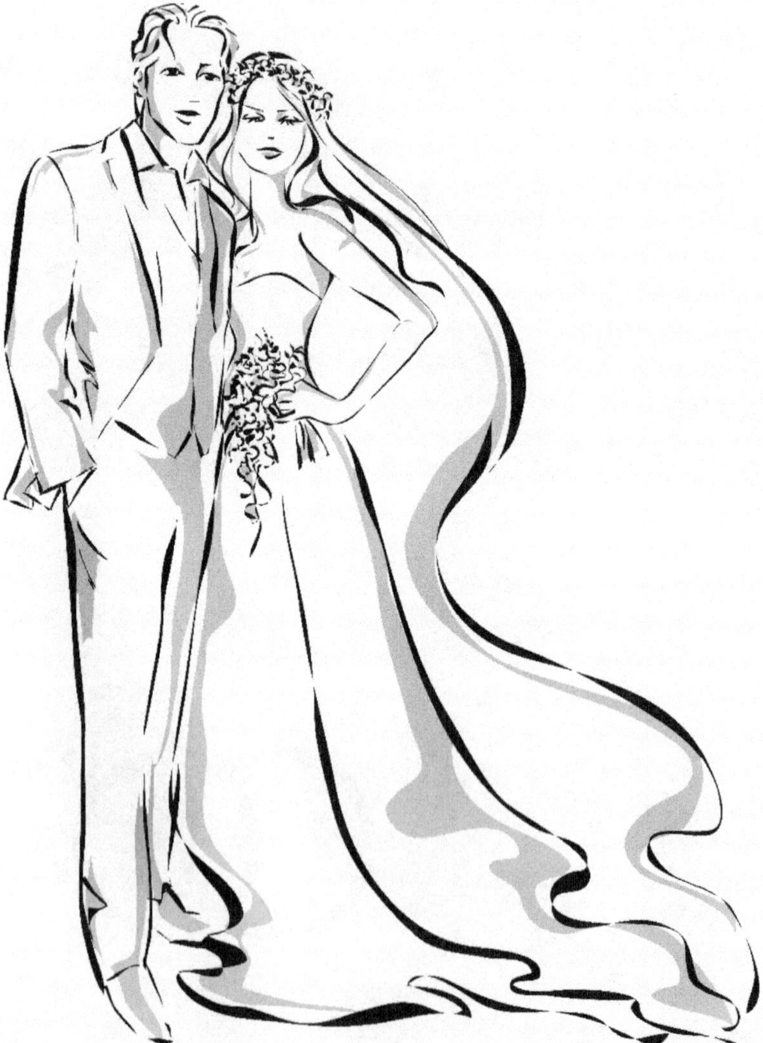

Eighteen

Clarabella

"You made your choice." My voice goes low as I fight back the fucking tears again. "And I wasn't worth a thirty-second phone call. Instead, I had to find out from Mikaela." Why can't my mouth just shut up? Why?

"You are worth more than that." His voice is soft, and I need to turn and look at him, but instead, all I can do is look down at my hands.

"I need a drink." My voice comes out shaky, and I reach for the bottle and take another sip. Maybe if I drink enough, I can forget everything.

"What did you eat today?" he asks, and I want to tell him it's not his concern.

"Breakfast," I answer him in one word.

"I'll make you food, and then I'll go," he says, and the lump in my throat fills up. I have to get away from him.

I grab the bottle and get down from the stool, then make sure my ass isn't showing when I walk toward the couch. "I don't think." I hear Luke's voice before I sit on the couch and sink into it. It's almost like quicksand.

"What the fuck?" I blurt, holding the bottle in the air to ensure I don't spill any of it.

"Shit," he says, rushing over to me, and it looks like he's going to grab me, and right now, after that talk, the last thing I want him to do is to touch me.

"Grab the bottle and turn around," I warn, and he grabs the bottle and just looks at me. "Fine, don't turn around," I say, moving to get out of the sunken hole. "But I'm not wearing your boxers under this shirt, and all these panties can be described as are string."

He glares at me, turning and walking away from me. I huff and puff, trying to get out, and finally, I roll out of the hole and end up on my knees. "What in the fuck?" I say, getting up now and feeling like I just ran a marathon.

"The raccoons made the base of the couch their home," he explains with his back still to me.

"Why in the hell would you not throw it out?" I brush myself off. "Can I get rabies from sitting on the couch?" He laughs. "It's all fun and games until I have to get a rabies shot from an infested couch." I look at his back and then to the couch. "I swear, I feel things crawling in me."

He looks over his shoulder, laughing. "Sit down and

let me make you food," he suggests, turning when he sees that I'm covered.

"Whatever." I roll my eyes, walking over to the stool and sitting again while he goes to the sink and washes his hands before coming back and grabbing the bag of food he brought in before.

I watch as he takes out the ingredients and then turns to grab a pan. "You have state-of-the-art cookware," I observe, grabbing the bottle of scotch. "But a couch that is rabies infested."

He just shakes his head. "I come here to get my inspiration."

"Did you cook the raccoons?" I ask with my hand halfway to my mouth, and he just glares at me.

"I like to come up here when a lot is going on and just find my peace," he explains as he takes the chicken out and pats it dry. "I come here and create dishes and then see if they are good or not."

"So, you come up here in the middle of nowhere." I cross my legs. "And cook for yourself and then eat the food." I want to puff out and tell him please spare me, but I don't.

"Pretty much," he says as he turns the stove on, and I just watch him cook. I don't know what to say. When I walked out of the room, the last thing I thought we would discuss would be him leaving. At least I told myself I wasn't ever going to bring it up and make him see how much it bothered me. But push comes to shove, and you get enough liquid courage in you, and all bets are off. Sitting in front of him, I'm trying to be snarky about it, but then my heart fell when he said that it was the best night of his life. I couldn't even look at him to see if he was telling the truth. Instead, I had to look to the side and fight through the need to let the tears come. I felt his eyes on me the whole time as I blinked my eyes furiously to make the tears go away.

"Can I use the bathroom?" I finally say, knowing that I should wash my face. "I'm assuming that you don't have makeup remover?" I ask as he looks up at me.

"Yes, it's next to the facial scrubs that is next to the hammam spa." I can't help but snort out at his comment.

"Where can I sign up for that service?" I ask over my shoulder and walk to the bathroom. I'm about to go in when I think about him not checking in there. "Is there a window in there?"

"No," he says, and I just nod my head. "Should be all clear."

"Great, just what you love to hear," I mumble, turning the door handle and stepping in to close the door behind me. The bathroom has one sink, a toilet, and a shower. It looks like it was updated at the same time as the kitchen. I walk over to the pedestal and turn on the water, looking into the mirror. Well, there are no black streaks down my face, so that's a plus. "They were not joking when they said waterproof." I take a second to wet my hands and then put them on my cheeks before walking out, and the smell just hits me and my stomach growls. "It smells amazing," I say, walking over to the kitchen as he whisks something in the cast-iron pan. "What are you making?"

"Chicken Alfredo," he answers, without looking at

me and I just stare at him. My heart is beating so hard in my chest I have to walk away from him in case he can hear it.

But then I stop and look over at him. "You were going to come up here on my wedding day, get trashed, and eat my favorite meal."

"I guess I'm a glutton for punishment," he says as he grabs two plates and puts food on them.

My mouth waters when I sit on the stool, and he walks over and puts a plate in front of me. "I know it wasn't on your menu for the wedding," he says, walking around me to sit down on the stool beside me. "Hope it passes your standards."

"Well, it looks like shit." I keep my face straight as I look at him and all he does is stare at me. "Kidding," I say, laughing, and he flips me the bird. This, this right here is what we do. We can hate each other one minute, and then it's back to normal. It's always been like that with him.

"Bon appétit," he says, grabbing his fork and twirling the pasta around it. I watch him take the first bite, and he nods his head. "Not too bad if I say so myself."

I grab my own fork, and the minute the pasta hits my tongue, I moan. "It's orgasmic," I say, and he just shakes his head. The creamy, buttery sauce just hits all the boxes as comfort food. "Was there anyone in New York?" The words leave my lips before I can kick myself. *Why the fuck would you ask him this? For what reason?* My head screams at me. I don't even look at him. Instead, I focus on the pasta in front of me.

"No one that I wanted to marry," he says, and I don't even know why it matters. I was going to get married. It's not like I waited for him. The rest of the meal is quiet, neither of us saying anything.

I look over at him as he finishes his last bite. "Why don't you just stay the night and leave tomorrow?" He just looks at me, and all I can do is stare into his eyes. They look as if there is a battle going on. "It's already late, and you look tired."

"There is only one bed," he reminds me, and I repeat the words so they can sink in my head.

"There is only one bed." I grab some pasta to keep my mouth busy from saying something that I shouldn't say.

"I would say, sleep on the sofa." I try to joke with him, but the nerves in my stomach make it feel like a fish flops when it gets out of the water.

"I'll sleep in the truck," he says, and I roll my eyes.

"That's stupid. We can sleep in the same bed," I respond and then grab the scotch, taking a gulp. "I can sleep under the covers, and you can sleep on top, and we can put some cushions in the middle of us."

"Like the wall of China?" he jokes, and I look at him.

"Yes, with a barbwire fence." I fake a smile as I take another sip. "Like shark-infested waters right out of Alcatraz."

He can't help but throw his head back and laugh. "I am going to clean up since you cooked."

"No, you don't have to do that," he says, leaning over and taking a long pull of the scotch.

"I'm assuming that means you're staying?" I ask,

getting up and walking over to the sink to see that he was cleaning as he went, and the only things left to clean are the two plates and the pan.

"Who is going to save you from the raccoons if I go?" He leans back, smirking at me, and the only thing I do is stick my tongue out at him, making him laugh even more. My head spins as I start to wash the dishes.

"I'm going to go shower," he shares, getting up from the stool and grabbing the bottle of scotch. I don't say anything to him. Instead, I finish cleaning up. My head spins even more now, and I laugh as I pull off the covers to the bed and climb under them. As soon as I lay my head on the pillow, the bathroom door opens, and he walks out just wearing his jeans. He looks around twice and then spots me in the bed. "Building the wall?" he asks, and I just laugh.

"I didn't turn off the lights." I close my eyes, taking in the spinning of the room. I open them up again, watching him walk to the wall and flip the switch. He steps into the room, and I see that his jeans button is undone. His feet are bare, and I can see his shadow coming to the bed.

"Permission to lie down on the covers," he jokes, and I can hear him chuckling before he lies down on his side of the bed.

"I didn't build the wall," I note. "My head was spinning." My eyes get used to the light, and the soft light from the moon comes into the window. "It's peaceful," I say, and he turns his head on the pillow and looks at me. "Did you mean what you said?"

"Which part?" he asks, his voice soft as he turns over

on his side to look at me.

"The part about our night together?" I ask, knowing that I shouldn't even care and there are other things to worry about. "Forget it," I say just as fast, getting ready to turn over and give him my back. I make a mental note to never ever drink scotch again.

His hand comes out, grabbing my hip before I turn around. "Clarabella." He says my name exactly like he did that night. "I'm a lot of things," he says, his voice coming out so clear. "I may be a coward for the morning after, but I'm not a liar."

I swallow, and I don't know why, but I feel like he's closer to me. "I never said you were a liar." The words come out, and my mouth is suddenly as dry as the desert. "I've drunk too much." I pretend as if I'm drunker than I really am.

"You didn't even drink that much." He calls me out on my lie. "You took sips the whole night."

"What do you want from me?" I wish the lights were on so I could see his face. So I could stare into his eyes and see what he's thinking.

The air feels so thick in the room. It feels like time is standing still. It feels like both of us know what is going to happen, but neither of us is sure it should happen. My heart starts to beat so hard I feel like it's literally going to come out of my chest. My tongue feels like it's getting heavy, and my hands are shaking with anticipation. My brain is finally catching up to what is happening in my heart when he says the words.

"I want this," he says, his voice almost growling. His

hand on my hip reaches up into the side of my hair, and in the blink of an eye, my hands are reaching for his face as his lips crash down on mine. The minute our tongues invade each other's mouth, we both moan. His tongue slides into mine, and I can taste the scotch on him. It's a moment that will forever stay with me, a moment that I guess was bound to happen. A moment that feels like it was always supposed to be like this. I move my head to the side so I can deepen the kiss, his tongue fighting with mine. We both want to win the battle as he pushes me onto my back. My leg moves up, but it's stuck under the cover.

"Wait." I move my head away from his, and he stops and doesn't move.

"I shouldn't have." He moves off me enough for me to throw the cover off me and then reach for him.

"This is better." I pull him back down on me, and my leg cocks up over his hip, my finger coming up and tracing his bottom lip. "Kiss me, Luke."

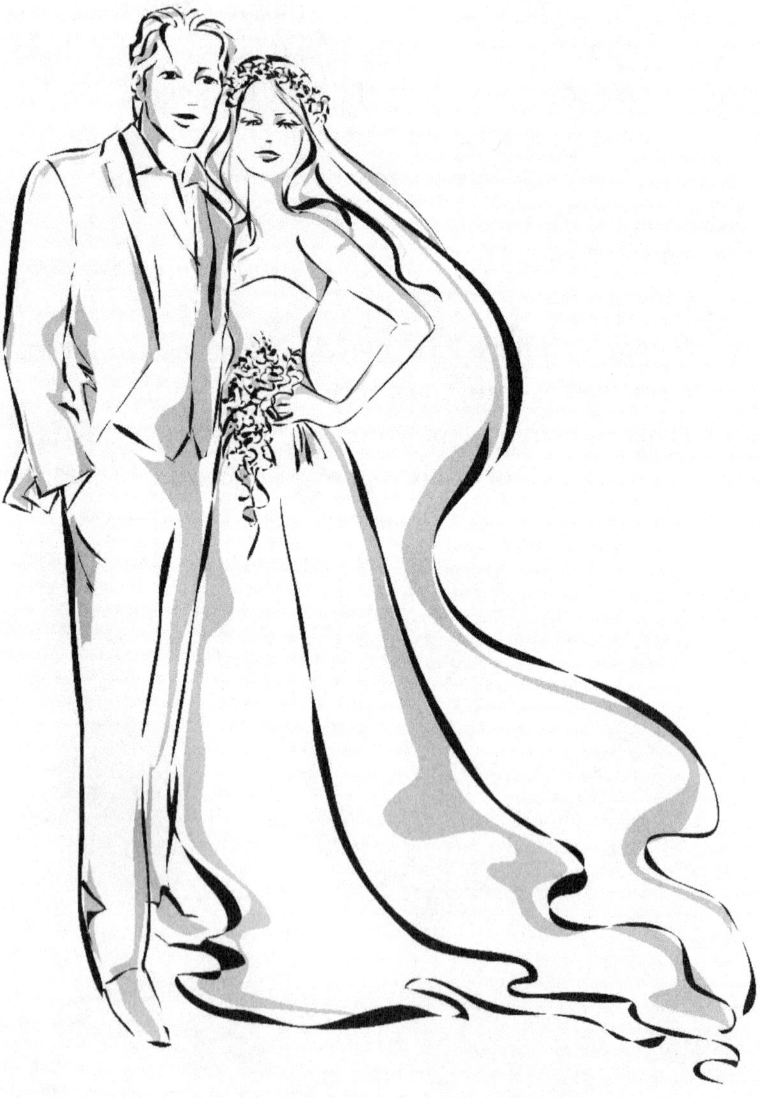

Nineteen

Luke

"Kiss me, Luke," she says as her fingers trace my lips. When she told me to stop before, I wanted to kick myself. I should have never kissed her; I was so out of fucking line. But lying in bed with her and just being near her does crazy things to me. Stuff that I've never felt before. With her, everything seems to come so naturally. With her, every single touch is like an electric shock. With her, every kiss feels like the first. With her, every single second I want to spend touching her, even if it's just her hand or to tuck her hair around her ear. It's fucking everything.

"With pleasure," I say right before my lips find hers

again. My tongue slides into her mouth, meeting hers. Her leg hitches over my hip, and my hand goes to her ass, finding it bare. The minute I squeeze her ass, we both moan. Her hips thrust against me, and I let go of her lips to move down to her neck. I trail kisses down her cheek, wrapping my arms around her tighter than I should. Her legs open for me, wrapping around my waist as I suck her neck. "Fuck," I say, closing my eyes as my tongue comes out and licks her neck.

"Wait," she says breathlessly, and I wish I'd kept the lights on so I could see how her eyes change colors when I slip into her. From the first time, I was mesmerized by seeing her eyes get darker every single time I took her. I loosen my grip on her, and she slips her hands between us. Grabbing the shirt and pulling it over her head, she shows me that she's completely naked under there. Well, the little panties barely hide anything. My mouth bends automatically, taking a nipple into my mouth.

"Yes," she hisses out as my hand comes up and I switch from one nipple to the other. I pinch the other nipple. "Fuck," she says, her legs becoming tighter around my waist. "You know how sensitive they are."

"Oh, trust me," I say, biting down on her nipple. "I remember." I move my head down her stomach. "I remember everything about that night." I look up at her, and I move down, and her legs fall from around my waist. "You know what else I remember?" I ask, kissing the inside of her thigh. "The landing strip that you have." My finger goes under the lace of the white panties, and her body shivers when I move the panties to one side, and it snaps under my fingers. "Oops." I laugh, and she just looks down at me.

"Nothing stopping you now." She spreads her legs even more but then sits up, and I get up on my knees. Her hands go to my pants, my cock rock hard under the zipper as she unzips me. "Because from what I remembered…" She pushes the pants off my hips. "You really liked it when…" She gets on her knees, the white string that she called panties falls down to her knees on the bed. "When you lie down." She pushes me back now and straddles my lap. "And I sit on your face." She bites my lower lip. "All the while I suck your cock."

My hands grab her ass. "My cock would like very much to get back into your mouth," I say to her as I fall onto the bed on my back. She puts her hands beside my head and bends down to kiss my lips, her tongue coming out to play with mine. She kisses me until I'm the one who is breathless, and when I open my eyes, she turns around.

"Now this." I lift my head, licking her slit and making her moan. "Is what I remembered." She falls forward. One of her tiny hands wraps around my dick, and I stop breathing for a second before she licks the head of my cock. "Fuck." I close my eyes for just another second before she takes the head of my cock into her mouth. "Are we going to race?" I challenge, licking her again. This time, my tongue circles around her clit. "First one to come is the bottom," I add. "You come, I pound you. I come, you ride me."

"Either way, I win," she says, her mouth swallowing

my cock while her hand continues to jerk it. I lick up her slit and suck in as she moves her ass from side to side.

One hand holds her ass in place while the other runs up her wet slit. "You are already wet for me." I observe as a finger slides right inside her, and she moans around my cock. "Slick." I add another finger inside her and move slowly, knowing she hates when I go slow. With Clarabella, it's always hard and always fast. "Your pussy tastes like heaven," I say as my tongue slides in with my fingers. "Fucking sweet." My finger gets buried inside her, my thumb circling around and around her clit, and she tries to move her hips, but my hand stops her. "Tell me what you need?" My fingers wiggle inside her as they slide out and then in so slowly, she lets go of my cock to moan. "All you need to do is tell me what you need, and I'll give it to you." I try to focus on her pussy, but her hand tightens on my cock as she jerks it.

"I need you to move faster," she declares, looking back at me. "And I need to…" She closes her eyes as I move my fingers faster than before. Her hand even stops moving, and as much as I love having her mouth on my cock, I love making her come more. I slip my fingers out of her, and she groans but not for long. "Luke."

"I know." I turn her over to her back and place my knees beside her, my cock next to her mouth. "But like this." I reach down, and my two middle fingers disappear inside her. "I get to finger fuck you and…" I bend down, taking a nipple in my mouth, knowing that the two together will set her off like a firecracker.

"Fuck," she says, lifting her hips off the bed and

trying to get me to go faster. "Stop torturing me." Her hand comes up to take my cock in it. "Or else I'm going to just take what I want."

"Oh, yeah?" I look up at her, my fingers moving in and out of her, and she's getting so wet. "And what are you going to do about it?" I move to the other nipple and bite down on it.

"Need more," she says breathlessly. "Need more." She lets go of my cock, and she moves at record speed. She sits up and pushes me down. I'm in shock, thinking maybe she changed her mind, but instead, she throws her leg over my hips and impales herself on my cock. "Yes," she cheers, and she rides my cock hard and fast. "That's what I need," she says with reckless abandonment and rides my cock. I let her set the pace, my hands on her tits rolling and pinching her nipples. Her pussy starts to tighten around my cock, and my balls get tight.

"I'm there," I share, and she closes her eyes as she moves up and down faster and faster. "Come on my cock," I say, and she nods her head, the words all stuck in her throat. "You wanted my cock, so I gave you my cock. Now come on it." I pinch both nipples at the same time, and it's what she needs to go over the edge.

"Yes," she says, over and over again, and my cock just explodes in her. She collapses on my chest and buries her face in my neck. My hands wrap around her. "That was what I needed." She kisses my neck softly. "Did you...?" She lifts her head.

"At the same time," I say, and she smirks at me.

"So, who won?" she asks, and I can't help but laugh.

"My cock is in you, so I think we can say we both won." I kiss her and turn her over on her back, and this time, I'm the one who fucks her.

I OPEN MY eyes for a second, the sun creeping into the room, before closing them again. I reach out my arm for Clarabella, but it comes up empty. My eyes fly open as I look at the side of the bed where she fell asleep. The pillow is still indented from her head as I get up on my elbow and look around the room. The covers are around my waist. "Clarabella?" I call her name, wondering if she is in the bathroom. I wait a couple of seconds to see if I hear any movement before I flip the covers off me, stand, and call her name again. "Clarabella." I grab my boxers and slip them on, but I have this dread in me that she left. My heart starts to go crazy in my chest, and my mouth feels like there is sand in it as I try to swallow. I rush out of the bedroom, looking around the empty cabin. The front door is open, and I can see her sitting down with the shirt I was wearing last night. She looks out into the trees, not moving. I look over to the kitchen and see that she started coffee.

My feet move before my head, and she looks over her shoulder. "Hey," I say, and my heart sinks when she doesn't look at me. Instead, she turns her head and just continues staring out into the horizon.

"I made coffee," she says loudly, and I turn to walk to the coffee machine before going out to her. The whole time I'm psyching myself, looking over at my shoulder to make sure she doesn't take off.

I fill up my white cup with the black coffee and turn to walk back outside, sitting right next to her. The birds chirping in the trees has her looking up. "It's so peaceful here," she notes. I bring the cup to my lips, trying to calm down that she hasn't looked over at me. Her hair is wild from the shower we took last night and from pulling it most of the night afterward. She takes a sip of her coffee, and fuck, if she isn't the most beautiful woman I've ever seen. The only thing that I can think of is boy, did I fuck up when I told her she was a mistake.

"When did you get up?" I ask awkwardly, trying not to get caught staring at her and making her think I'm a weirdo.

"A while ago," she says. "I didn't want to wake you."

"Not going to lie," I start to say and then stop nervously. "When I opened my eyes and found the bed empty, I sort of had a slight panic attack thinking you took off on me." I take a gulp of the hot coffee, hoping that it burns my throat, and I stop talking.

She laughs. "Nope, I only run away when I'm wearing a wedding dress." I can't help but chuckle at her joke.

"What were you thinking about?" I ask, turning to see that she is looking at a tree with a bird in it.

"Everything," she says. "And nothing."

"Regrets?" I finally say, and her head whips to look at me. "Do you regret last night?"

"Should I?" she hisses, her teeth clenched together.

"I was just making sure that you know." My voice

trails off as I think for the right words. "Yesterday was a roller coaster of emotions, and today, the day after your wedding, you wake up naked, not next to the person you probably thought you would be next to, so I was just wondering."

"Definitely didn't think I'd wake up with you this morning." She laughs. "If I'm honest."

The burning starts in my stomach, and I try to convince myself that it's from the hot coffee that I just drank, but it's not. It's from the thought that she could have been married this morning. "What's that look about?" she questions, and I look back at her.

"Do you remember the first day we met?" I ask, and she just smiles.

"No," she lies, but I can tell from the way her eyes light up that she does. "Oh, wait." She puts her finger to her nose and pretends to think about it. "It was at a party." I bring the cup of coffee to my mouth. "You pretended you liked me and then dated my best friend."

I shake my head. "I didn't pretend I liked you." I side-eye her. "Besides, I wasn't the one who stopped talking to the other person."

She gasps. "I didn't stop talking to you."

"Really?" I put my coffee cup down. We never really spoke about what happened in college, not even when we were friends again after she stopped hating me. "We were friends." I hold up my finger when she looks like she is about to say something. "I used to come over early just to talk to you."

"But," she says, and I shake my head, and she just

glares.

"Then one day, you just stopped talking to me." I shrug. "So you were the one who hated me."

"Are you done yet?" she asks, and I know that she's ready to argue because she puts her cup down beside her. "Okay, one, I thought we had a connection." She points at me and then her. "And then I walk out, and you are all tongue down my best friend's throat."

"She stuck her tongue down my throat the minute you left to go to the bathroom," I admit to her. "So I figured that she knew something I didn't know." She glares at me, and I smile and lean in to kiss her lips softly. "Sorry, go on," I say, but the need to touch her is greater than getting this story straight, at least for the next thirty minutes. "Wait." I hold up my hand before placing it on her cheek and then kiss her softly. "Now you can continue."

"I don't know what I was saying." She smiles and kisses me again. Her eyes are so much lighter than when I walked out, and if I did anything right this weekend, the fact that I made her smile is everything.

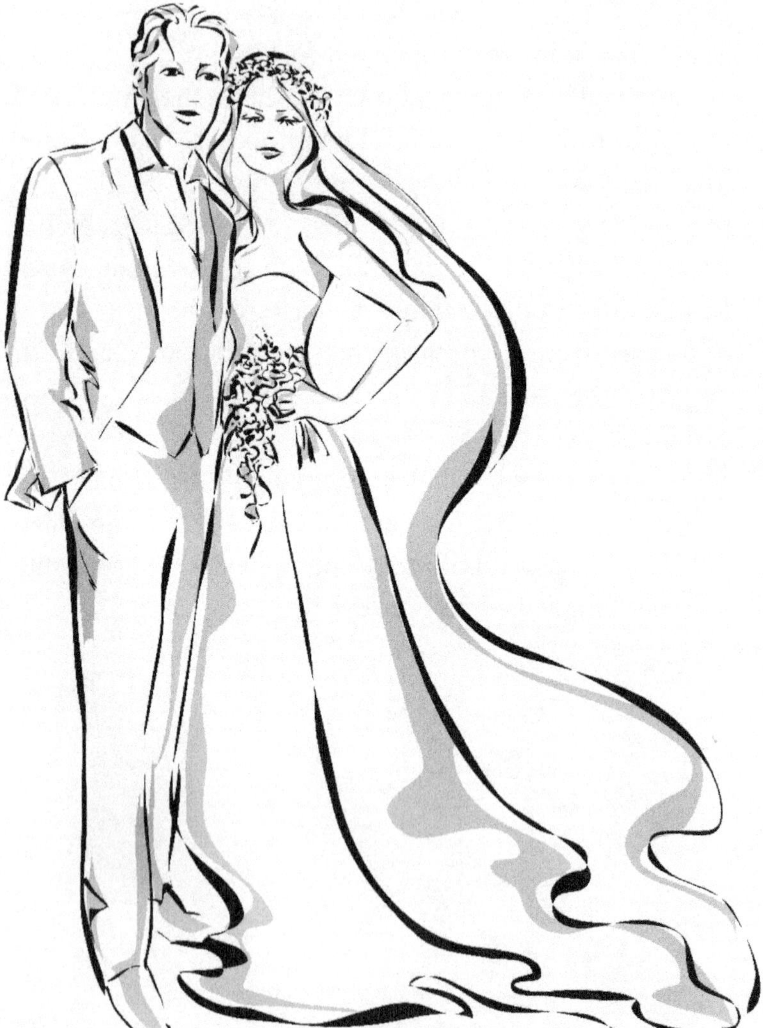

Twenty

Clarabella

"I don't know what I was saying," I admit and lean forward to kiss him again. I can't help but smile. "Oh, I know, when you started dating my best friend and would taunt me."

"I never taunted you," he says. "I thought you hated me."

"What?" I respond, shocked. "How can you say that?" I watch him as he shakes his head, and his hand falls from my face. He takes the same hand and puts it around my shoulders.

"She told me so," he says, and I look at him, shocked. *That fucking bitch*, is going through my head.

"Okay. One, she knew I had a crush on you. I told her." I hold up my hand. "And two, I stopped talking to you because my crush was becoming deeper than I wanted it to, especially since you were banging my roommate."

It's his turn now to move away from me. "I never banged her." He holds up his hand, and I'm shocked to say the least.

"She told me," I mumble.

"Well, this is awkward," he says. "One, we dated for two months, and well, it was weird." My eyebrows press together. "She was all touchy-feely when you were there, and then it was like a switch went off when you weren't."

I laugh. "And this is why I'm not friends with her anymore." I shake my head. The minute she started dating Luke, I started distancing myself from her. Who dates the guy your roommate likes? Oh, I know, a bitch. One you don't need.

"So that's why you hated me?" he asks, and I roll my eyes.

"I didn't hate you," I say, ignoring his laughter. "I just didn't like you." I drink the cold coffee. "Much."

"You literally stopped all communication with me, and when you saw me again four years later, you refused to even talk to me." His arm pulls me closer to him. I don't say anything, and neither does he. I just rest my head on his shoulder. When I woke up this morning, I got out of bed as quietly as I could. I thought he would wake up again and tell me it was a mistake, so I got myself ready for it. Plus, my head was spinning with everything that happened yesterday.

"Clarabella," he says as he kisses my head. "We should maybe talk a bit about last night." *Here we go*, my head says, expecting him to say something I don't want to hear, but he doesn't. "We didn't use protection."

"I have an IUD." I turn in his arms to look at him. His arm falls from my shoulders, but he holds my hip. "And I'm clean. I got tested." He looks down at me. "It was for insurance. Edward and I always used protection."

"I've been with one person besides you, and I wore protection," he says, and I hate the way my stomach goes tight. *I was engaged*, my head tells me. "What do you want to do?" he asks, and I look at him.

"About life?"

He laughs. "No, about today. Do you want to go back home?" My head starts to shake before he even finishes.

"Would it be okay if we stayed the weekend?" I ask, and he just smirks.

"There is no Wi-Fi or television. What will we do to pass the time?" He winks at me. "I mean, I can think of a couple of things."

I can't help but throw my head back and laugh out loud, the sound echoing in the middle of the trees. I stand beside him, and he looks up at me. His hair still has the spots that my fingers were pulling last night. "I think it's best if you show me." I tilt my head to the side.

He stands up, wrapping his arm around my waist to

pick me up. "I like that idea better than mine," he says, walking back into the cabin where he spreads me on the counter and eats his breakfast.

"I CAN'T BELIEVE that you didn't bring any other clothes," I gripe, putting on his boxers and a black T-shirt. "If we get pulled over, or we have a flat tire, they are going to think you kidnapped me."

He looks over at me, laughing. "Not with those shoes." He smirks as I slip my feet into my wedding shoes. "Fuck," he swears, and I look over at him. "Should have made you wear the shoes last night."

I don't even bother answering him. Instead, I just roll my eyes and head toward the truck. "We literally can't even stop and get out of the car." I look down at my exposed legs.

"I can." He closes the door to the cabin behind him and walks out with his dumb backpack in one hand and my wedding dress in the other. "I have enough gas to get home." I watch him walk down the steps toward the truck. He's always been hot, but now with the scruff on his face a touch longer, he looks even hotter. This whole weekend has been somewhat of a blur. There was a lot of sex, but then there were times that he just let me be. He let me sit in the silence of the cabin as I gathered my thoughts. He places my wedding dress down in the back seat gently before getting into the front. "You good?" He looks over at me, and I just nod my head. He did that a lot this weekend when he saw me sitting outside and just reflecting. I would go outside when he was in the shower or when he was cooking, and he let me have the time to reflect. He never once intruded, even during morning coffee when he would come outside and sit with me. He would wait for me to say something.

"Not in the least." It's the first time I answer him anything but yes. My fingers tap on the middle console where my phone is charging. I have no doubt that once it gets a signal, it'll be going off like fireworks on the Fourth of July. "But you have to face the music at some point."

He slips his hand in mine as he starts the drive home. We don't say anything, and I know right away when we get a signal. The pings are every single second. "Well, that was nice." I slip my hand out of his and grab the phone, not sure what is going to be waiting for me. I see that I've missed more notifications that I don't even want to read at this point. So instead, I just send a text to the family chat.

Me: On my way home. Should be there in two hours.

I power down the phone and place it back in the cupholder. The closer that we get to home, the more my stomach sinks. At one point, I open the window because I feel like I'm going to throw up. I lean my head against the door and close my eyes as the wind blows on my face.

When the truck stops, I open my eyes to see that I'm parked in my driveway. "You have arrived at your destination," Luke quips. "Your destination is on the right." He tries to make a joke about it, and I even laugh before turning to see my sisters pull in behind us. "And here comes the cavalry." I look over at him and wonder what he's thinking. I also know that with my sisters here, we aren't going to be able to talk freely.

"Well, well, well," Presley goads, getting out of her car and slamming the door. "Look at what the cat dragged in."

"I'll get your stuff," Luke says quietly from his side of the truck.

I pull the door handle open and step out. My sisters both look at me. "What the hell are you wearing?" Shelby shrieks.

"It's the only thing he had." I point over to Luke.

"Are you wearing anything under that T-shirt?" Presley folds her arms over her chest, her eyebrows going up.

"Boxers," I admit. Their mouths hang open, and I throw up my hands. "These are the only clothes he had." I look over at Luke as he carries my wedding dress over his shoulder.

"I was only going away for the weekend." He tries to defend himself, but nothing he says will make this okay.

"And you brought no clothes?" Shelby asks, shocked.

"That's what I said." I walk toward my house, looking around to see if any of my neighbors are out. We got home just before lunch on a Monday, so it's no surprise that most of them are at work.

"I wasn't planning on going out." Luke shakes his head and walks behind me.

"I'm sorry," Presley says, not moving. "I just can't wrap my head around the fact that you went away without packing clothes." She puts her hand to her head. "Like what if you had an accident and shit yourself." Luke looks at her like she has two heads.

"That's what I said." I look over at them when I put the code to the door in, and it doesn't open.

"Oh, we changed the code," Shelby shares. "We thought that Edward would come and camp out." She gives me the new code, and I put it in. The minute I walk in, I cough at the smell.

"What the hell is that smell?" I look around, seeing if maybe something is on fire. I wave my hand in front of my nose.

"Mom came by yesterday and saged the house." Presley laughs. "To take out the bad juju. She wanted to torch the bed, but we stopped her. You're welcome."

"Well, that might be my cue to leave," Luke says, looking at me. I want to say something to him, but my sisters are right there. "Where do you want the dress?"

"Just throw it on the couch," I reply, pointing over to the living room off the entrance. He walks over and places it on the couch gently. "Thank you," I mumble to him as he walks back to the door.

"Ladies." Luke nods at them and then looks back for a second before walking to his truck. My sisters look at him and then back at me

"I'm going to change." I avoid them. "And when I come back, you can fill me in on everything."

"I'll get some coffee going," Shelby states.

"Coffee!" Presley gasps. "We're discussing her doomed wedding. Cut her some slack."

"Fine," Shelby says, and I ignore them while I walk to the bedroom, stopping and then turning on the step.

"Um," I start to say, not sure how to ask if Edward came to collect his things.

"Gone," Presley says. "Threw everything in a black garbage bag and dropped it off on the hood of his car." I just nod, then turn to go change. I put on a pair of yoga pants and go back downstairs. I'm not ready to take Luke's shirt off yet.

"Okay." I slap my hands together. "Tell me what I missed." I sit down on the couch as my sisters come to sit with me. One's holding three shot glasses, and the other one is holding a bottle of scotch. I'm surprised that I don't even take one shot while they fill me in. People were shocked to say the least. My mother was furious, Edward was calling them nonstop, and his parents threatened to sue us if the deposits were not returned. It was a nightmare, and the more and more they spoke about it, the worse my headache became. The phone in my lap beeped a couple of times, and I avoided looking at it because I thought it was Edward or my mother.

"Are you going to be okay to come to work?" Shelby asks quietly after they stop talking for ten minutes. "You don't have to because you were already scheduled off."

"What am I going to do, sit at home and wallow?" I shake my head, putting it back down on the couch.

"Okay, so are we discussing what we are going to tell people?" Presley is the one to ask.

"I mean, we can always go with he didn't satisfy you sexually." Shelby winks at me.

"Or his dick was too small," Presley adds. "Was his dick small?"

"His dick was fine," I tell them, feeling numb. "I don't know what I want to tell people." I wipe away a tear that escapes. "I'm pissed because I'm not even sad. I'm just tired. I'm emotionally drained, yet I have to put a smile on my face and pretend that I'm the bad guy."

"You are not the bad guy," Shelby says.

"What the hell am I going to say? He cheated on me and had a child," I say angrily.

"Well, it's the truth." Presley shrugs. "You aren't lying."

"I can't do that to the child. If I say something, I'm a bitch, but if I don't say something, I'm a selfish bitch for running out on my wedding day." I look at both of them. "I need one of you to call Edward and tell him that if he doesn't rein in his parents, I'm going to have no choice but to tell them the real reason I took off."

"I'll volunteer as tribute." Presley holds up her hand as my phone beeps again, and I look down and see that it's Luke.

"I know I should be the one to do it," I admit, "but I'm just not ready to talk to him or see him yet. If I do see him, I won't be able to hold myself together enough without wanting to physically assault him." I get up now. "With that being said, I need a shower."

"Oh my God, did he not have a shower?" Presley asks, putting a hand to her chest, and I laugh at her.

"He did," I assure her, walking away but not turning around, just in case they can see in my eyes that we shared the water each and every time.

"Oh, Clarabella," Presley says, and I look over at her. "We will be discussing this whole taking-off-with-Luke shit."

"I don't know what you mean. I walked out and had to escape. He was there."

"Is that your story?" Shelby gets up, tilting her head to the side.

"That's my story, and I'm sticking to it." I look at both of them, who share a look before they walk out the front door. I drag my ass up the stairs, going straight for the bathroom. I peel his shirt from my body and step into the shower.

When I get out, I slip on a pair of shorts and a matching tank top. My phone rings, and I see that it's Luke. I look down at the phone, and I want to answer it, but I'm not going to lie, I'm scared of what he is going to tell me. The minute the phone rings, the phone pings, and I see it's a text from Edward, so I turn my phone down on the counter. When a soft knock comes from the door, my whole body goes tense. I walk through the house, tippy-toeing to the front door. I look out the peephole and see Luke there, so I turn the lock and open the door. He's wearing a white T-shirt with dark blue jeans. His hair looks like he just got out of the shower and ran his fingers through it. His scruff is untouched from this morning.

He stands there in the middle of the porch, and my heart goes to my throat. His blue eyes light up when he sees me. "Hi," I mumble. "What are you doing here?"

"Figured you wouldn't make yourself something to eat." He holds up the brown takeout bag. "And then I brought this just in case." He holds up a bottle of scotch, and I can't help but laugh. "I called you," he says, and I can tell he's nervous. "But you didn't answer me, and I don't know why but I decided to just show up."

"You took a hell of a gamble," I reply, leaning on the doorjamb. I'm not even going to justify the way my heart is racing or the fact that I can't help the smile on my face. I also am not justifying that this is exactly what I needed after today.

"I'm a gambling man." He smirks at me, and my stomach fucking flutters. "May I enter?"

"I don't know." I fold my arms over my chest. "Depends on what's in the bag." I point at the paper bag. "And if it will taste just as good reheated?" He takes two steps in, kicking the door closed behind him before turning me and pushing me against the door.

"Hi," he says right before his mouth finds mine. His tongue slides into my mouth, and my hands roam over his chest. He lets go of my lips to ask, "Where can I put these?"

"Kitchen." I point over to the kitchen, and he walks over to put the bag and the scotch on the counter. "Let me show you around," I suggest, knowing in my head there is only one place I want to show him, and that's my bedroom. I walk to him, grabbing his hand and turning to walk up the stairs, wiggling my hips a bit more than I should. "This is my bedroom," I say and feel him behind me, holding my hips in his hands. He bends his head and attacks my neck. My hand comes up to his head.

I turn my head, watching him kiss my neck. "You have a nice bedroom." He turns me around to face him. My hand grips the bottom of his shirt, and I pull it over his head. His hands go to the spaghetti straps of my tank top, peeling them down my arms. My tits spring free as he bends to take a nipple in his mouth. I close my eyes as he backs me up against my dresser, only stopping when my ass hits it. He picks me up, placing my ass on my dresser. My whole body is on fire from his touch even though he barely touched me.

"I missed you today." His face is buried in my neck before he moves his hands down, peeling my shorts off me. His hand around my waist picks me up, placing my bare ass back down on the cool dresser. "It's crazy, right?" he says, getting to his knees and coming face-to-face with my pussy. He sucks my clit into his mouth, and my back falls against the wall as I put one foot on the dresser and the other on his shoulder. "It's fucking crazy," he quizzes, and at this point, with his tongue on me, I can't even focus on anything else. "You are so wet for me," he says, licking up his fingers, and my hand grabs his hair, wanting to keep him right there. "All day." He slides his two fingers inside me as he sucks my clit. His fingers move so fast, and I can't help but moan. "I can't get enough of you." His eyes look up at me as his tongue flicks my clit. "I can't wait," he admits, standing and kissing me. I taste myself on him as my hands go to the button of his jeans. "Put me in you," he says when his cock springs free after I push down his pants and boxers. "I need to be inside you."

"I need you inside me, too," I agree, gripping his cock in my hand and jerking him twice before rubbing it up and down my slit.

"Fuck," he hisses out when the head of his cock slides into me. "I was going to go slow with you."

"Later." He stops to look at me. "Round two can be slow."

"Is that so?" he asks, sliding inside me just a touch more. "And how is round one going to be?" He licks his thumb and rubs my clit, and I swear I'm going to cry out in ecstasy. "You like that?" He does the circle again. "I can feel you squeeze me." All I can do is nod because I'm afraid I'll cry out if he doesn't start to move.

"Luke." I pant out his name in a whisper.

"Yeah, baby?" He looks into my eyes.

"More." That's the only thing I can say, and he looks down at his cock halfway in me.

"Tell me," he says, and I bite my lower lip, trying to control myself.

"I just need you to slam into me and make me come," I reply, trying to move my hips.

"You going to watch?" He looks down at his cock as he slides into me some more. His cock is now half buried. "Your pussy is so tight." My eyes fixate on the way he's slowly sliding into me until he's buried all the way in. We both moan as he pulls all the way out until the tip of his cock slides out, and then this time, he slams right into me.

"Like that?" he asks as he repeats the move over and over again. My hand moves to the middle of my legs as I start to play with my clit. "You are almost there," he says. The sound of skin slapping is now filling the room louder than the two of us panting. "You get so fucking tight," he grits between clenched teeth. "I can barely pull out." I can't look away from his cock, and when I know I'm coming, I finally close my eyes and yell his name. "Fuck, one more before I come," he orders, pounding into me over and over again as I come. He grabs my nipple in his mouth, biting down on it and making me come again. I wish I could close my legs to stop him from moving. "I'm there," he says.

"My mouth," I say, pushing him off me as I push off the dresser and fall to my knees. I take his cock into my mouth just as he comes right down my throat.

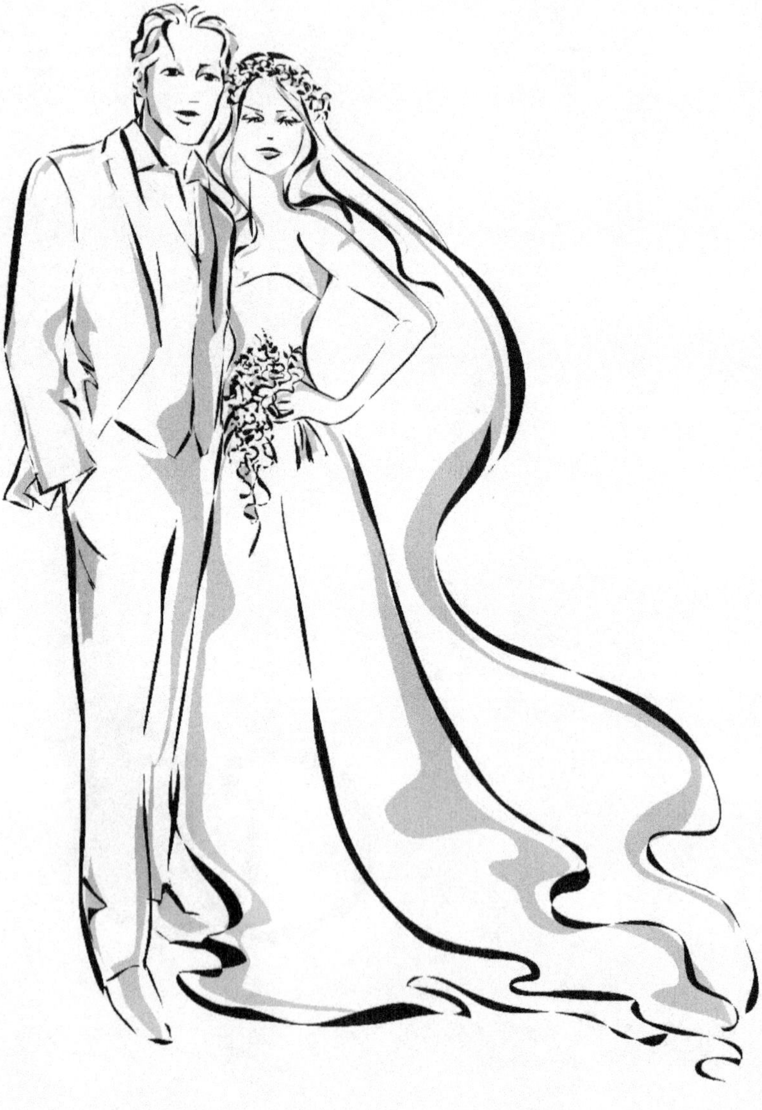

Twenty-One

Luke

"Holy shit." Those are the only two words that can come out of my mouth at this moment. I'm actually afraid that my knees are going to give out and I'm going to fall to the floor.

"That was," Clarabella states, while she still sucks my cock, jerking it a couple more times. "Exactly what the doctor ordered." She looks up at me as she drops my cock from her hand. My cock cries out in protest, wanting to immediately get back into her. She gets up from her knees, the only thing she is wearing is the tank top around her waist.

I lean in and kiss her lips. "Where is the bathroom?" I

ask, and she points at the door in the corner.

"You want me to come with you?" she asks and winks while she pulls up her tank top.

"I think I'm good," I reply, walking to the bathroom and not bothering to close the door. "Are you hungry?" I turn on the water and hear her laughter.

"Is that code for you want me to suck your dick?" I hear her voice coming closer and closer to the bathroom. "Because I think I just did that." She leans against the doorjamb. "And I think you ate dessert as well."

I finish cleaning up and walk to her. The need to keep kissing her is becoming very, very fucking strong, just like the need to see her again today, even though I knew that I should give her some space. I just couldn't. Plus, when she didn't answer me, I hated to think she was feeling down and I wasn't there. "Is that a yes, you're hungry, or a no, you're full?"

"I haven't eaten anything besides dick today," she says, and I can't help but laugh. I slip my hand in hers, turning to walk out of her bedroom and head to the kitchen. "Don't you need a shirt?" I look over my shoulder at her. "What?" she asks, walking down the steps. "I just don't want you to get burned in my house and then sue me."

"I'm sure we can come to some sort of arrangement." I kiss her neck as I get the paper bag. "Now, before we spend the night making out on your couch."

She throws her head back and laughs at me. "Is that what you think we are going to do?"

"It's not what I think we are going to do. It's what I

know we are going to do," I assure her. "How does a nice grilled salmon and vegetable medley sound?" I ask, and she just looks at me.

"I love when you talk dirty to me," she says. "What can I do to help?"

"You can sit your sweet ass on that stool and tell me about your day," I suggest. "Maybe have a glass of wine."

"Listen, if you are going to keep talking dirty to me, I might have to take off all my clothes." She walks over to one of the cupboards, grabbing two glasses and placing them on the counter next to me.

"If you take off your clothes, we really are never going to eat," I admit as she comes over and grabs a bottle of wine from the fridge, then pulls out the cork. She stands just close enough to me for me to lean over and kiss the freckle on her back that I love so much.

"You always kiss me on the same spot." She looks over at me as she pours a glass of white wine.

"You have a freckle," I say, kissing the spot again. "It calls to me." I smirk at her, and she brings the wineglass to her lips.

"I can hear something else calling for you," she says, and this time, it's my turn to laugh.

"Go." I point at the chair, and she kisses the underneath of my chin.

"Fine," she huffs, pouring a glass of wine for me and then grabbing the bottle to go sit down. "So how did it go with your sisters?" I ask, and I see the change in her eyes. "Forget I asked. It's really not my business."

"Did you go to the restaurant today?" she questions.

I nod, grabbing a pan and turning away from her. I hope she doesn't see that it bothers me that she isn't sharing with me. "What is the word on the street?"

I put the pan on the stove. "There is some chatter about the wedding," I answer her honestly. "But I didn't ask."

"What sort of chatter?" she asks, and I know it bothers her just from her tone.

"That you took off," I say, making sure that the heat is high enough before turning and starting on the veggies. "It's like the town secret as to why."

She rolls her eyes now. "Oh, here we go."

Hating to see how much it bothers her, I make sure to change the subject. "If it makes you feel better," I say as I slice and dice, "they started a side bet about Presley."

She claps her hands. "I want in on that one." She raises her hand.

"It's twenty-five to one that she makes it down the aisle the first time." I look up at her as I add salt and pepper to the top of the salmon.

"Out of all of us, she's the only one who is actually going to make it down the aisle the first time," she says, taking another sip of her wine as I add the salmon in the pan.

"She's not even dating anyone." I chuckle.

"No, but she's in love with Bennett, and he's in love with her." I stand here shocked at this news. "It's supposed to be a secret, but anyone who spends ten minutes with them can see it."

"No kidding," I agree, shocked, and for the rest of the

meal, neither of us talks about anything but her would-be wedding.

The two of us work side by side cleaning up. Every time she passes me, her hand goes from my back to my ass. Her touch was so soft. If I wasn't looking at her, I wouldn't believe it happened. Just like when I walked past her as she was drying the dishes, I stood behind her and pushed my cock into her ass. A touch for a touch is how the game was played until we couldn't wait one more minute, and I bent her over the stairs and had my way with her. The two of us collapsed into bed not long after.

THE SOUND OF a ringing phone wakes me up. "Ugh, what time is it?" I ask, looking over to the right finding the side of the bed empty. I hear the phone again. Looking over at the door, I hear that it's coming from downstairs. "Clarabella?" I say her name and then hear the sound of the shower at the same time as I hear the doorbell ring. "What the fuck?" I look over at my own phone at the side table, seeing it's just after seven o'clock.

I rub my hands over my face. The sound of her phone rings again, and I reach for my jeans. I'm pulling them over my hips when the doorbell rings again. "Holy fuck," I curse, buttoning my jeans as I walk downstairs. The bell rings again, and so does her phone. "Oh my God," I say, unlocking the front door and swinging it open.

"What the fuck?" Edward says, standing there wearing

jeans and a shirt. "Who the fuck are you?"

"Me?" I say, shocked. "What the fuck are you doing here?"

"My fiancée lives here," he replies, and I just laugh at him. My whole body fills with anger seeing him standing there at her front door. "Clarabella!" he shouts her name over my shoulder because there is no way in fuck I'm letting him in the door.

"I think it's a good idea if you get the fuck out of here," I growl through clenched teeth. "Before."

"Before what, you imbecile?" He takes a step closer to me.

"Oh my God." I hear Clarabella from behind me. "What the fuck are you doing here?" She pushes me out of the way, standing in front of me. Her hair is wrapped in a towel as she holds the robe she is wearing closed.

"What the fuck am I doing here?" Edward hisses at her, his face getting red. "What the fuck am I doing here?" He points at his chest. "What the fuck is he doing here?"

"That is none of your business," she says to him.

He throws his head back and laughs. "You are doing this to get back at me because of Louise." He shakes his head.

"Yeah, because the only way I would sleep with him is because you were sleeping with Louise." She snorts. "Idiot. You need to leave."

"I'm not leaving until you talk to me," he responds, and she just nods her head.

"Fine by me." She grabs the door. "But if you don't

get off my step in one minute, I'm calling the police and telling them that there is an intruder trying to break in."

She takes another step into the house and slams the door shut in his face. "Clarabella." He pounds on the door.

"Fifty seconds, Edward, and trust me, it would give me great pleasure to see you carted away in handcuffs." She turns to look into the peephole. "Forty-five seconds!" she shouts. "Lying sack of shit," she mumbles. "Thirty seconds!" she shouts yet again. "I can't wait to see your mug shot." She pushes away from the door.

"Is he gone?" I ask, and she just looks at me.

"What the hell were you thinking?" She glares at me, and I'm standing here shocked. "Why would you answer the door with your shirt off?" She storms past me.

"You have got to be kidding me," I say. "How is any of this my fault?" My stomach burns as she slams the cupboard door. "I was sleeping when your phone started going off and then the doorbell."

"And you thought, let me go downstairs and answer the door." She laughs bitterly, and my stomach sinks as I watch her make her coffee. "You didn't even think that, I don't know, maybe I shouldn't answer her door?" She turns, and I can see the anger in her eyes. She's pissed that she got caught with me.

"You are completely right," I agree, turning and jogging up the stairs to grab my shirt and phone from the side table. The whole time, my body is shaking with anger. I jog back down the steps, seeing her in the middle of the kitchen with her head hanging down. How the fuck did the last couple of days go from being the best days of my life, and then in the blink of an eye, it's all over? Poof. Gone. In a blink of an eye. "I'll see myself out." I don't even wait for her to say anything before I storm out of the house, slamming the door behind me.

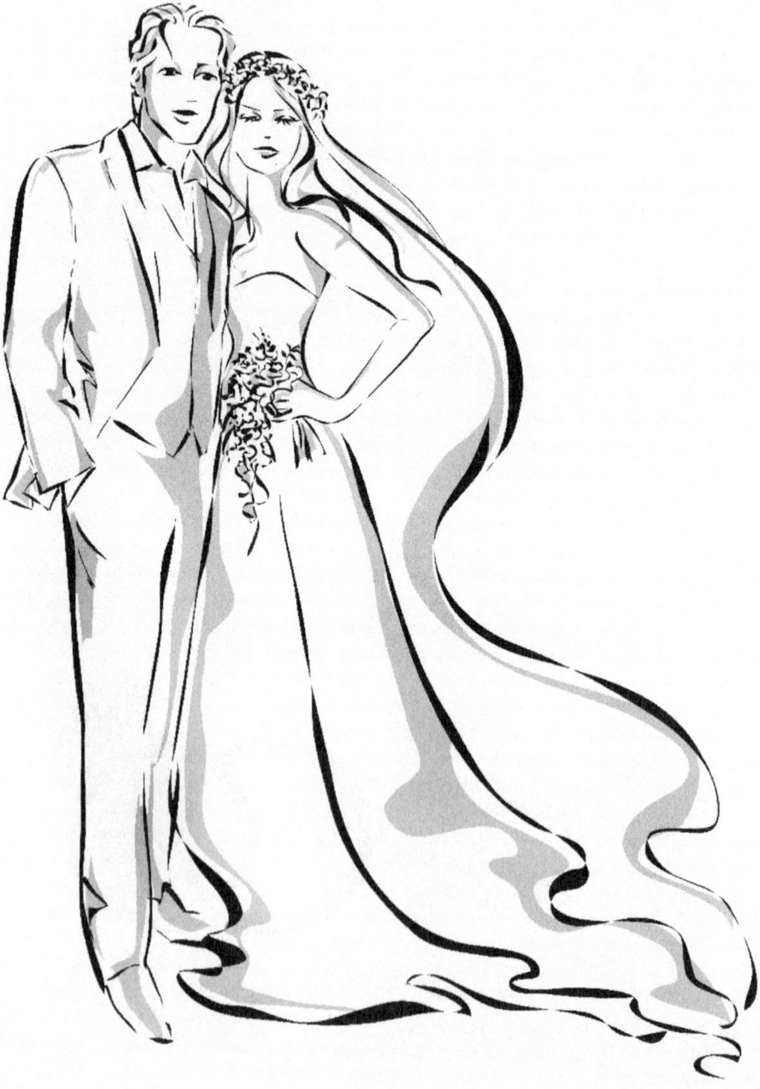

Twenty-Two

Clarabella

"I'll see myself out." He doesn't even give me a chance to say anything before he walks out of the house and slams the door behind him.

"What the fuck just happened?" I ask the empty room and myself as I look around. I woke up this morning in his arms and slipped out to take a shower. When I got out of the shower, I heard the bell, but then I thought it was just my imagination until I heard yelling. I can't even put into words how I felt walking down the stairs and seeing Luke and Edward face off. My stomach lurched into my throat, and I thought I was going to be sick all over the stairs. My feet moved before my head could process what was going on.

Did I think Edward would show up at my house? No, I did not. Did I think that Luke would answer the door in just jeans? No, I did not. Was it apparent that he spent the night here? You bet your ass it was. Should I care that Edward saw? No. Do I care that Edward saw? No. Do I care that someone else saw? You bet your ass I do.

The phone beeps on the counter, and I finally grab it looking down and see that it's Edward. I don't even bother opening the text before going upstairs and getting dressed. The bedcovers are thrown all over the place, and I can still smell Luke in the room. I don't even bother making my bed before stepping into the walk-in closet. I grab my one-piece, sleeveless pantsuit, tying it at the top of my neck and then putting a gold belt on with gold sandals. I blow-dry my hair quickly, tucking it behind my ear on one side before grabbing my purse and phone. I walk out of the house, and my heart sinks, seeing that his truck isn't here. Which is stupid since he left. "What did you think was going to happen?" I ask myself as I get into my car. "That he would be waiting for you after you shit on him for doing absolutely nothing."

I stop for coffee on my way to the office, and I get there later than I normally do. I put my sunglasses on top of my head as I pull open the door. I look around, seeing that no one is lurking, and I try to sneak in without my sisters asking me questions. "You look like shit," Presley states when I take five steps toward my office, and she stands in her doorway. "What is up with you guys and looking like shit after your non-weddings? This is why

mine to CHERISH

I'm never getting married." I roll my eyes at that last comment.

"I know why I looked like shit," Shelby says, pointing at herself as she stands in front of me with a cup of coffee in her hand.

"And why was that again?" I try to get the focus off me and onto literally anything else at this point.

"I was banging Ace, and I wanted to continue to do it, but we said once we got home, it would stop." She takes a sip of her coffee, smirking. "What's your excuse?" she tilts her head to the side and asks me.

"Found out my fiancé had a kid with someone else." I walk past her to my office, hoping that they don't follow me, but then again, I'm an idiot because there is no way I wouldn't follow either of them.

"Are we still harping on that?" Presley says, coming into my office and going straight for the chair and sitting down.

"It's been three days," I reply, annoyed at them. "Shelby took a week." I point at Shelby who walks into the office and goes to sit next to Presley.

"And I see we are still in mourning." Shelby points at me and my outfit. "Which is why you are still in black."

"Oh my God," I say, pulling out the chair behind my desk and sitting down. "Don't we have anything else to do?"

"No." Presley shakes her head.

"Same," Shelby says, and I look up at the ceiling. "It'll be easier and faster for everyone if we can cut to the chase of the bullshit." I just stare at her. "We saw you yesterday, and you didn't look like this."

"Yeah, you had this sort of glow," Presley shares, raising her eyebrows as she looks at me. "Must be all that fresh air." She turns now to look at Shelby. "You had the glow because of the sun. She had her glow because of the fresh air."

"I had the glow from the sex." Shelby laughs and then stops midlaugh when she thinks about what she said and looks at me. "You slept with Luke!" She gasps, pointing at me with her mouth hanging open as if she just solved the world's biggest mystery.

"Can't put nothing past this one," Presley deadpans. "She's like Sherlock Holmes."

"You knew?" Shelby shrieks, hitting Presley's arm.

"The question is, how didn't you?" Presley shakes her head. "He got there, and they both had this glow, and he was walking with a skip in his step from his balls being drained. Almost like a ballet dancer."

I hold up my hand. "Can we not do this right now?" I say. "I have had quite the morning, and it's not even nine." They both look at me, and I know that if I want them to be gone, I have to just get it over with. "Edward showed up at my house this morning."

"Called it," Presley gloats, holding out her hand to Shelby. "You owe me fifty bucks."

"Shut up." Shelby pushes her hand away from her. "I thought he would respect her wishes."

"Like he respected her enough not to fuck someone on the side." Presley throws her head back and laughs. "The guy is a liar and a fraud. How can you trust anything he says? Don't piss on my leg and tell me it's raining." She folds her arms over her chest.

"How did that go?" Presley asks with a soft voice.

"Well, considering Luke answered the door with only his pants on…" I put my thumbs on my temples. "It did not go well."

"Hold the phone." Presley leans forward as if she didn't hear what I just said. "Did you just say Luke answered your door with pants on?"

"I believe she said only his pants on." Shelby puts in her two cents. "So he was shirtless."

"And at what time was this?" Presley asks.

"Now look who thinks they are Sherlock Holmes." I look up at the ceiling, and I just have to come out with it. "I was in the shower," I start, and now both of them are looking at me with shocked looks. "When I came out, I heard the bell, but I was like it can't be, who the hell rings someone's doorbell at seven o'clock in the morning?"

"A narcissist," Shelby says, and I just look at her. "Sorry, go on. In the shower while Luke is in your bed naked. Got it."

"I heard shouting, and when I walked down the stairs, there they were." I throw up my hands. "Face-to-face, both of them shouting at the other."

"Oh my God," Presley says with glee as she claps her hands. "This is so much better than I thought."

"What happened then?" Shelby asks, all intrigued.

"Then I told Edward that if he didn't leave, I would call the cops."

"Why does it sound like you are leaving something

out?" Shelby inquires.

"Because she is." Presley just stares at me. "What happened after that?"

"Well, I sort of yelled at Luke," I mumble, avoiding looking at them. "And then he stormed out."

"You sort of yelled at Luke?" they both say at the same time. "What the hell did he do wrong?"

"He answered the door." I get up, needing to move. "Who does that?" I look at my sisters, and they both stare back at me. "Like, why would he even think of answering my door?"

"The doorbell rang," Presley says. "What did you want him to do?"

"Nothing," I answer. "I wanted him to stay in bed and let me handle it."

"But did he know that Edward was coming over?" Shelby asks, and I glare at her midstep. "I'm just asking."

"Hold on one second," Presley adds. "Are you mad because he answered the door, or are you mad because he went toe-to-toe with Edward?" She shakes her head, leaning back into the couch. "Because I'm a little confused here."

"I was going to get married three days ago!" I shout at them. "Now I have this naked man answering my door."

"So what?" Shelby says. "What difference does that make who answers your door? You don't have to answer to anyone."

"So what?" My voice goes louder and louder. "So what? My neighbors could have seen him. I'm already the topic at the deli counter. You really think I wanted to add to it?"

"I think that you shouldn't give a shit what anyone thinks," Presley declares, getting up. "But that is just me. Did you discuss this with Luke?"

"No," I say, my voice going soft. "He stormed out."

"Oh, fuck," Shelby says. "You know what this means, don't you?" She gets up, leaving me hanging. "You have to go and apologize."

"For what?" I throw my hands in the air.

"For being a dickhead," Presley points out, shaking her head and walking out. "I did not expect this from you."

"Yeah." Shelby nods. "She expected it more from me since I'm anal about everything, but you…"

"I was not being a dickhead," I say in defense.

"You were being an asshole, then." Shelby tries to find another word. "Put yourself in his shoes."

"I don't want to." I pout, the stubborn side coming out.

"What would you say if you were at his house and his ex-whatever came to the door, and you answered it, and then he got mad at you." I open my mouth to say something and then close it.

"Can you two get the fuck out of my office?" I point at the door, and they both laugh.

"Are we not discussing that you had sex with him on your would-be wedding night?" Shelby asks, not sure if she should walk out or not. "Were you drunk?"

"No," I admit to her. "I mean, I drank a bit, but I wasn't drunk."

"Let me know how it tastes!" Presley shouts from the hallway, and I just walk over and stick my head out.

"How what tastes?" I look at her, confused.

"When you eat crow." She laughs and starts to walk away from me.

"I hate her," I mumble to Shelby, who is rolling her lips to keep from laughing. "And you, too, get the fuck out."

"Gladly," she agrees, walking over to the door. "Just for tomorrow, will we be having another meeting to tell you how wrong you are or is, like, this the last time?" I flip her the bird. "So tomorrow it is."

I walk over to the door and slam it after them, and I can hear laughing when the intercom goes off. "Was that what it sounded like when he left?" Presley's voice fills my office.

I don't answer her. Instead, my head just hits the desk. "Holy fuck," I mumble. "They might just be right."

"We are right." Shelby's voice fills my office now. "I suggest luring him with scx." I close my eyes, praying that they just stop talking right now. I spend the whole day looking out my window and wondering how the fuck I'm going to handle this.

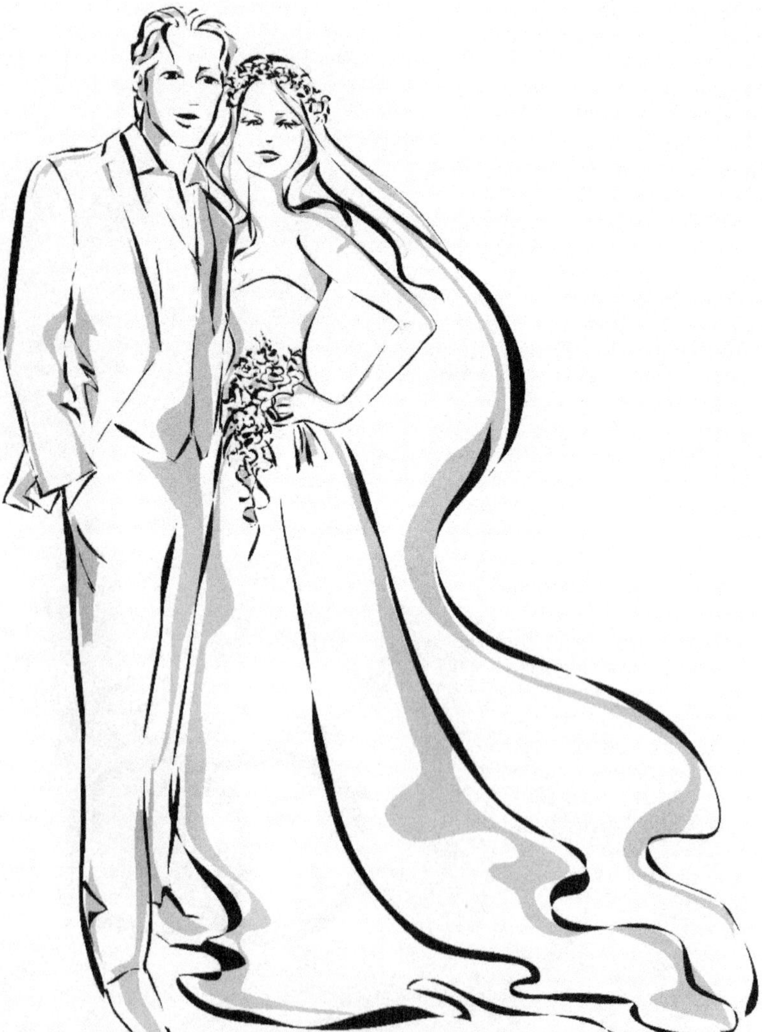

Twenty-Three

Luke

I park my truck in the driveway, getting out and slamming the door behind me. The sun is just going down as I jog up the two steps to the front door. Unlocking the door, I grab the mail lying on the doormat before walking in and kick the door shut with my foot, tossing my keys and phone onto the table by the front door. I don't turn on any lights as I make my way from the entryway past the kitchen and finally to the back room where my bedroom is.

I kick off my shoes before reaching behind me to pull my T-shirt off as I start the shower. I've been in a bad mood since I walked out of Clarabella's this morning. I mean, I didn't exactly walk out. It's more like I stomped out like a child, even slamming the door behind me. I knew the minute I got behind my wheel and took off that I made a mistake. I should have discussed it with her. I should have relaxed for a minute. But the thought that she didn't want to be seen with me just hit home in more ways than one, and I just couldn't escape it.

When I pulled up to the restaurant, Mikaela was there having coffee, and the day just turned shittier and shittier as the hours went by. I want to say that it was everyone else who was the problem, but it was all me. And it didn't get any better because I kept checking my phone, wondering if she was going to text me or call me, but it was radio silence. There was no missed call, no text, no nothing, and it just ate away at me.

The shower doesn't even help, and when I walk into the kitchen twenty minutes later, I'm wearing just gym shorts. I turn on the television, putting it on *SportsCenter* before walking to the kitchen and pulling open the fridge. "Fuck," I hiss when I find it empty. I'm about to walk over to the phone and order something when I hear a soft knock on the door. I look over at the door, not sure if it was actually a knock, when I hear it again. I don't even bother checking to see who it is before I swing open the door, and my heart stops in my chest. Or maybe it starts, but whatever it is, I feel a sense of calmness run through me as she stands there wearing a black outfit.

"Hi," she says, standing there nervously as she smiles shyly. "I come bearing a peace offering." Her voice cracks at first as she holds up a bottle of scotch in one hand. "And figured that food would sweeten the deal." She holds up the brown bag in the other hand. I stand here in front of her, holding the door, and all I can think is that she got even more beautiful since I saw her this morning. "Can I come in?" Her eyes shine, and I see her eyes blinking furiously as she blinks away tears.

I don't say anything to her because the only thing I want to do is yank her to me and wrap my arms around her and just be with her. But instead, I move out of the way, giving her the space she needs to walk inside. The minute she steps inside, I hurriedly close the door behind her, making sure she can't leave. She doesn't move from beside me. "Hi," she says softly, and I can smell her lavender scent, and my hands itch to hold her hand.

"Hi," I greet just as softly to her standing in front of me, my hand coming up to cup her face without even thinking about it. I bend my head to kiss her lips gently. I don't know if she is going to kiss me back, but I couldn't go another minute without kissing her. My hand drops from her face as she looks up at me.

"I'm sorry." Those two words make all the anger just melt away. Her even showing up here, I don't even remember why I was mad to begin with. Nor do I care.

My hand slides around her waist as I pull her even closer. "Me, too." My voice is but a whisper before I kiss her again. This time, my tongue comes out and slides with hers round and round until we are both breathless. "Come in." My hand falls from her as I walk her into the house.

"I went by the restaurant to see if you were there," she

says when we both stand by the island in the kitchen, and I look over at her. "Mikaela said she kicked you out."

"She didn't exactly kick me out." I roll my eyes, and her eyebrows go up. "Okay, fine, she kicked me out," I confirm, and she laughs. "It seems I was a negative Nancy." I pull out a stool for her to sit on. She sits on the stool, and I walk over and grab two glasses for the scotch before sitting next to her. "What did you bring?" I ask, looking over at the brown bag.

"Burgers," she says, grabbing the brown bag and putting her hand in it, taking out one container and handing it to me. "I figured it was a safe bet."

I grab the container from her, and I can't help but lean forward to kiss her lips. "It's safe." This time, she is the one who leans into me for another kiss, but her tongue slides in with mine, and I can't help but turn and grab her. I open my legs, pulling the stool in the middle of them.

"We should talk," I say when she lets go of my lips, and she nods her head.

"We need to talk about what is going to happen going forward," she shares, looking down at her hands.

"I agree." I take her hand in mine. "I just want to say that I want to be with you." My heart speeds up in my chest as I admit it out loud.

She is very quiet, and she just looks up at me. "Who's to say you won't take off again?" she asks, and I know that she has a valid point in being scared.

"From when I was a young kid," I start, "I've always been taught that nothing lasts forever. I've also been taught that the minute you get used to something or admit that you want something, they turn around and show you that nothing is guaranteed. It's why I never had a serious relationship. It was just easy not to get attached. It's why the only friends I truly have are Mikaela and Francois in New York." She looks down, and her hair falls in her face. I put my hand under her chin and lift her eyes to see me, tucking her hair behind her ear. "For the first time in my life, I've let myself want something," I admit. "The first time we were together, it was like this whole thing was a fucking dream, and I had this voice in the back of my head telling me that it was a mistake." As I admit this to her, the lump in my throat grows bigger and bigger. My heart beats so fucking fast I think it's going to come out of my chest. My hands are so fucking sweaty I feel like I need to wipe them down. But Clarabella just squeezes my hand, making it feel like it's okay. "I've let my guard down when it came to you, and slowly, you've crept past all these defenses, so taking off was the only thing that I thought would be right. But with that said, going to New York was also a dream come true, and I just couldn't say no to that."

"I would never want you to choose me over your career," she says softly, and I can see the tiny teardrop escape from her right eye. "Never. I would never tell you not to go away for six months either. All I ask is that you just talk to me."

"Fair enough, and for the record, I can't even tell you how sorry I am," I say, and then I lay it all out for her. "My parents never thought I would amount to much. It's not like they were the nurturing kind, and for some crazy reason I can't even explain to myself, I want to make a name for myself. I want to become the best person I can be so that I can say *look at what I did*. It's stupid, and it's sick and twisted, but this is me." I smirk at her. "And if you give me a chance, I promise to make it up to you."

"All I ask of you is to talk to me," she reaffirms, and I nod my head. "And that goes for me also." Her hand comes up, and she holds my face. "This morning, I was just shocked that Edward showed up and..."

"And I should never have answered your door," I admit. "It wasn't my place."

"I don't want people to think that I just ran off because of you," she admits. "I don't want people to talk more than they are."

"And me answering your door half-naked didn't help." I smile sadly. "I promise if you have me over again, I won't answer the door."

She leans forward and kisses my lips, and I can't help it, but the nerves settle. "How about for the next little bit, we just be me and you?" she suggests softly. "Before we tell the world."

"I'll take you any way I can get you," I say as I turn my face in her hand and kiss the palm of it.

"Okay, so now that I told you what I want from you." Her voice is soft as I bring her hand to my lips, kissing her fingers. "What do you want from me?"

I chuckle. "You, I just want fucking you."

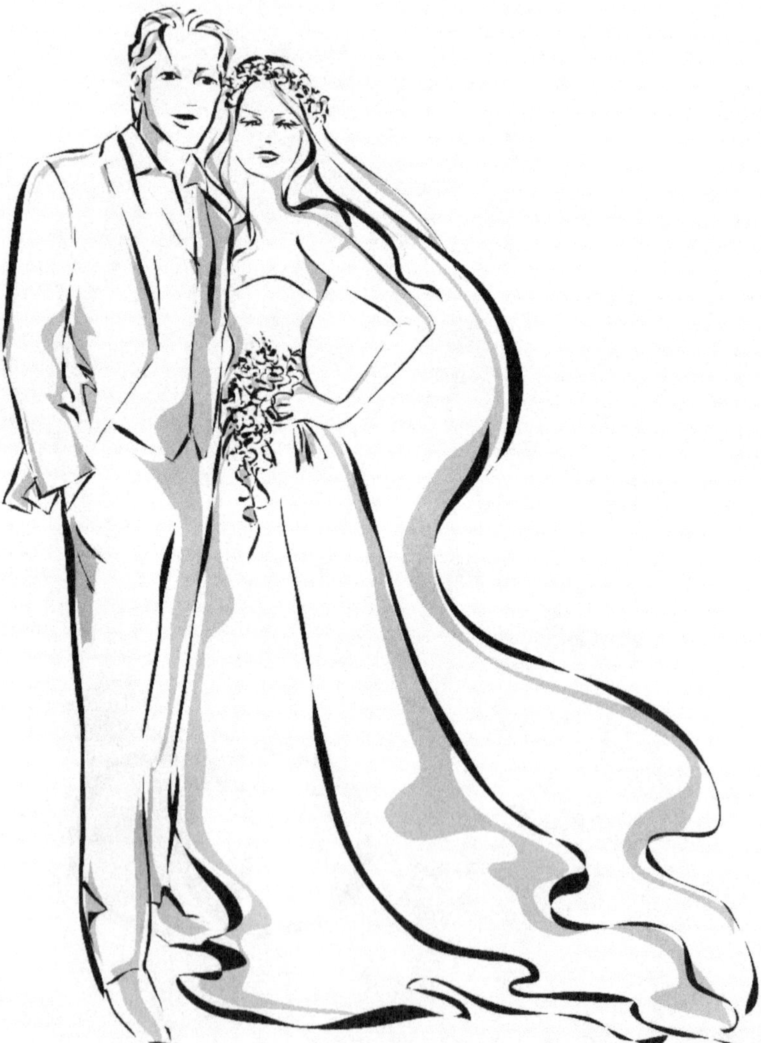

Twenty-Four

Clarabella

I lie in the middle of the bed on my stomach as I feel little butterfly kisses starting on my naked shoulder. "Morning," Luke grumbles from beside me as he kisses the freckle on my back three times before asking me, "Do you want coffee?"

"What time is it?" I ask, sinking deeper into the bed.

"It's a little after nine." I feel the covers move, and I know he's gotten out of the bed. I open one eye to watch his naked ass walk over to the bathroom. "I feel you staring." He looks over his shoulder and chuckles. "Want me to come back to bed?"

"Yes," I grumble. "But first, go make coffee."

He looks around my room now. "Is it safe to go downstairs in just my boxers, or will I come face-to-face with one of your sisters again?" He picks up his boxers from the floor where he tossed them last night.

"It's a fifty-fifty chance." I turn over on my back now, holding the sheet to my chest. "But if it makes you feel better, I've already seen Ace's junk." From the look on his face, this does not make him feel better at all.

He just stares at me. "Why would that make me feel better?" he asks as he puts his boxers on, and I can't help but look at him. His body is perfectly sculpted, which is due to him lifting weights and running four times a week. Something that came as a shock to me when I woke up one morning and he was gone, only to return a sweaty mess thirty minutes later. I mean, I'm not going to complain about it, especially since he dragged me to the shower and fucked me against the shower wall.

"I don't know." I laugh, grabbing one of the throw pillows from the floor and putting it behind my head. "You were a little freaked out a couple of days ago when my sister saw your ass." I point at him.

"We were having sex on your kitchen table." He throws his hands up. "And they just came waltzing in. They didn't even knock, or I don't know, call."

"I think there was some screaming and then Presley turned and pushed Shelby down." I roll my lips, thinking about the scene. "They were also not the only ones yelling." I wink at him, which just makes his jaw tense as he bites down.

"I was midorgasm." He glares at me.

"I bet they never do that again." I can't help the laugh that escapes my mouth.

"Good to know." He turns and walks out of the bedroom. I throw the sheet off me and walk into the bathroom to pee and then wash my hands and face. It's been two weeks since we've had the talk at his house. Two weeks since everything has gone down, and besides my sisters, no one knows about us. I can't even put into words how easy it is with us. We've started to alternate where we stay at night. With our schedules, it's hard to spend that much time together. He usually gets in later in the evening, but I always wait up for him. Then I'm up early in the morning, and he always makes it a point to get up and have coffee with me before going back to bed. I put my toothbrush back in the holder and see his toothbrush next to mine, and I can't help but smile.

Walking back out of the bathroom, I contemplate putting on a robe and joining him downstairs, but I hear him walking up the stairs. He stops at the doorway, staring at me with a cup of coffee in each hand. His blue eyes light up when he looks at me from head to toe. "Like what you see?"

"No." He smirks, walking into the room and coming straight for me. "I don't think like is the proper word for it." His lips fall on mine, and my whole stomach gets butterflies.

"Thank you," I say when I grab a cup from his hand and walk back to the bed, placing it on the nightstand. He follows me and is about to get back in bed when I tilt my head. "Are you coming into bed with clothes on? What happened to your rule that one must always be naked in the bed?"

"And the living room," he adds, and I just laugh as he slides his boxers off and then slips into the bed next to me. He sits up with his head to the headboard. "How was last night?" he asks about the wedding that took place. He got home before me, which was a first, and was waiting for me as soon as I got home.

"It was eventful." I fill him in on the drama. "But it's over." I lean over and kiss his shoulder. "What are your plans for the day?" It's my first day off in two weeks, and I hope he has nothing planned so we can spend the day together.

"I'm going to hit up the food and drink festival," he replies, taking a sip of his coffee.

"Oh." I sit up now. "I want to go. Can I come with?" I ask, and he just smiles.

"I was hoping you would say that." The smile fills his face, and thirty minutes later, we are both getting out of bed and getting dressed. I slip on blue jeans with a light blue T-shirt, and when I walk out of the closet, he's sitting on the bed that we made together.

"You look nice," he compliments, getting up and coming to kiss me.

"Right back at you," I say, looking at him with his black jeans and a white shirt, I lean in and kiss his neck. There is just something about him that I always want to kiss him. It's so strange, and I'm not sure if it's normal since I've never been this touchy-feely before.

We get to the festival, and he parks as I look over to

where the row of white tents are set up. "Have you been to this festival before?" I ask as we make our way toward the entrance.

"Not this one," he says. "But I went to one in New York." My stomach gets tight when he says that. There are questions I want to ask him about New York, especially about the girl he was with, but I never feel like it's my place. I mean, who am I to say anything? I was engaged, for fuck's sake. "Have you?" He looks over at me, and I just shake my head.

When we get to the entrance, a person is handing out the map layout. "How do you usually tackle this?" he asks, and I just laugh.

"I usually just put one foot in front of the other and walk." He shakes his head as we walk past the first tent, grabbing some samples. "So if you had to choose one meal for the rest of your life, what would it be?" I ask as I grab a wine sample that someone just handed to me.

"Probably steak and potatoes," he says. "You can't go wrong with that." I nod, and then he takes a sip from the water bottle he just bought. "What about you?"

"Pizza. Hands down, it would be pizza."

"Really?" He smiles at me. "I was going to say that, but I thought you would laugh at me."

"Why would I laugh at you?" So many people are bustling around us, but the two of us are in our own world. We walk almost at a snail's pace, taking our time enjoying being out in the sun.

"Well, I'm a chef, and all I can come up with is pizza," he says as our fingers graze each other's, and my belly flips again. It's really becoming annoying that it happens every single time he touches me. I make a mental note to google how long it lasts when I get home.

"But pizza is a mix of everything," I observe as our fingers touch again. This time, his pinky comes out and holds mine for a couple of seconds before letting it go. "It's got carbs, cheese, veggies, and meat. I mean, you can't go wrong."

"Exactly," he agrees and then looks at me. "Can I hold your hand?" he asks, and all I can do is smile at him. Another thing I've only done with him is I'm constantly smiling. Or not constantly, but the majority of the time he's around, I have a smile on my face.

"Why wouldn't you be able to hold my hand?" I ask as I slip my hand into his, and our fingers fold together.

"I don't know. We are out in public," he reminds me, looking down. "And we may see people you know."

I can't help but stop the way my heart is beating at the fact that he sleeps with me every single night, yet he's afraid to hold my hand in public. "I would very much like to hold your hand," I confirm, and he lifts our joined hands up to his lips as he kisses my fingers.

"So I was thinking," he starts, and I can tell he's nervous. "That maybe one of these days we can go out on a date."

I roll my lips to keep from laughing. "Is that what you were thinking?" I ask, leaning closer to him. His finger unlocks from mine as he gently puts his arm around me, pulling me closer to him. "I don't know about you." I slip my own arm around his waist. "But I consider this to be a date."

"Is that so?" He looks down at me as I look up at him and nod. "If this is a date, should I be able to, I don't know, say kiss you?"

"I don't know the rules of Dating 101." I try not to laugh. "But I think there should definitely be some kissing."

"I agree with that." He nods his head, and we aren't even paying attention to any of the tents we're passing by.

We're fixated on each other, our feet moving at the same time. "What else is there on a date?" I ask.

"I mean, if it's a good date, there should be some making out in the car." I nod when he says this.

"It's always a good date when there is some heavy making out in the car." I look ahead at everyone. "What about groping?"

"Ohh, second base." He laughs. "That's a good base to be at."

"I mean, it is a good base, but third base." I look up at him. "Now, third base, that is where it's at."

"What is third base exactly?" he asks as his eyes meet mine, and we basically stop in the middle of the pathway. He turns to look at me, his hand grabbing one of mine.

"Oh, that base consists of below the belt." I laugh. "Sometimes, one can slide into the base."

"With their mouths?" He winks at me.

"I mean, is there any other way to slide into third base?" I ask, and I look down below his belt to see that his cock is starting to get into the action. I step into him.

"I mean, I like third base and all but…" I step in a touch more, my head tilted back, waiting for him to kiss me. "But nothing is better than knocking that hit out of the park and getting a home run."

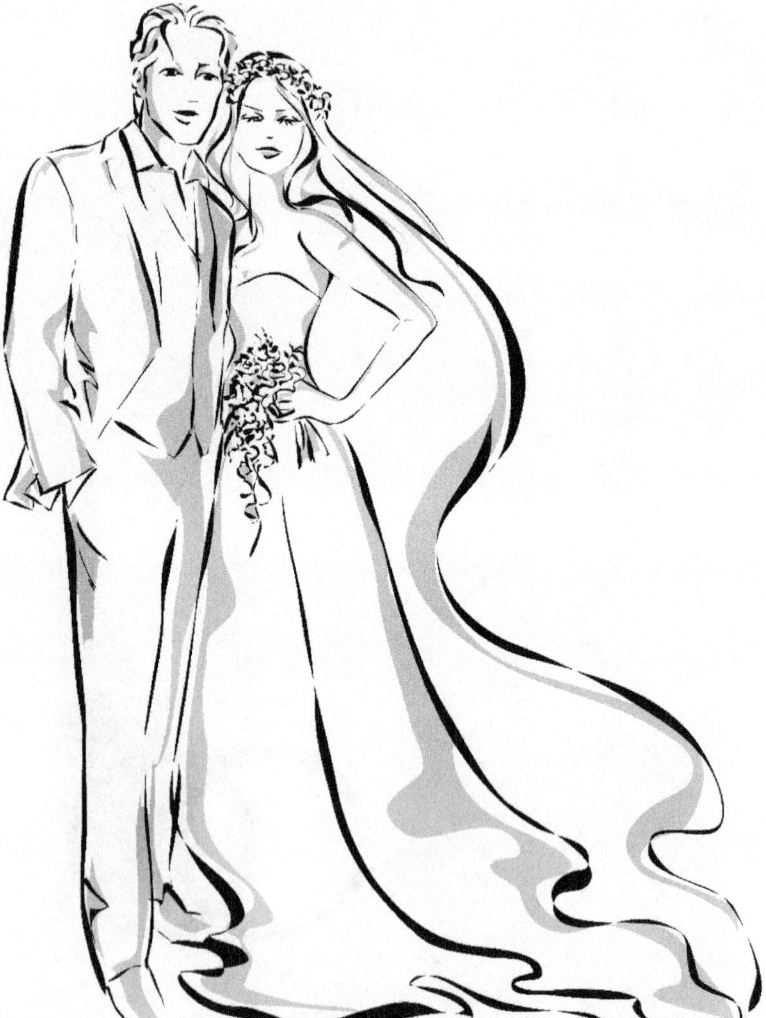

Twenty-Five

Luke

"I need to order a couple of things." I look over at Mikaela as I do inventory, closing the produce fridge. The phone rings from my back pocket. Reaching around, I take it out and see that it's Clarabella calling. My whole face fills with a smile, and I can't help it.

Turning around, I walk out of the kitchen before I press the green button. "Hey, beautiful," I greet softly, looking around to make sure no one hears me.

"Hi." She sounds like she is rushing around, the sound of her heels clicking in the background. "Um."

"Um," I repeat after laughing at how nervous her tone

comes out. "Are you okay?"

"No," she says, and my heart immediately stops in my chest. I feel the color draining from my face, and the only thing going through my mind is to get the fuck to her.

"What happened?" I ask, and I'm already walking to the back door. I cover the bottom of the phone and look over at Mikaela. "Mikaela, I have an emergency." Her eyes go wide, and she nods at me so I know she's going to handle this when I get into the truck. "Where are you?"

"I'm at the venue," she says, and I can't even control the way my heart is beating. I literally think I'm going to be sick as I peel out of the parking lot.

"I'll be there in five minutes," I say into the phone. The past three weeks have been a complete dream with her. There has never been any other time in my life when I have felt so settled and so fucking complete. There has never been any other time in my life when I felt like I deserved this before and put someone before me. Ever. I make sure that I schedule myself off when she has the days off. There has also never been any other time in my life when I smile more than anything. Every night I go to bed holding her and wake up next to her, and I keep waiting for the other shoe to drop.

"I'm fine," she assures me, her voice coming out soft. "It's just…"

My hands grip the steering wheel so tight my knuckles turn white. "It's just what, Clarabella?"

"I'm in a little bit of a predicament," she says, her voice hushed, and I literally can't get there fast enough.

"Are you honestly on your way here?" she asks as soon as I pull into the parking lot of the venue.

"I'm at the back," I say, and now I can hear her mumbling something to someone. The sound of her heels in the background lets me know she's on her way to the kitchen. I hang up the phone, putting it back in my pocket as I walk up the steps to the kitchen, and I pull it open.

I look around, seeing things on the counter but no one in the kitchen, when the door swings open and Clarabella comes in. I smile when I see her wearing cream-colored pants that fit her tight with a bright cherry-red sleeveless silk top. The matching red shoes make my mouth water, and I can't help but stare at her. My eyes meet hers, and I give her a once-over, making sure she is okay. I don't even notice that her sisters are two steps behind her. "I'm so happy I came in early today," Presley says, and I look at them confused.

"I'm just pissed that we can't capture this on camera." Shelby pouts, while my eyes go to her and then back to Clarabella.

"What the hell is going on?" I ask, relieved that she's okay.

"Yes, Clarabella," Presley urges, looking at her. "What the hell is going on?"

Clarabella glares at her as she wrings her hands in front of her, and I can tell that whatever she is going to tell me, she's nervous about it. "Nothing is going on. It's just I'm stuck." I tilt my head to the side. "And I need your help."

"Oh my God," Shelby says, putting her hand to her mouth. "How the mighty have fallen."

Clarabella's head whips around as she looks at her. "Don't you have somewhere else to be?"

"No," Shelby states at the same time as Presley says, "I wouldn't leave this room even if the room was on fire."

"Okay." I hold up my hands. With the three of them together, you can't understand anything since they have this special bond. It's like they know what the other is thinking just with their eyes. "I don't know what is going on, but someone better tell me why the hell I rushed over here."

"You rushed over here?" Presley says, clapping her hands. "So you have no idea why you are here? Brilliant." She laughs and turns to Clarabella. "Clarabella, why don't you tell Luke why you called him and why he rushed over here."

"I hate you," she mumbles to Presley and then takes a step toward me. I don't know if she's hoping that her sisters don't follow her, but they move with her. "So the chef for today who was supposed to come in…" She avoids looking at me. "And well, he decided that he isn't coming in." I can tell that her face is filled with worry.

"And the event starts in three hours," Shelby shares, and I get it now. I step closer to her now, and I can smell her lavender scent. I want nothing more than to kiss her lips.

"Hold on," I say softly as I put my finger under her chin to lift her eyes to me. "Are you saying that you hired another chef to replace me?"

"That would be a yes," Presley confirms, and Clarabella just takes a deep inhale.

"In my defense, it was six weeks ago." Clarabella throws up her hand, and my hand falls from her face.

"So six weeks ago, you fired me?" I put my hands on my hips, enjoying that she is dying inside at this moment.

"I didn't fire you," Clarabella defends.

"Yeah, she didn't fire you," Shelby says. "She was weeding you out."

Clarabella slaps her hands together. "Okay, everyone out," she orders, turning to look at her sister. "You and you." She points at her sisters. "Go do something else."

"Ugh, fine," Shelby says, turning and walking out.

"The damage is done anyway," Presley declares. "Luke, thank you for the entertainment as always." She smirks. "I'm just happy you aren't naked this time." She turns and walks out.

"I will never live that down." I look up at the ceiling, then look back down at Clarabella, but this time, I walk closer to her and wrap my arm around her waist. "So you were weeding me out?" I say, my heart suddenly calmer now that I have her in my arms. She puts her hand on the arm around her. "Isn't that interesting?"

"I was not weeding you out," she lies, and I can tell she's lying because her chest gets blotchy when she does. "It was complicated."

"I don't think it's as complicated as you say it is." I bend and kiss her lips, not waiting another minute. "You didn't want to work with me."

"No," she answers. She wraps her arms around my

neck and closes the gap between us. "I did not want to work with you."

"Why?" I ask, bending my head and kissing her again. This time, the kiss lingers for a second longer than it did before. "I had no trouble working with you."

"Yeah, well, I didn't want to work with you," she answers, looking at me. "I was mad, and I became petty."

"And you hired another chef," I point out. "And how is that working out for you right now?"

"Well, considering I'm about to swallow my pride and beg you for a favor." She rolls her eyes. "Not great."

"Well, what terms are we discussing?" I ask.

"How about a blow job twice a day?" she offers, and I roll my eyes at her.

"I already get that," I joke with her, and now it's her turn to roll her eyes at me. "Let me see what I need to do, and then we can talk terms." I kiss her lips, walking over to the folder on the table. I see the list of food that needs to be prepared and how many people it's going to be for. "This should be okay," I say. "But it will cost you."

"She'll pay double." I hear Shelby from behind the closed door.

"Are they really out there?" I whisper, pointing at the door as she just nods her head. "Were they out there the whole time?"

"Probably." She shrugs.

"They heard what we said." I close my eyes.

"I think they know we have sex." She laughs. "They caught you plowing into me." I close my eyes and put my hands on my face. "Now get to work," she says, and

I can see that she is back to her relaxed self.

I shake my head, walking over and washing my hands before starting to prepare the food. The waitstaff arrives, and then Clarabella comes in. "How is it going?" she asks, and I see that her red heels are changed to black flats.

"I'm almost done," I reply, looking at the clock. "I'm going to get ready to plate in five minutes." She turns and grabs the stack of plates and comes over, placing them down for me. She makes sure that all plates are taken out as soon as they are plated. She rushes back and forth to make sure that everything is okay. The second service is pretty much the same as the first.

She directs the staff perfectly, and a plate never sits for longer than five seconds. The staff all respect and listen to her. I take a second between courses to see her pull a couple of waitresses aside as she explains things to them. Each time, she does it quietly and respectfully, and I'm in awe of the way she handles things. Three hours later, I'm wiping down my area when the three of them come into the kitchen.

"Well," Shelby says. "I'm going to say that I think that is the smoothest service that we've ever done."

"Hands down one of the easiest," Presley agrees. "There wasn't one complaint that we had."

"Do you usually have complaints?" I ask them as I walk over to the sink to wash off the rag before tossing it into the dirty linens basket.

"No," Clarabella replies. "My sisters are just trying to butter you up so you don't fire us."

"With that," Shelby says. "I'm out." Presley salutes me before turning around and walking out with Shelby.

"Are you done?" Clarabella asks, and I look around at the busboys loading another round into the dishwasher.

"I'm done," I say, and she smirks at me. "Come with me." She motions with her head, and I follow her out into the venue place. I look around the room, seeing the empty tables as she walks to the bar area in the corner. She walks around the counter, grabs something from behind the bar, and then comes back to my side. I sit on the stool, and she sits on the stool beside me, putting down two glasses she was holding in her hand. She fills the glasses with scotch, then puts the bottle down and picks up one glass in each hand, handing me one.

"To teamwork." She holds her glass up.

"Teamwork makes the dream work," I joke with her and click her glass with mine. She's about to bring the glass to her lips before I say something. "Oh and to paying off debts." I wink at her, and she just looks at me without taking a sip of her drink. "I hope you saved your energy. I plan on making you pay for trying to weed me out," I tease, taking the shot of scotch and placing the glass down on the bar. "So, Clarabella…" I say her name, leaning into her. My cock is hard as fuck, and I can see that her eyes turn a darker blue. "The only thing you get to decide tonight is your place or mine?"

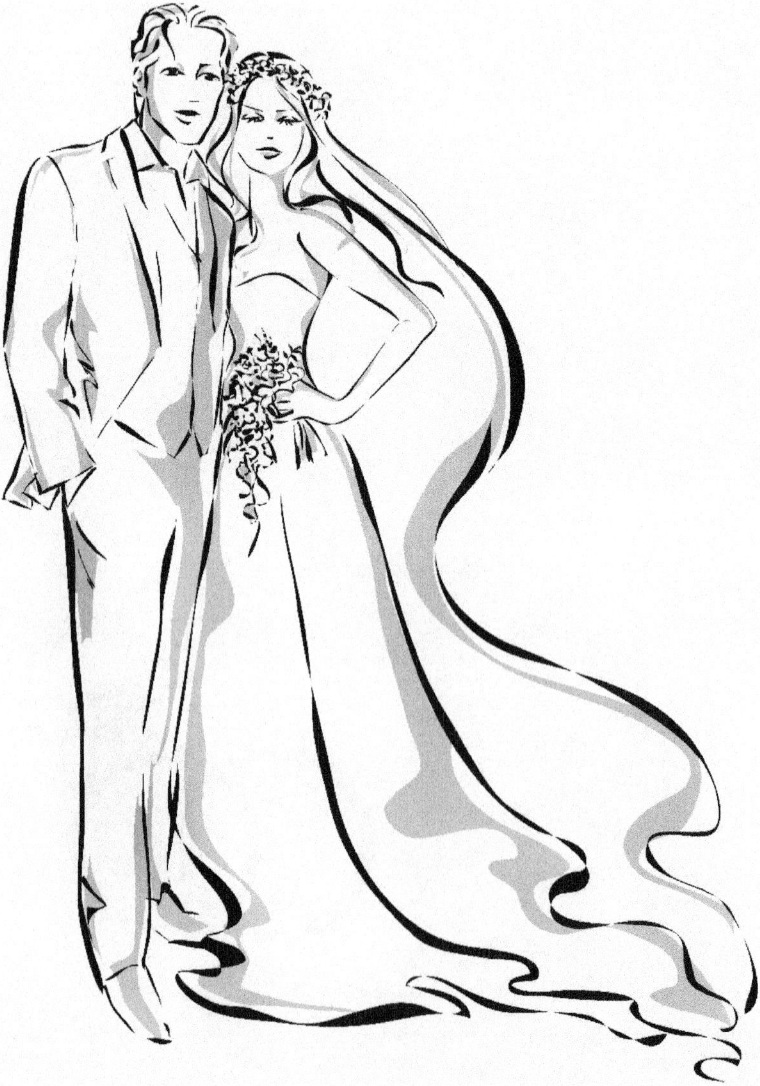

Twenty-Six

Clarabella

"Hey." Presley sticks her head into my office. "Shelby and I were going to go grab some dinner. Did you maybe want to come with us?" she asks, and I nod my head.

"That sounds great," I say, pushing away from the desk and looking down to see that it's just after six o'clock. "Where do you want to go?" I ask, walking around the desk and going to grab my purse.

"What the hell are you wearing?" Presley asks, and I stop midstep to look down and make sure I didn't get something on my outfit today. "Are those jeans?" She puts her hands on her hips, and I see that she is wearing jeans, so I don't know why she's giving me such a hard time. Especially since none of us had any appointments today.

I get to my purse and put my phone in it. "These jeans cost me three hundred dollars," I huff, looking down at my white jeans.

"Oh, trust me, I know how much they cost," she states, putting her hands on her hips. "What I'm asking is why are you wearing clothes that aren't black?" I open my mouth to say something but nothing comes out because I didn't even notice. When I can't come up with any words, all I do is roll my eyes at her.

"I don't know what you're talking about." I pick up my purse, avoiding looking at her when she laughs out loud and claps her hands together.

"Are we going for dinner or what?" Shelby asks, coming into my office and looking at me standing here looking at Presley. "What's going on?"

"We are discussing the fact that Morticia here"—Presley points at me—"is wearing white pants and that she hasn't been wearing black for a while."

Shelby gasps and glares at Presley. "I thought you said we were going to discuss this at dinner." Shelby huffs, "You are the worst."

"I couldn't help it." Presley shrugs. "She's even wearing a peach shirt."

"Ugh, you suck," Shelby says. "Now, where are we going to eat?"

"Is that even an option anymore?" Presley says. "Imagine we went to another restaurant and Luke found out."

I roll my eyes. "He'd be fine," I assure them, and my heart starts to speed up a touch when I think about seeing him. The three of us walk out of the office and head over to the restaurant, all of us hopping in one car.

"I love the summer," Shelby says as we make our way to the restaurant. The sound of live music fills the air, and the sound of kids' laughter is off in the distance as families walk together down the main road.

Walking in, I see that some of the tables are free, and it's not as busy as it is on the weekends. I look around as Shelby and Presley talk to the hostess, who nods her head and grabs three menus as she leads us to the corner booth. I slide into one side while Shelby and Presley slide in front of me. "Is Luke here?" Shelby asks while I look around and see the kitchen door open as a server comes out.

"He should be here," I say, ignoring the way that my heart is beating. "But it's not like we keep track of each other." I ignore their looks by grabbing a menu that I know by heart, just to avoid looking at them.

The server comes over, and she recognizes me from when I've come in beforehand with clients. I smile at her as I order a wine, and not two seconds later, I see him come out of the kitchen. I try to hide the smile that fills my face, but I can't. If I see him, I smile. If he walks into a room, I smile. When he kisses my neck in the morning, I smile. It's the smile each and every time. "I heard we had special guests." His eyes light up when he sees my sisters and then slides in beside me. "Hi there," he greets and leans in to kiss my lips.

"Hi," I say, putting my hand on his leg. He slips his fingers in with mine, and I can't even put into words what I feel. It's the strangest thing every single night we slide into bed together, and it feels like it's always been like this. Like he was always holding me to sleep, like he was always waking up with me and making me coffee while I got ready.

He talks to my sisters, and nothing feels forced, and it's probably because we worked together before, so they know him. He gets up, going to the kitchen to continue working, and when it's time to get the bill, the server tells us it's taken care of. My sisters get up to leave, and I follow them but stop instead of walking out of the door. "Are you not coming with us?" Shelby asks me when I look over my shoulder.

"I think I'm going to just wait here for him." I hold my bag in front of me nervously.

"Of course you are." Presley winks at me. "Also just so you know, car sex is not all it's hyped up to be."

"Well, he has a truck," I counter, and they both just laugh. "I'll see you both tomorrow." I hold up my hand before turning and walking back over to the bar. I pull out an empty stool by the end of the bar.

"Hey, what can I get for you?" the bartender asks as soon as he spots me.

"I'll have a soda water," I say, and he nods at me before walking away.

He comes back over a couple of seconds later, placing a napkin on the bar and then my drink on top of it. "Let me know if you need anything else." I nod at him, picking up the glass and taking a sip of it when I feel a hand on my back. I turn around and see him there smiling down at me. "You waited?" he says, sitting on the stool beside me, turning his body to face me. "You didn't have to wait." His legs open.

"I know I didn't have to." I smile at him. "I wanted to." I turn on my stool to face him, my legs inside of his legs. He moves his hands from his legs to mine. "What time are you done?"

"I can get out of here now if you want." He winks at me, getting up from his stool, holding out his hand for me so I can get up. "Besides, I think you have to work off a certain tab."

I laugh as I slip my hand in his and get up. "Is that so?" I ask, and he just nods his head.

"That is so," he confirms and looks over at the bartender. "She's with me," he tells him, and he just nods his head. "Let's go out the front." He puts his hand on my lower back as we walk toward the front door. The hostesses smile at us as we walk out. He opens the door for me to step out. The heat hits me right away as he walks out with me. "So my place or yours?" he asks in the middle of the crowded street. More people are outside walking around than when we arrived. The ice cream store two doors down has a line forming outside.

"You're pretty sure of yourself," I joke with him when I start to walk and come face-to-face with Edward. My whole body goes stiff as he glares at me. He looks at me and then over at Luke beside me. The warmth of Luke's hand on my back stops me from shivering.

"Well, well, well." His voice goes a touch louder when he comes closer to us, and I see that some people have looked over. "Isn't this a nice surprise?" My mouth is suddenly dry, and there isn't any way I can say anything, nor do I want to say anything. The last thing I want is to bring attention to myself. My heart is hammering so hard in my chest I don't know if he's yelling or it's just the echo. "My runaway bride with the hired help."

"Watch yourself," Luke warns, his voice low as he stands up straight beside me, and he's advanced just a touch, so he's almost in front of me.

"Watch me?" Edward sneers. "Watch me?" He points at his chest, and I can't help but look around and see that people are not only looking but I also see a couple of them pointing. The back of my neck starts to get hot, and I want to just walk away from him.

"Luke." I say his name, putting my hand on his arm. "Don't bother." Luke looks at me, his eyes dark with anger.

"Yes, Luke, why should you bother?" He laughs bitterly. "I mean, she left me at the altar!" he roars. "Without even giving me a second to explain myself." I just stay quiet, not even willing to give him anything. "In the end, you left me for this piece of shit. You are a cheater." He points at me, and I swear my head flies back as if he hit me in the face.

He takes one foot to advance, and Luke steps in front of me. "I think the pot is calling the kettle black." Luke takes another step forward, their chests almost touching. "You had everything you could ever have, and what did you do?" Luke asks. "And what did you do? You fucked around and had a baby with someone else. Instead of telling her that, she has to hear it from the woman who knocks on her door a minute before she is supposed to walk down the aisle." I can hear gasps from around me, and I want the street to open up and swallow me. My stomach turns, and my eyes just look down at the ground to avoid everyone looking at me.

"There is no one else to blame for anything besides you." Luke points at him. "So you better check yourself. You coward." Luke slips his hand in mine. "And if you ever come at her again." His voice goes low. "I'm going to put you to the ground." Edward just looks at him, his chest moving in and out as he pants. His nostrils are flaring. "I'd love nothing more." Luke smiles at him, then turns to look at me before leading me to the back of the building and away from the prying eyes.

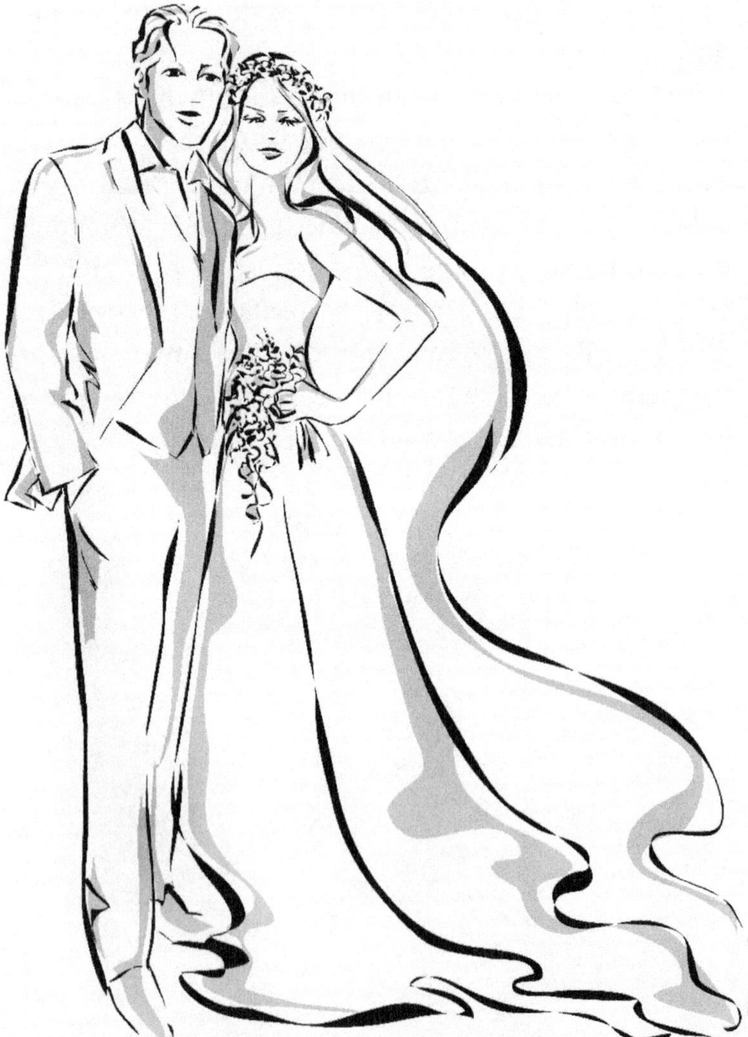

Twenty-Seven

Luke

My hand grips hers as I walk around the restaurant toward my truck in the back. The minute we are away from the prying eyes, she slips her hand out of mine. My whole body is filled with fury, and I want nothing more than to walk back over to that piece of shit and put my fist in his mouth. "You okay?" My voice is soft as I open the truck door for her. She never looks at me, nor does her head come up, and all she does is nod as she steps into the truck. I wait for a second to see if she is going to look at me, but all she does is grab the seat belt. I close the door and walk around but stop at the back for a minute, looking up at the sky before getting into the truck. I want to get her as far away from the restaurant as I can. I look over at her a couple of times on the way to her house. The only reason I go to her house is that it's closer than mine, and right now, I want to sit down with her and make sure she is okay. After I pull up in the driveway, I turn off the truck, and she is out of it in a split second. She jogs up the front steps, never once looking behind her as she unlocks the door.

I step in and watch her put her purse on the table at the front door before walking in. She makes her way straight to the kitchen, opening the cupboard on top of the fridge and then taking down the bottle of scotch. "Are you okay?" I ask as she walks to the island and just looks up at me. I can tell she's pissed. This is the same look she gave me when I stupidly opened her door that other time and came face-to-face with Edward. "Wait for a second." I hold up my hand suddenly, not sure what the fuck is going on. "Are you pissed at me?"

"I don't know what I am." She unscrews the top of the scotch bottle and brings it straight to her mouth, taking a gulp. She puts the bottle down and then wipes her mouth with the back of her hand.

"I'm sorry." I stare at her, never taking my eyes off her. "Why the fuck are you pissed at me?" I point at my chest. The nerves are now making my body shake even more. "What the fuck did I do?"

She looks down at the scotch and then looks over at me. "You told everyone my business!" she shouts. "You literally just told them everything. In the middle of fucking Main Street, you just told everyone everything, without even batting a fucking eye."

"What the hell are you talking about?" I say, confused again. "He was standing there spewing shit from his mouth, and all you did was stand there."

"Because I didn't need any more shit being said about me." She throws her hands up. "Everyone was looking at us!" she shrieks. "Everyone was looking at us, whispering and pointing." She shakes her head and looks down at the counter.

"Yeah, I know." I put my hands on my hips. "Looking at us and listening to the shit he was saying. The lies that were coming out of his mouth." I shake my head. "He's so lucky that there were people there, and I couldn't throw him into a wall or throat punch him or anything that would have stopped him from talking." My hands form fists by my sides.

"Who cares?" she yells. "Who fucking cares what he says about me?" She closes her eyes, and when she opens them, I can see the tears in them, and it guts me. My stomach feels like someone is stabbing it over and over again as the burning starts to build, moving throughout my body.

"I fucking care!" I roar. "He's not going to talk about my woman like that." I shake my head. "I tried to remain calm, but then he called you a cheater, and there was no way in fuck that I was just going to let him have that. No fucking way." I stare at her, and she doesn't say anything to me. Her mouth opens and then closes and then opens again.

"Your woman?" she repeats that part, and I suddenly

think that maybe I should have worded it better.

"Um, yeah," I say like *duh obviously*. "I don't know what people call each other when they are with each other every single day and share a life together. We are both thirty. Is calling you my girlfriend not too young? So yeah, my woman sounds about right."

"What about the girl in New York?" She stares at me, and my heart stops in my chest.

"What?" I whisper, and I think that perhaps I need to take a step back and just let things calm down. Maybe I should have made her work through things before I just jumped right into it.

"The girl in New York," she says again, and this time, the burning in my stomach spreads to my chest, then my throat. "What about her?"

I take a second to think about what she is asking me exactly. "What about her?" The only words that can come out of my mouth at this point.

"Well, where does she stand?" This whole line of questioning is so out of the blue. My head is spinning around and around as I try to wrap my head around everything that happened tonight.

"She doesn't stand anywhere." I just shake my head. "Stop with this runaround and little questions here and there. Why don't you ask what you need to ask?" She looks down at the bottle of scotch, and instead of giving her a chance to ask the questions, I just come right out. "She was nothing." I don't take my eyes off her. "She was less than nothing." I feel pressure on my chest, wondering how long she's had this festering inside her.

"Will you see her again?" she asks, still not looking at me, and I can't even fathom how long she's had this idea in her head.

I walk over and stand next to her, putting one hand on the counter and the other on her hip. "Clarabella." I say her name, and she looks up at me, and I can see the tears in her eyes and the way that she is blinking to fight them back. "I don't even know what her name was." I tell the truth. "We met at the restaurant when she came in with friends. She flirted with me, and I stupidly went home with her. I spent maybe two hours with her before I walked out and said I would never do that again."

"You don't need to justify yourself to me," she says, and I snap. The space I was giving her was gone when I took another step into her. Turning her to face me, I tighten my hand on her hip to make sure she doesn't move farther away from me.

"I don't need to justify myself to you," I say softly, turning her and making her look at me. "I want to justify myself to you." One of my hands comes up as I brush her hair away from her forehead. "Look at me, Clarabella," I urge, and she lifts her eyes to look at me. "I don't know what you put in your head or how long you've been thinking about this, but I need you to know that there is no one but you. Not now and not before." My thumb rubs her cheek. "I fucked up six months ago letting you go." My voice comes out softly. "And I'm not even going to be sorry that Edward fucked up the way he did. I can't because if he hadn't, then I wouldn't be standing here right now in front of you." I can't help but bend and kiss her lips. "Tonight, when he came at you and called you a cheater, there was no way I was ever going to let people think that. Because that isn't you. You aren't that person."

"I know I'm not," she says, and I can't help but lean down and touch her lips with mine. "I know who I am and what went down. I know in my heart that the truth will come out." She takes a deep breath. "I just didn't want it to come out in a shouting match in the middle of Main Street. The chatter about me being a runaway bride is starting to die down." She closes her eyes. "And now with that, it'll just be more shit people will talk about."

"I'm sorry," I say softly, looking into her eyes. "I'm sorry for not thinking of that, but I just couldn't let him pull a scene and be the wounded party when he's not." I swallow down the lump that has formed in my throat. "You would be married to him right now." I can't even fathom that thought. "But I can't be sorry for standing up for you. I won't apologize for that because I would do it over and over again." I hold her chin with my thumb and my forefinger. "So you are just going to have to get used to it."

"I mean…" She smiles now, and I can't tell you how happy and relieved I am to see it. "I am your woman, apparently, so there are things I need to get used to." She laughs, and I lift her and place her on the island, moving the bottle of scotch over to the side.

"You are my woman." I try not to laugh, but I can't help it. I've never had the need to care or have anyone attached to me.

"What does that entail exactly?" She jokes with me. "So that I know what to do as someone's woman."

"Well, for one," I start, moving her hair behind her shoulder. "I think it gives me the right to kiss you whenever I want."

"You do that already." She leans back on her right hand.

"But this allows me to do it in public," I say, the tightness in my stomach coming now. "And not just in private."

"You kissed me today in public," she says softly.

"But you tensed up when I did it." I try not to make it sound like it hurts me. "It's fine. It's just I'd like to do it more."

"I'm sorry." She sits up straight, our chests touching. "I didn't even notice. So noted." She kisses my lips. "What else does being your woman do?"

"Well, I get to bring you flowers because I want to," I say, just winging it at this point, and she knows it when she rolls her lips and falls when she chuckles. "I don't know. I just want to be able to call you my woman."

"Luke, I've been your woman from the time you put me in your truck on my would-be wedding day."

I tilt my head to the side. "Is that so?"

"No idea." She laughs. "Maybe it was a couple of days after. Maybe it was the time you showed up here with a bottle of scotch and food." She leans in and places a kiss on my throat. "Maybe it was when I showed up at your house." She moves the kiss up to my cheek. "Maybe it was the time that you held my feet in your lap as you told me about your day." She kisses the side of my lips. "Maybe it was the day that you took me out at one o'clock in the morning because I wanted a milkshake." She puts her hands on my shoulders. "Regardless of when, I've been your woman for a while."

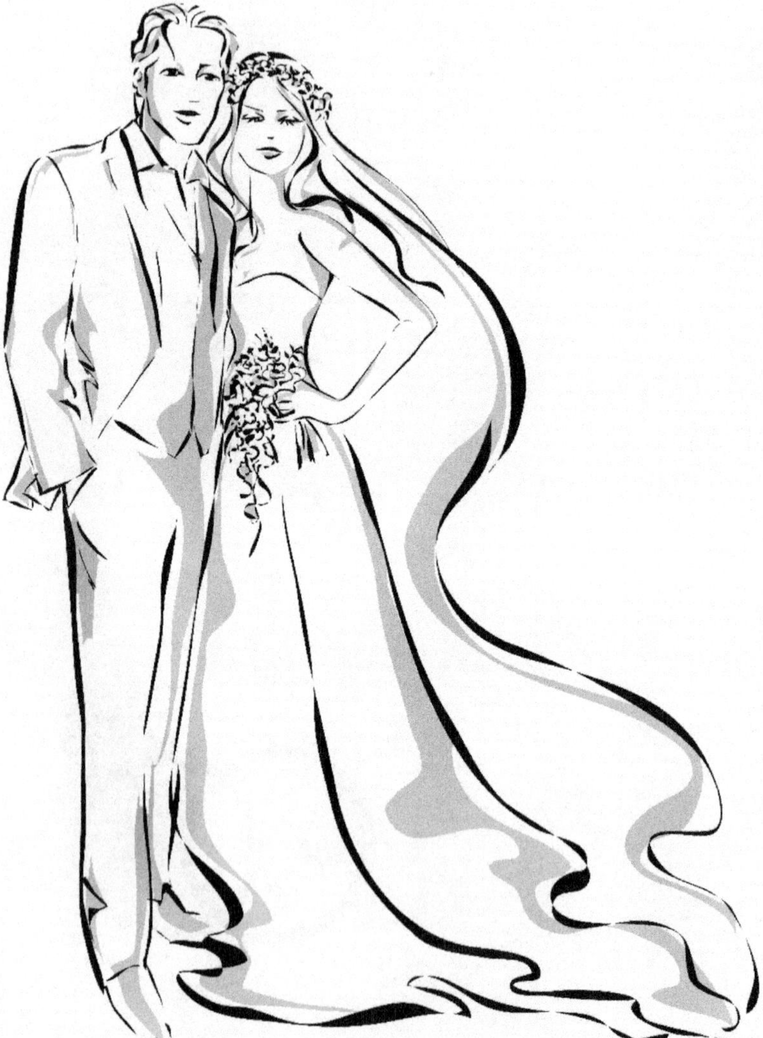

Twenty-Eight

Clarabella

"No idea." I laugh as a lightness fills me. The nerves and anger from tonight are gone without a second thought. "Maybe it was a couple of days after. Maybe it was the time you showed up here with a bottle of scotch and food." I lean in and kiss his throat, exactly where I kiss him when he's on top of me. The same spot where I can feel his heart beating on my lips. "Maybe it was when I showed up at your house." I move up, kissing him right where he has a little dimple. "Maybe it was the time that you held my feet in your lap as you told me about your day." I move my mouth closer to his mouth, kissing the corner of his lips. "Maybe it was the day that you took me out at one o'clock in the morning because I wanted a milkshake." I put my hands on his shoulders as I think of all the little things he's done for me in the last month. Things that he didn't have to do, things that seemed like nothing but were everything. "Regardless of when, I've been your woman for a while." I finally kiss his lips, and his tongue slides with mine as my legs wrap around his waist tighter, pulling him into me. "So does that mean you're my man?" The way my heart beats in my chest, I'm thinking that I'm going to fucking throw up right now.

"I was your man the minute you smiled my way," he says, and I can't help the butterflies in my stomach. His hand goes into my hair like it always does as he tilts my head to the side, his tongue slides with mine. His hand goes to my waist as he picks me up. I lock my ankles at the base of his back and wrap my arms around his neck. He lets go of my lips, walking me up the stairs. "You know what we never did?" He kisses my neck.

"We aren't doing that," I say, making him laugh, and he just shakes his head.

"Not that." He kisses my lips again. "We never went slow."

"Because it's overrated," I say, my stomach fluttering when he lets me go and stands behind me.

"But it can be so much fun." He pushes my hair to the side, bending his head and sucking my neck. "Taking my time with you." He sucks my neck again. This time, both his hands come up to cup my tits. His fingers pinch my covered nipples through my shirt. "Worshipping every single part of your body." He trails soft kisses across my shoulder. His hands still massage my breasts. My eyes close as I take in the feeling of him. I turn in his arms and take off his shirt, leaning down and kissing right in the middle of his chest.

He moves my hair to the side again with one hand as he uses the other one to raise my chin so he can kiss me again. My hands go for his belt as he slides his tongue into my mouth, his hand now going for my jeans also. The both of us work the buttons and zippers at the same time. He pulls my jeans down to my ankles and then kisses my legs as he makes his way up to me, stopping right where my lace panties show him how wet I am for him. He places a soft kiss there, and then I step out of the jeans at the same time as his jeans hit the floor. I turn to walk to the bed, and I'm stopped when he comes up behind me, and his hand grips my hips to stop me. "Not yet," he whispers in my ear before his tongue comes out, and he licks down my neck. He wraps an arm around my chest, and the other slides into my panties. "Wet for me." I don't know if he's asking me or telling me. My hand moves to the back of me as I take his cock into it. "Fuck," he hisses when my hand starts to jerk his cock slowly at the same time that he slips the tip of his finger into me, teasing me. I hold my breath, waiting for him to slip the whole finger into me, but he doesn't. He takes his hand out of my panties and then pulls the shirt over my head. My hand goes back immediately to take his cock as he unclips my bra.

Turning me in his arms, he bends his head to take a

nipple in his mouth. I moan as he bites down on it and then makes his way over to my other nipple. Flicking it with his tongue before sucking it into his mouth. "Luke," I say breathlessly as he moves his mouth up to mine. His mouth covers mine at the same time both his thumbs and forefingers pinch down on my nipples. His mouth swallows my moans as he picks me up and walks me over to the bed, laying me down on it gently. His mouth lets me go as he looks down at me before he takes off my panties, tearing another pair. He gets on his knees as my legs open for him, waiting for his warm wet tongue. He kisses the inside of my thigh, sucking in as my eyes watch him get closer and closer to my pussy. He kisses right next to my hip and then trails kisses up my stomach. His tongue comes out and trails up to my nipple as he sucks one in his mouth before licking to the other one. My whole body is on edge, needing him. "Luke," I say again as he licks his way up the middle of my chest and then to my mouth again. I open my legs, thinking he is going to slide into me, but he doesn't.

"I'm going to lie on the bed." He looks into my eyes. "And you are going to straddle my face." I close my eyes for a second. "And I'm going to eat your pussy." From the first time, sex with Luke has been on another level. It's as if my body was made for him.

He lies down on the bed, and I throw my leg around his head, facing his cock, "No, the other way. You aren't touching my cock until it's in you." I move again, and this time, the minute my knees fall beside his head, he lifts up, and his tongue slides into my pussy. I can't help but fall forward. He licks up my slit, twirling his tongue around my clit. "I want you to come on my tongue," he says, sucking me into his mouth and then sliding his tongue into me. "Just with my tongue fucking you." I close my eyes as he devours my pussy. "You are dripping wet," he declares, and I want him to slide two fingers inside me, knowing that the minute he does that, I'm going to go off. I can feel the orgasm at the tip of my toes as his tongue fucks me twice before he sucks my clit. Over and over, his tongue flicks my clit, and I'm lost. I can't even focus, but I do know that I need his cock even if it's in my mouth. I turn around, and when he's about to say something, I sit on his face. His tongue slides into my pussy at the same time that I take his cock into my mouth. "Cheating." I don't care what he says, to be honest. My hands grip the base of his cock, moving it with my mouth. Finally, he slides a finger into me, thrusts it twice before taking it out, and replaces it with his tongue. "How bad do you want to come?" he asks, sucking in my clit, and I move my hips from side to side.

"So bad," I confirm as I try to get some friction going when he pushes me off him, and I think I cry out.

"I want to watch you ride my cock," he says, lying on the bed, holding up his cock in his hand.

"Finally," I say, going over to him and bending my head to kiss him. The both of us make the kiss needy. I'm about to straddle him when I turn around. "You want to watch me ride," I throw over my shoulder as my hand grips his cock, and I slide down it. "Fuck," I swear when I have him all the way inside me. I look over at him, his eyes dark as I bend forward, and his hand grips my ass. I move up and down his cock. "Oh my God," I say each and every time, and I'm about to come when his hands grip my ass, stopping me. "Luke, so help me God," I warn as he pulls out of me, my hand going to my pussy as I finger myself.

My ass to him now, and he gets on his knees. "If you make yourself come, I won't give you my cock." I move my hand, looking over at him as he slides his cock into me slowly at first, and then he pulls out and slams into me.

"More," I urge, pushing back on him. "Please, more."

"My woman wants it hard." He slams into me, his balls slapping my clit.

"Yes," I hiss, my hand going to play with my clit.

"Then I have to give it to her hard," he says, gripping my hips and now fucking me hard. The both of us don't last. I come within seconds over and over again. I'm close to the end of the orgasm when he stops moving, and I cry out, wanting him to move. "My woman wants to come again." He slams into me, and all I can do is nod my head.

"Your woman wants you to come inside her," I urge, as I squeeze my pussy around his cock. "Come to think of it," I say, trying to focus on my words and not on the way he's fucking me. "I want you to fuck me and then come in my mouth." I can feel his cock getting bigger in me, his hands gripping my hips so hard he's going to leave a mark. "I want to suck the cum from your cock, lick you clean, and then fuck you again."

"Clarabella," he hisses. "I'm going to." His hands leaves my hips now, and I turn, taking his cock into my mouth as he comes down my throat. Over and over again, I swallow him, my fist working with my mouth. "Fucking hell," he says when he slips out of my mouth. "That was."

"That was," I agree, turning and lying on my back, spreading my legs for him. "That was just the beginning." I put one hand under my head, and the other hand moves to my pussy as I finger myself. "Your woman wants to come again. Now the question is are you going to watch me make myself come, or are you going to help?"

I TURN OFF the car and look over at the house. My heart slams against my chest when I open the door and step out. Once I walk up the pathway, my hand shakes when I press the bell. I can hear footsteps, and I wonder if maybe I shouldn't have come, but I can't back out now because the door opens. "You have some nerve showing up here," Edward's mother says as she stands in the doorway of his house. The last person I thought I would see today was her, but I guess this is how it has to go.

"I'm looking for Edward," I say, not backing down nor willing to let her see me nervous. I did nothing wrong.

"For what?" She sneers at me. "To gloat about moving on."

I swallow down the hurt and then think about what he must have told his mother. "To gloat?" I ask, and everything in me snaps. "Is that what you think this is?" My voice goes louder, and I think I even scare her with my tone.

"Mother," Edward says from behind her. "Close the door," he snaps.

"Yes, close the door so I can't tell you the truth," I say, not even caring if people are staring at me. I guess the saying *let's give them something to talk about* is right. "Yes, why don't you so you won't know why I actually left your son at the altar."

"Mother, close the fucking door," he snaps, and I see his face is white.

"Yes, Mommy," I mock him. "Close the door, so I don't tell you what a spineless coward of a son you have." Edward's mother's face matches her son's now. "I met Louise," I say, and her eyes go big.

"That whore." She laughs and folds her arms over her chest. "So what? Everyone has a past."

"They do." I nod my head. "But not everyone's past comes with a future." I look past her to Edward. "Not everyone's past comes knocking on my door with a baby." His mother gasps. "So if you are looking for the real reason as to why I left your son, you should ask him about Edward Jr." I clap my hands. "Fuck, this feels good." I smile at her. "Now, down to the nitty-gritty. If you don't stop harassing my family with frivolous lawsuits, I'll have to tell them my truth. I don't think you can sweep a child under the rug that easily. Especially since I'm sure Louise would love nothing more than to tell the world. Also, I want you to fuck off," I tell Edward.

"You see me walking down the street, go the other way. You see me come out of a restaurant or a store, turn the other way. Bottom line, you see me, you make sure I don't see your fucking face." I nod at the both of them as they stand there, not saying anything. "Have a great day," I say, turning and starting to walk down the stairs with a skip in my step. "Have a great life."

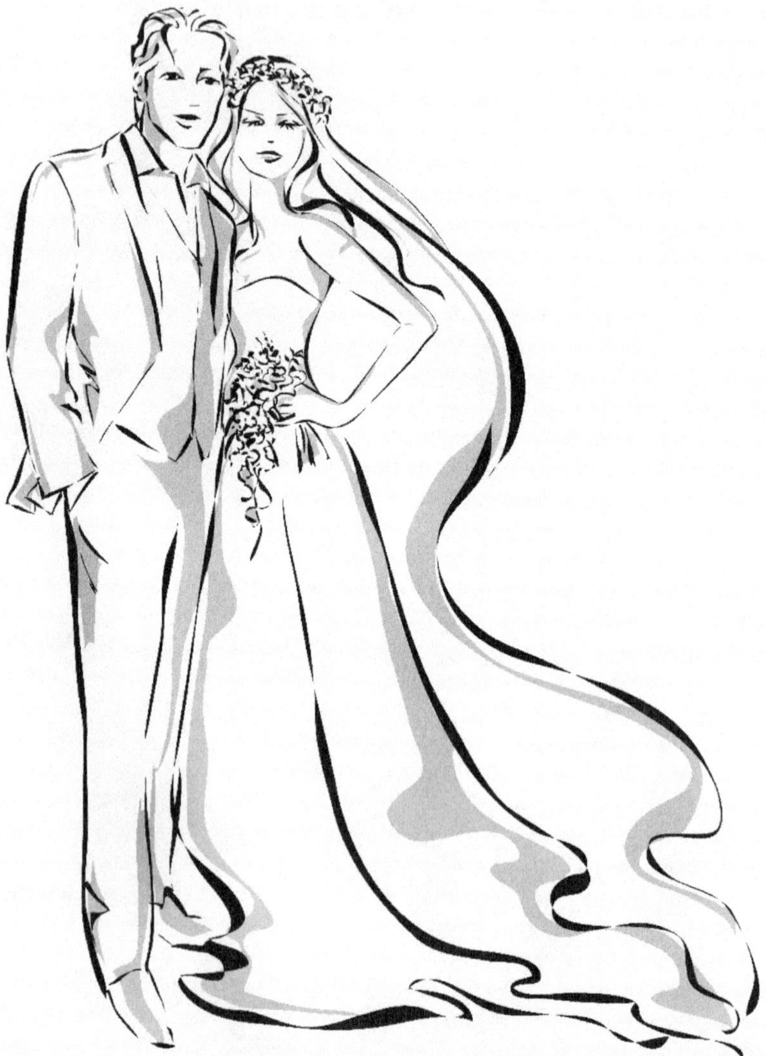

Twenty-Nine

Clarabella

I walk up the steps to the office and pull open the door, the cold air hitting me right away. I get two steps into the door before I hear mumbling in the kitchen. "Morning!" I yell down the hallway toward the kitchen as I make my way to my office.

"Well, well, well." Shelby sticks her head out of her office, looking at me walking out now. "If it isn't the talk of the town." I turn and roll my eyes at her, waiting for the dread to come in, and I'm shocked when I feel nothing, nothing at all.

"How bad is it?" I look at her and see Presley come out of the kitchen with a coffee cup in her hand. She looks at me and smirks.

"On a scale of one to ten?" Presley says, taking a sip of her drink. "I'm going with a million."

I open my mouth while Shelby hits Presley. "She's only saying it's one million because you didn't call and tell us. And she's bitter that she found out through me and thought I was lying."

I look over at Presley, who just nods her head at me and points. "That is correct," Presley confirms to me. "Imagine if you might." She glares at me. "Getting a phone call informing me of this whole scene that went down."

"I didn't really have time to call you." I shake my head, thinking about the showdown that happened in my kitchen not long after the showdown that happened on the street that then proceeded to a whole other showdown in the bedroom.

"It's been what, ten hours since it happened?" Shelby glares at me. "Ten hours." She holds up both hands, wiggling her fingers. "And you couldn't pick up a phone and be like 'hey, I'm alive and I'm okay.'"

"Why would I be dead?" I fold my arms over my chest and chuckle.

"Well, you are dead to me," Presley declares, doing a fist in front of her with her thumb sticking out and running it against her neck. "So I don't even care what happened."

"Seriously, ten hours. Ten." Shelby gasps. "What the hell were you doing?"

"It's not what she was doing," Presley says. "But who

she was doing it with."

"Can we focus on what's being said, please?" I hold up my hands, trying to make them change the subject.

"The word on the street is that Luke looked like he was going to body-slam Edward into the ground like the Hulk," Presley informs me, and I just close my eyes.

"It wasn't that bad," I tell them and turn to walk into my office with the two of them following me. They sit down, and I tell them my side of the story, and when I look up, they both have their mouths open.

"Wait," Presley says, holding up her hand at me. "What did he call you?"

"His woman." I hold up my hands, thankful I'm not the only one who is wowed by that declaration.

"What does that even mean?" Shelby asks, amazed. She's looking at Presley to see if maybe she has the answer, and I can tell she does not.

"Like, do you get a crown?" Presley sits back in the chair and puts her hand in front of her mouth. "Like, is that an elevated position? Do you skip dating and be like boom, his woman?"

"I have no idea." I look over at Shelby to see if maybe she has the answer, and she just looks at me with her eyes big.

"Does he walk in front of you and beat his chest?" Presley rolls her lips. "With a bat over his shoulder wearing a loincloth and grunting?"

I can't help the laughter that comes out of me. "That's what I thought would happen."

"Bet you he gave you his bat all right." Presley

winks at me. "You know, since you're his woman and everything."

"Can we focus on what is going on and not about what happened after?" I look at both of them. "How bad is this gossip?"

"Is it gossip, though?" Presley asks me. "I mean, it's not like what he said was a lie."

"I know that, but..." I look up at the ceiling, trying to steady the way my heart is going nuts. "It's like before I was the runaway bride, and that just started dying down. Now I'll be the poor girl whose fiancé had a kid with someone else."

"Fuck what anyone thinks." Presley is the first one to say something. "Like, for real, think about it. No one cares. By tomorrow, it'll be old news." I just stare at her. "Okay, by like next week for sure."

"What does this mean now?" Shelby asks me, and I just look at her, not sure what she's asking me. "Are you with Luke or not?"

"Well, considering that I'm his woman." I try to make a joke but then look at them. "Yes."

"Another one bites the dust," Presley jokes, getting up and grabbing her cup. "This was fun. I'm still pissed at you, but I will let you know that I called Mom and complained about it, so you should be getting a phone call from her any minute."

I groan. "Thanks." I flip her off as she walks out of the room with Shelby right behind her. It's one thing to go face-to-face with my sisters; it's a whole other ball game to go face-to-face with my mother. "I hate you!"

I scream at the door, and then I pick up my phone and FaceTime my mother, biting the bullet.

"So she's alive." That's the first thing she says when her face fills the screen after one ring, and all I can do is roll my eyes.

"And we wonder where we get our dramatics from," I say, turning in my chair and looking outside at the sun shining into the office on the flowers. Then looking back at her as she picks up a cup of coffee.

"You get that from your father." She points at the screen and then goes quiet. "Are you okay?"

"I'm fine," I assure her, and she just laughs at me, clapping her hands.

"You are one hundred percent most definitely not fine," she huffs. "And it's okay not to be fine, Clarabella."

"Okay, I'm not fine fine," I admit to her. "But I'm not like 'woe is me' not fine."

"Interesting," she says, and I can see her tapping her finger on the table. "Does this have to do with Luke?"

"Probably." I look at her. "I was so pissed that he just told everyone my business."

"Hold on one minute." She puts her hand up. "Edward came at you in public and tried to humiliate you by turning the tables on you." Her voice goes louder. "And you got mad at Luke?"

"I didn't see it at first," I huff. "But I did when we spoke about it."

"Good." She nods her head. "When are you bringing him to meet me?"

I laugh. "No idea."

"Clarabella Baker, I will show up at his restaurant on Friday to meet him with or without you," she warns. "I'd rather it be with you."

"So when you said when are you bringing him to meet you, what you forgot to say is you have until Friday." I look at her, and she shrugs.

"You take it the way you want to." She smiles at me, and I fill her in about Edward, something that I didn't tell my sisters. "You are lucky I wasn't there." She leans back in her chair. "Those mofos." I can't help but laugh out loud at her slang, and the phone shows me that Luke is calling.

"Mom, I have to call you back," I say, and she just hangs up on me. "Hello," I answer the phone, not bothering to hide my smile.

"Hey," he greets softly. "Are you busy for lunch?"

"No," I say right away, and even if I was, I would make time, which is crazy. Since I would never have before.

"Good, I'll pick you up at eleven," he states, and I laugh. "Also, it might be safe to say you might not go back to work this afternoon."

"Is that a fact?" I can't help but shake my head and look over at my schedule in front of me, seeing that I'm free. "Well, considering I'm your woman and all."

"I see you know your role," he says, laughing. "Pick you up at eleven." He doesn't even give me a chance to answer him. He just hangs up.

"What the fuck?" I say to myself, looking down at the phone.

"That must be part of being his woman." Presley's voice comes on the intercom, and all I can do is laugh.

"I guess so," I mumble to myself as I try to keep busy until eleven.

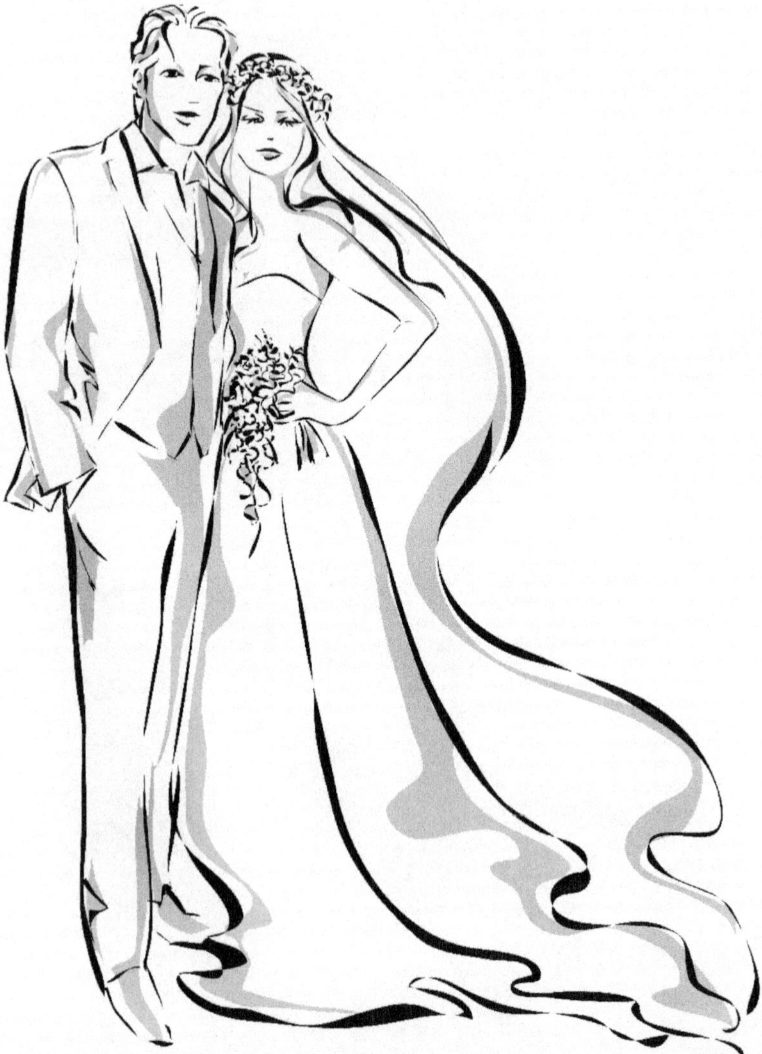

Thirty

Luke

I slam the truck door and walk up the front steps to her office. I don't think I've ever gone in through here, and as soon as I walk in, I put my sunglasses on the top of my head. I look around the room and see Presley sitting down at the front desk. "Hi," I say to her. She smiles, picks up the phone, and I hear her voice come out on the speaker.

"Luke is here to pick up his woman," she says, smirking at me, and I shake my head.

"I guess you heard about that." I put my hands on my hips.

"Oh, did we." She leans back in the chair. "We even

googled what does being his woman mean."

I nod my head at her. "And?"

"There were a couple of things," she says, trying not to laugh. "One said that you wanted to be the only man in her life, and the other—"

"Said something about a tiara and a sash," Shelby says, coming into the room now, trying to hide her smile.

"I'll look into that," I say, putting my hands in my back pockets and hoping like fuck that Clarabella gets her ass out here fast.

"Go away." I hear her voice and look over at her, seeing her walk into the room. I can't help but smile when she tucks a strand of hair behind her ear. She walks to me, and I'm expecting her to stop in front of me, but instead, she comes chest to chest with me and kisses my lips. I put my hands on her hips, bringing her even closer to me. "Hi," she says, once she lets go of my lips.

"Hi." I smile at her and kiss her again. "Ready to go?" She nods her head. "It was a pleasure." I look at Shelby and then Presley.

"Don't do anything I wouldn't do," Shelby teases.

"Yeah, and that says a lot from the woman who had sex at the side of her house last weekend." Presley shakes her head.

"Can I get any privacy in this place?" Shelby throws her hands in the air and turns to walk out of the room.

Clarabella slips her hand in mine as we walk out. "Should I follow you or…?"

"Nah," I say, opening the truck door for her. "I can bring you back to work tomorrow."

mine to CHERISH

She gets in the truck, and I lean in and kiss her. This time, my tongue slides in to meet hers. "As much as I love kissing you," she says, pushing me away. "We are on camera." I step back as if someone tossed cold water on me, and I look up and see the camera pointed at me. I wave my hand before walking around the truck and getting in. I grab her hand, bringing it to my lips and then holding it between my legs as I drive away to the secret place I picked out.

I open the door and then grab the picnic basket from the back seat, and she meets me behind the truck. "This is so nice." She looks around. "I've never been here."

"Good," I say, grabbing her hand and walking with her up the hill to the top where we can look down at the field in the distance. I pick a spot under the tree that gives us some shade. I open the basket, taking out the blanket, and put it down for her as she kicks off her ballerina shoes and sits down. My heart starts to speed up when I sit down and take everything out.

"What's going on?" she asks, looking at me. "You became quiet all of a sudden."

I sit down and look over at her. "My business partner called me from New York this morning."

I can tell right away that it bothers her when her eyes get darker.

"Oh," she says, moving the basket to her so that she can keep her hands busy.

"Clarabella," I call her name, and she looks up at me. "What do you want out of life?"

"Um…" she says. "That's a loaded question."

"Is it really?" I laugh nervously.

"What do you want out of life?" She turns the question on me.

"Um, that's easy," I say, and if you would have asked me four months ago, it would have been the hardest question to answer. "A successful business."

"Same," she agrees, smiling.

"So, we got that one. We can put a check next to that." I pick up my hand and put an invisible check mark in the air. "I want someone to come home to." I swallow down, looking at her.

"I didn't know," she starts to say. "But I want the same." She looks down and then looks up again. "When Edward asked me to marry him, I felt like a deer in the headlights. But then I don't know." She shrugs. "I got excited about all the things that came with it. Even when I thought I was getting cold feet."

I laugh. "When did you think you had cold feet?" I ask, my stomach tight when I think about her with someone else.

"When you showed up in town." She smirks at me. "Maybe a bit before then."

"What else do you want?" I ask, and she stares at me dead in the eyes.

"I want to eventually have children." She smiles, and her whole face lights up. "I'm not saying tomorrow, but I want to have them in the next five years." A tightness forms in my chest, and all I can see is her with a baby in her arms. "Are you going to go to New York?"

"Do you want me to go to New York?" I put my arms

behind me and lean back on them.

"I don't want you to choose between me and your dreams," she says, not skipping a beat. "I would never ever make you choose."

"But what would happen to us?" I ask, the two of us tippy-toeing around the main question.

"Nothing." She shakes her head. "We could commute," she offers, optimistic. "I could come there for a couple of weekends, and you can come here."

"So we would do long distance?" I ask, and at that moment, it's the worst idea she's ever had. At that moment, I know I don't ever want to do that. I also know that her whole life is here in this town. She has her business here, and she has her family here. She planted her roots here, and I would never take her away from here.

"Lots of people do it." She smiles, trying to convince me and maybe herself. "It'll be an adjustment, but I think as long as we communicate and put each other first, it can work out."

Sitting up, I hold out my hand for her, and she comes over to me and straddles my lap. Her hands go to the middle of my chest. "What if I told you that it's not good enough?" I swallow down the lump in my throat. She looks down, and I see her blinking fast, putting my finger under her chin and lifting up her face.

"I can't believe you're doing this," she says, pushing away from me, and I grab her waist before she jumps up, but she's faster than me.

"Clarabella," I call her name, and she just starts to

walk away before stopping and turning around.

"Literally, it's been less than twenty-four hours since you called me your woman!" she shouts, and I try not to laugh at her. "Twenty-four fucking hours. You literally stood in the middle of fucking Main Street and basically peed on my leg, marking your territory." Fuck, she's beautiful. "And then one phone call, and it's like, see you later."

"Are you done?" I ask, and she glares at me. "One, you're fucking beautiful." I hold up my hand with one finger up. "Two, you are mine." I hold up another finger. "And three, I turned it down already." I hold up the third finger, and her mouth opens to say something and then she closes it, nothing coming out of her. "I turned him down."

"Why the fuck would you do that?" she shouts at me.

I walk over to her and wrap my arms around her waist. "Well, for one," I explain. "I like waking up with you. I love that you are there when I come in at night. The thought of not doing that every single night or even every other night is just not worth it."

"I don't want you to not do it just for me," she says, wrapping her arms around my neck.

"I'm not doing it for you," I admit to her. "I'm doing it for me."

"Well, that's good to know," she replies, and I laugh.

"I have to say, you really are hot when you're pissed off," I growl and bend to kiss her neck. "I thought you were going to throat punch me, and I've never been so turned on in my life."

"You are a sick, sick man." She shakes her head.

"Must be sick in love," I offer, and for the first time in my life, I'm in love with someone, and I want to shout it from the rooftops. "With you." She goes stiff in my arms. "Breathe," I urge. "Just take a deep breath in and then out."

"Luke," she whispers.

"Can we go home now?" I ask, and she shakes her head.

"You can't just throw out that you are sick in love." She sniffles, and I see the tears in her eyes. "It's not okay."

I chuckle at her. "It's more than okay," I inform her.

"My mother wants to meet you," she blurts out.

"Okay." I smile.

"I think I love you." She takes a deep breath. "Like, I knew I liked you a lot since we were in school, and then when we got close again, I felt something, but I told myself it was nothing. Then you left, and it hurt so bad even though I pretended it didn't." She palms my face in one of her hands. "And now when you told me you were leaving, I really fucking hated the idea." I can't help but laugh. "I mean, I would support you and do whatever you wanted, but I didn't like it, and then it hit me like a kick in the vagina that I love you." She wipes a tear that rolls down her face.

"It's good to know." I grab her face in my hands and kiss her. "Now can we go home and have make-up sex?" She looks at me and then looks at the blanket under the tree. "Are you insane? You know that being my woman means no one gets to see you but me." She rolls her eyes.

"And that means we have sex where no one can see or hear you."

"Buzzkill," she retorts, letting go of me and then walking back to the blanket and shoving everything in the basket. "Shelby has sex everywhere," she mumbles. "Maybe I'm good with being a girlfriend and not a woman." This woman makes me crazy one minute and then just makes me laugh the next one, and I'm going to have so much fun having make-up sex with her.

Dearest Love,

Another wedding season is behind us. Our very own Clarabella tied the knot. It was in the middle of nowhere with no cell service, and it was just the way it was always supposed to be.

It looks like Cupid is aiming his bow at Presley. Except Presley has shielded herself with body armor. But nothing could protect her from the stork.

Looks like that plus sign will have her walking down the aisle, or will she still be the lone wolf she thinks she is?

XOXO
NM.

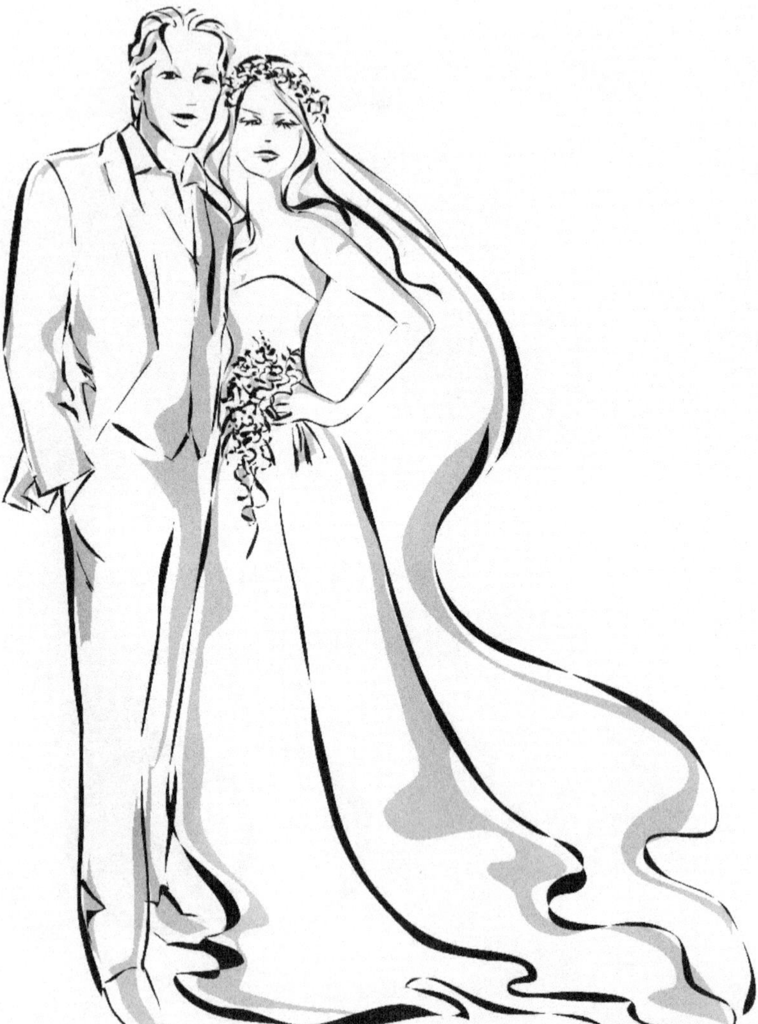

Epilogue One

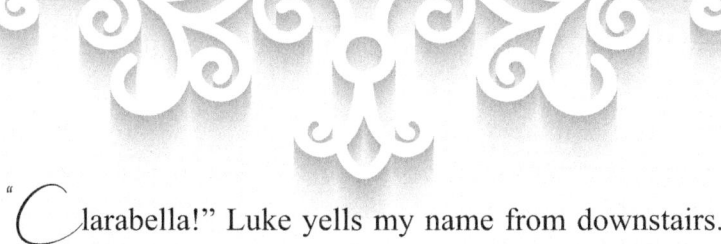

Clarabella

"Clarabella!" Luke yells my name from downstairs. "Let's go."

I grab my bag on top of the bed and walk to the hallway. "Clarabella," he repeats my name again.

"Oh my God," I say, walking down the stairs and seeing him standing there with both hands on the banister as he calls my name. "Would you hold your horses?" I look down at him, and he looks so handsome in his black jeans and a black T-shirt. "What is the big rush this morning?"

"It's the first time we've had off in weeks." He grabs my hips as I stand on the step in front of him, looking down at him. "And I want to get going so we can start naked weekend."

"One." I hold up my free hand. "You said we are leaving by nine." I turn my hand over and see that it's nine ten. "I'm ten minutes late, and that's because you decided that you wanted to shower with me."

"Hmm." He pulls me closer. "That was fun." He smiles up at me, and my heart speeds up in my chest, and my stomach feels like a wave hitting the shore every single time. It's been over six months now, and honestly every single time he kisses me it's like the first time all over again. "And it's always a good decision to get you naked and wet." He kisses me again. "Now can we get on the road?"

"We can." I take a step down as he grabs the bag from me.

"Why is this so heavy?" he asks, ushering me out of the house. "It's naked weekend. You don't need all these clothes."

I laugh at him. "I'm going to leave some clothes there," I explain, and he just shrugs.

"I don't know why; it might be naked day every time we are there," he says, opening the back door and throwing my bag on top of the seat.

"Where is your bag?" I ask when he opens the passenger door for me.

"It's naked weekend." He pffts. "Why do I need a bag?"

I look at him. "I got nothing," I reply, closing the door and watching him walk around the truck. I take my phone out of my pocket and text my sisters.

Me: Heading out right now.
Presley: BYEEEEEEEE.
Shelby: Enjoy naked weekend.
Me: How did you know about that?
Shelby: I have to admit the walls are really thin in this place.
Presley: Yes, please keep that in mind the next time you think you want to talk about getting it hard. At this point, I'm surprised I'm not a raging alcoholic.

I can't help but laugh. "What's so funny?" Luke asks when we back out of the driveway.

I look over and reach out to run my hand through the hair at the back of his head. "Presley heard us talking about naked weekend."

"Is there anything that your sisters don't know?" he asks me, and I roll my lips.

"They don't know that." I try to think. "They don't know that we live together," I say, and he whips his head around. "I mean, they know we live together, but they don't know you officially moved in and will be selling your house."

"We've been living with each other since your almost wedding day," he jokes with me and shakes his head, laughing. "Well, after today, there is going to be a for sale sign, so it won't be a secret for long." His hand finds mine at the back of his neck, and he brings it to his mouth, kissing my fingers. I lean my head to the side as I watch the trees as we drive up to his cabin. We try to get away and come here at least a couple of days a month, but the past two months have been crazy busy for the both of us. Especially since we just partnered together with a property that he was looking at out by the lake. It is a great space for a restaurant during the week, and then the weekends will be amazing for weddings. He will be the in-house chef, and we will run the events. We didn't know what to expect, but it is now fully booked for the next three years.

He pulls up to the cabin, and just like the first time, I let him walk in first just in case we have special visitors that I'm not okay with. He comes out smiling. "It's all clear." He walks down the steps to me. "I love you." He kisses my lips, then moves to the side so I can walk into the cabin. My head is down, and when I step inside, I look up at the glow of candles and stop in my tracks.

The whole living room looks like it's been cleared out, and painted in the middle of the wall is "You have my whole heart for my whole life," and under it is fairy lights that hang down, and pictures of us fill the whole wall. My feet move on their own as I look at the pictures we've taken in the past six months. I turn around seeing white, peach, and ivory roses that fill the room. A massive vase sits in the middle of the room with a sign in front of it that says, *it has always been and will forever be you.*

I put my hands to my mouth and turn around to see Luke in the middle of the room down on one knee; the sob rips out of me, and I bend down, trying to laugh and smile while I cry tears of happiness. "Wow, this is a lot easier than I thought it was going to be," Luke says to me, and I see his own tears in his eyes. "When I went to ask your mother for your hand in marriage, I was so nervous." I put my hand to my chest that he went out of his way to ask her, knowing how hard it must have been for him but knowing that it was what I would have wanted. "And the whole time leading up to this minute right here has been a roller-coaster ride to say the very least." He laughs. "But kneeling in front of you, knowing that I'm going to ask you to spend forever with me, is the calmest I've ever been. Clarabella, there is not one day that goes by that I don't have a smile on my face. There is not one day that goes by that I'm not thankful for so many things." He looks down. "Especially since I didn't have much to be thankful for. There is not one day that goes by that I don't think I'm the luckiest guy on earth because I get to come home to you. Because I get to wake up with you. Because I get to kiss your lips when I want. Because I get to hold your hand. Because I get to cheer you on when you become the boss lady. Everything about you makes me love you even more. I know that you don't need someone to make you whole." He laughs. "But I need you to make me whole. Without you, I'm a shell." He takes the black box out of his back pocket. "Clarabella, will you be my wife?"

I can't help but laugh. "Is that above being your woman?" The question makes him laugh.

"It definitely gets you a tiara," he says, opening the top, and to be honest, I don't even fucking care what's in the box. It could be from a Cracker Jack box.

"I mean, if I get a tiara," I say, laughing as the tears pour down my face. "Yes."

The minute I say yes, I hear commotion behind me and look over to see my family coming out of the bedroom. "About time," Presley says, coming over to me and hugging me.

"What are you guys doing here?" I ask them after I hug my mother.

"Sorry to intrude on your naked weekend," my mother says, and I can hear moaning coming from Luke. "But I couldn't not be here."

"Can we just go outside so we can sit down?" Presley says, looking at us.

"We can bring the couch in from the bedroom," Travis suggests, and she just shakes her head.

"They have naked weekends here." She points at me and then Luke. "There have been ass cheeks and ball sacks all over this place." She puts her hand in front of her mouth. "And I, for one, am not touching anything."

"You helped decorate," I point out.

"She wore gloves and a mask," Shelby shares with Ace beside her, his arm wrapped around her shoulders.

I look over at Travis, who has Harlow beside him as she hugs his waist. "Um," I say, looking at everyone in the room and then back at Luke. "We're engaged, right?" I ask, and he just looks at me, and the only one who is thinking what I'm thinking is Presley, who groans. "How hard would it be to get married here?"

"I knew it," Presley gloats. "I fucking called it."

"What are you talking about?" Luke says, and I take a deep breath.

"I had the big wedding planned," I remind him.

"I know, I drove you away from it," he says, putting his hands on his hips.

"What she's trying to say is that she had the big wedding, and now all she wants to do is get married," my mother says, stepping forward, smiling at me with big tears in her eyes.

"I mean, we already have food for the engagement party," Luke says, and I just stare at him in shock. "And your sisters already had the decorations brought down."

"And I might have snuck in a dress," Presley admits, and all I can do is stare in shock.

I hold up my hand. "Where is this celebration taking place?" I ask.

"Come this way." Luke holds out his hand for me, and I walk to him, and he slips the ring on my finger. "Now it's official." I shake my head as I follow him out and walk down the stairs as he walks toward the path that we hike in, an arch of white and green flowers leads into where the reception is supposed to happen. "What the fuck?" He gasps, and I look around the clearing in the middle of the forest surrounded by trees, and tables are set up. Huge moss-like flowers sit in the middle of the tables surrounded by white roses, and what looks like tree branches are in the middle of five round tables with dark green tablecloths that fill the empty space. White place settings are set up with sage-green napkins on each plate. White vine leaves drape over us as if they are falling onto lanterns to light up the area. It's the most romantic thing I've ever seen. "You told me that you would handle it."

"And we did," Presley confirms. "You are lucky that we couldn't put candles all around this place." She puts her hands on her hips. "We also have enough flowers left over to make a nice archway."

"We need to get someone to marry you," Shelby states. "And there is no service."

"I'm ordained." Presley sticks her hand up, and Luke just stares at her in shock. "Two years ago, the officiant was in a car accident, and well, I had to save the day."

"There isn't anything we can't do," Shelby declares, and I clap my hands.

"Then let's get married," Luke says.

"Are you sure?" Harlow asks me. "This may delay naked weekend by like eight hours."

"That's a deal breaker for me," I joke. "We could get married naked."

"I just threw up in my mouth," Travis says, putting a fist to his mouth. "And now I need booze to take the image out of my head."

"Oh my God, are you really doing this?" my mother asks. "Not the naked part." She shakes her head. "But are you really, really going to get married here?"

I look over at Luke, and everything in me calms down. "There has never been anything that I have been surer about in my life." I smile at him.

"Really?" Presley says, and Shelby slaps her arm. "What? I'm just asking. She literally was going to get married this year to someone else."

"Presley," my mother scolds between clenched teeth, but nothing could stop the smile that fills my face.

mine to CHERISH

"Let's go, people. You have thirty minutes!" I shout and turn to walk back to the house.

"How are we going to do this?" Travis says, and in three minutes, Shelby and Presley have given out orders.

"The dress is in the bedroom hanging in the closet," Presley explains when we walk into the bedroom. She walks over and grabs a couple of black garment bags and turns to Luke. "You can have the bathroom, and then you leave." She looks at him. "Immediately leave." Then she hands one to Travis and Ace. "You follow him." Then she motions with her head to Harlow and my mother. "If you don't have a vagina, you are not allowed in this room." She slams the door in the guys' faces. "Now, where were we?" She looks at me. "I want to say, thank God you washed your hair."

Everything is a blur after that moment and the only moment I will remember is when she takes my dress out, and I get tears. "How did you know?" I ask my sister.

"You spent way too much time looking at it when we went to the store last month," Presley replies.

"It was the only dress that you went up to and touched," Shelby adds, smiling. Last month, we had to go and help a bride pick out a dress, and the minute I saw this dress hanging, I envisioned myself wearing it. "Now, let's get you dressed."

I walk over to the dress and step into it as I pull it up and hold the front to my chest. It's got a sweetheart neckline, and the top half is an ivory satin. I slip my hands into the off-the-shoulder big puffy chiffon sleeves. My sisters tie the three buttons in the back, and when I look down at the multi-layered chiffon bottom, I feel like a princess. My mother buttons one cuff at my wrist, and Harlow buttons the second one. "This is the one," I say, putting my hand to my stomach.

"We are just missing one thing," Shelby notes, looking at Presley and trying to hide her tears.

"A husband," my mother says, and we all laugh as I turn to walk out of the bedroom and stop when I see Luke there waiting for me. He's wearing black pants and a white button-down shirt untucked. The sleeves are rolled up to his elbows, his hair is pushed back, and you can see where his fingers ran through it. He's never looked hotter. His face is filled with a smile when he looks at me.

"Oh my God." Those are the only words he says as he wipes a tear away.

"You have one job," Shelby warns. "One."

"I…" Luke starts to say.

"It's not like you've never seen her in a wedding dress before," Presley says, and my mother moans. "What? It's true."

"I can't wait until it's your turn," Harlow says to Presley, and she throws her head back and laughs.

"Please, after you three?" She points at us. "I'm dying alone with my ten cats."

"Why would you get ten cats?" Shelby asks, shaking her head.

"We are going to wait outside," Harlow says with a smile. "Please keep all clothes on."

I can't help but chuckle as she walks out, and my

heart speeds up when it's just the two of us. "You look beautiful."

"Better than the first one?" I ask, and he nods his head.

"This is you," he says, coming to me. "And you are mine."

"I am yours," I confirm to him, and he kisses my lips. "Now, can we go and make me your wife?"

"We can," he agrees, kissing my lips one more time. "All this time," he continues, holding my hand as we walk out of the house, "you were always going to be mine." I look over at him as he brings my hand to his lips. "And I'll cherish you forever."

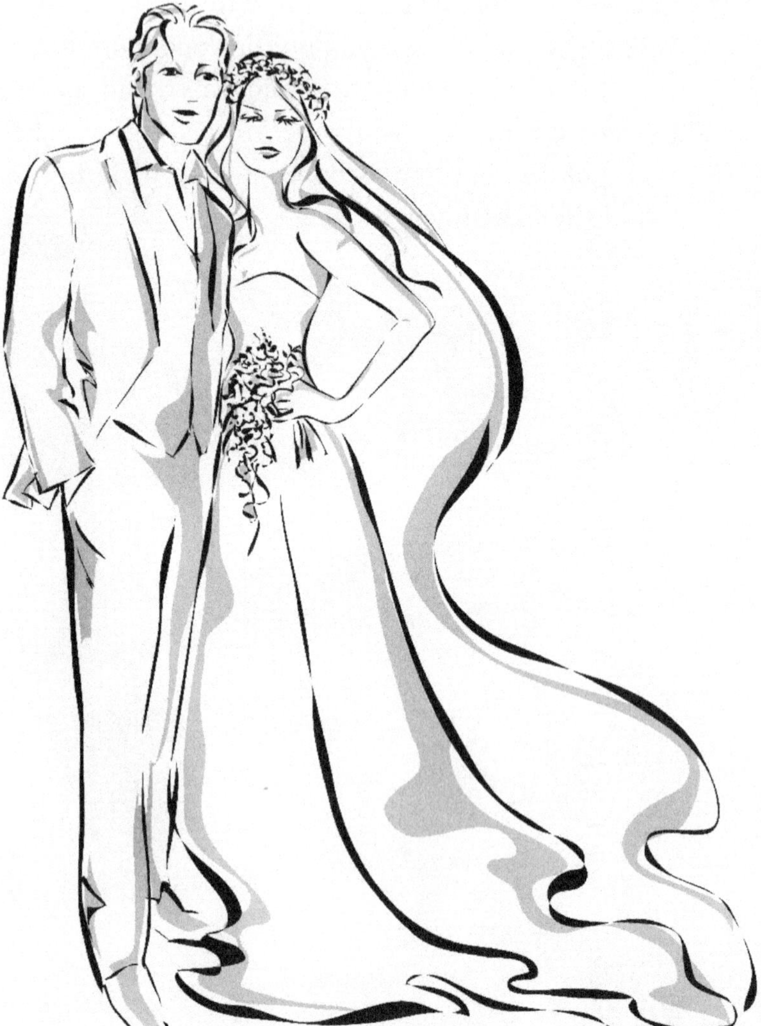

Epilogue Two

Luke

One year later

"Honey, I'm home!" I shout as I walk into the house and slam the door behind me. Walking to the kitchen, I expect to see Clarabella sitting at the island, but all that is there is her purse. Her shoes are kicked off beside the island. "Hello!" I shout up the stairs, and after a minute, when I don't hear anything, I walk up the steps. I go straight to our room and see the bed is still unmade from the morning, the picture of us from our wedding above the bed, and every single time I see it, I smile. "Clarabella?" I call her name and see the bathroom door is closed.

"In here." Her voice comes out soft, and I walk over and open the door, expecting her to be in the bath. She isn't. Instead, she is sitting in the middle of the bathroom with her legs crossed and a brown bag beside her. There are open boxes next to her and in front of her are what look like five or six white markers.

"What are you doing?" I ask and see the worry on her face.

"Do you know what these are?" She points at the things in front of her.

I walk over and squat down in front of her and see a tear rolling down her cheek, and my whole body goes stiff. My stomach is in my throat, and my whole body goes on alert as every single possible scenario goes through my mind. "I have no idea," I say to her and reach out to pick up one. I turn over the white stick in my hand and see the word Pregnant in the middle of it. My eyes fly back to her.

"I know," she says softly. "I mean, I didn't know, which is why I decided I needed to take six. I don't know how it happened."

"Well, we do have a lot of sex," I remind her. "Are you sad about having a baby with me?" I can't even swallow the lump in my throat.

"No." She gets up on her knees. "I was scared you would be sad."

"What?" I say, shocked. "Why the fuck would you even think that?"

"I don't know. We never really discussed it," she says,

getting up and pacing in front of me.

"Did you or did you not tell me you want babies?" I get up, still holding the test in my hand.

"Well, yeah, I told you that I wanted babies." She puts her hands on her hips. "But you never said you did."

"I married you." I chuckle. "Which means that I accepted everything you wanted." She just opens her mouth, and then I take the steps to her. "It's an honor for you to have our babies. There is no one else in the whole world I want to have kids with. There is no one else in the whole world I want to do life with except you." I hold her face in my hands and kiss her lips.

"That was sweet," she says. "But I peed on that stick, and it's now on my face." I drop my hands and laugh just like I always do.

"Everything with you is laughter and joy." I look back down at the stick in my hand. "And I can't wait for our children to feel what it is to be loved." My eyes come back up to find hers. "Not going to lie, I'm scared that I'm not going to know what to do."

"Please." She rolls her eyes. "All the babies love you. It's like you're a baby whisperer."

My whole chest feels like it's going to explode. "This is crazy." I shake my head. She comes to me and wraps her arms around my chest.

"And just like that." She smiles.

Printed in Dunstable, United Kingdom